The GLORIOUS RACE of MAGICAL BEASTS

ALEX BELL

Illustrated by Tim McDonagh

faber

CHAPTER ONE

All sensible people know that libraries are wondrous and magical places. Not only are they bursting with words and stories, facts and figures, delightful glimpses into other lives, but they're also full of cosy corners in which visitors can tuck themselves away for an hour or two. Some might want to read, or study; others might just wish to be quiet for a while, somewhere warm, and friendly, and safe. All libraries are special, of course, but none more so than the Royal Library in the port city of Harmonia. It had the honour of being the largest library in the world, and was home to more than two hundred thousand books, which were carefully looked after by a dedicated team of fifteen librarians.

There was the Head Librarian – a much admired person at the very top of the hierarchy. Then there were two deputies, and below them were three managers, followed by four higher and four lower librarians. And right at the very bottom of the chain was the apprentice librarian. The one currently in position at the Royal Library was a twelve-year-old boy named Elijah Cassius Dewey Fleet – but most people called him Eli. Getting accepted as an apprentice a month ago had been the happiest day he could remember. It was his dearest wish to work in the library for the rest of his life, perhaps even making it to Head Librarian one day.

That morning, just like every other, he arrived bright and early, before anyone else was around. In fact, it was *so* early that there was still a sliver of pale moon in the sky and the sun was only just beginning to rise. Eli didn't mind getting up at dawn. He liked being useful, and it fell to the apprentice librarian to perform a very important task at the Royal Library – namely, to tidy up after the library bats.

Most visitors never saw them because by the time the doors opened to the public, the little winged creatures had long since tucked themselves away and were fast asleep behind the stacks, or dangling upside down from their roosts in the library's courtyard.

Each time he arrived, Eli paused at the bottom of the steps for a moment, set down his briefcase and gazed up at the building to admire its beautiful marble pillars and domed roof. From the corner of his eye he noticed a bat swoop in through one of the open windows. Most of them would be back by now, but it wasn't unusual to see one or two stragglers.

The doors opened to the public in exactly two hours, so there was no time to waste. Eli picked up his briefcase and climbed the steps. A pair of marble lions guarded the front doors, and he patted them both on the head before taking a heavy gold key from his pocket and letting himself inside.

The Royal Library was home to many rare and precious books, including the world's very first encyclopaedia, the largest bestiary of magical animals and an ancient scroll containing the original city plans for Harmonia. It was an impressive collection, but the problem with old books was that there was always a host of bugs and bookworms wanting to feast on them. And that was where the library bats came in. Each night they emerged to hunt among the stacks, gobbling up all the insects they could find.

It was an ingenious solution, but it had one significant downside – the bat droppings, or guano, left behind each night. Someone had to tidy up the mess, and that task naturally fell to the lowliest staff member – the apprentice librarian. It was a famously unpleasant and time-consuming job, but Eli was perhaps the first apprentice in the library's history who didn't mind, and even got a sense of pride and achievement in making everything spick and span once again.

The front doors led straight into the library's famous Long Room, but the dimness made it difficult to see very well that early in the morning. Fortunately, Eli had a solution for this and was pleased that he didn't need to waste expensive fuel in the library lamps. After setting down his briefcase, he shrugged the straps of his tortoise bag from his shoulders and carefully put it on the floor by his feet. He had designed the bag himself. It was somewhat bulky and awkward, but there was no easy way of transporting a tortoise. The bag had to be large enough to contain a plastic tank, which in turn had to contain a little heat lamp, a tortoise cave, a shallow dish of leafy salad and one or two favourite toys. And Humphrey himself, of course. There was even a small mesh window, although this was currently covered with a knitted curtain.

Eli crouched beside the bag to unzip it, and long beams of moonlight immediately poked through the gap. He reached inside with both hands to take out Humphrey – who was asleep in his shell. He set him down on the library's marble floor, and at once the entire space was bathed in a silver glow. The effect was both beautiful and ghostly. Eli doubted there'd ever been a moon tortoise in the Royal Library before he'd brought Humphrey. They were extremely rare creatures, with only a few hundred left in the world. Their shells shone with the pure silver light of the moon – a light strong enough to illuminate even this large space.

The Long Room was, indeed, long, lined with many dozens of bookcases that held almost half of the library's vast collection – some ninety thousand books. Each case was so tall that a ladder was required to reach the upper shelves. The books continued up to a second floor with an ornate wrought iron balcony running all the way around it. The ceiling had three domes – known as cupolas – decorated with astonishingly beautiful paintings, each depicting one of the three muses. And at the end of the room was the famous Book Spiral – a unique, twisting structure that contained the library's collection of forbidden books – because no books were forbidden in the Royal Library of Harmonia.

Eli loved it when the library was open to the public and some of the country's best writers and wisest philosophers and most eloquent poets wandered its halls, looking for inspiration and knowledge. As one of the librarians, he was pleased and proud to share it with the public – but he also especially liked this early part of the day when it was only him and these thousands of ancient books.

'Good morning, Humphrey,' Eli said, giving the tortoise a little pat on his glowing shell.

Humphrey had been a gift from Eli's parents, and he treasured him greatly. Slowly, the tortoise's stubby legs emerged, followed by his head. He peered up at Eli with wise black eyes and stretched his neck out so Eli could give him a chin rub. Then his gravelly voice appeared inside Eli's head. 'If you need me, I'll be in the poetry corner.'

Eli was the only person who could hear Humphrey talk, and this was how he knew that his tortoise had an especial love of poetry. Ancient, romantic, classical, modern – Humphrey adored them all. He'd requested a poetry party for his hundredth birthday, which was coming up in a couple of months, but he was having a little trouble narrowing down the particular poems he wanted read out. So he stumped off to the poetry section to browse the shelves for inspiration. He wouldn't be able to take the books from the shelves, of course, but that didn't matter to a moon tortoise. They only had to sniff a book to immediately know all the words contained inside.

'Remember not to try to climb the shelves!' Eli called after him. 'You don't want to flip yourself over again.'

'I won't,' Humphrey replied.

Eli snapped open his briefcase and took out an apron, a set of knee pads and a pair of rubber gloves. The apron was rather on the frilly side, having once belonged to Eli's nana. It was covered in a cheerful pattern of bright yellow rubber ducks all wearing different hats. Fortunately, no one ever saw Eli in his apron, or else he feared he might struggle to be taken seriously. There was no set dress code for the librarians, but Eli always took pride in dressing smartly in a tweed suit and tie. He had three other suits at home, all of which he'd found in second-hand shops. They were patched and mended, and a little shabby around the cuffs, but Eli made sure they were always clean and pressed. It may not have been a conventional choice for a boy his age, but Eli had always thought that a smart, orderly appearance helped lead to a calm and orderly life. He slipped his protective gear on over the top of his suit and set to work.

His first task was to remove all the leather sheets placed over the tables and chairs every evening. Several of these were stained with guano and Eli set them by the door to be scrubbed outside later. The clean ones he folded up and put away in a storage cupboard, before taking out a bucket and mop, and starting on the floor.

There wasn't too much guano – after all, the bats were quite small, and spent a large part of the night out in the city – but their droppings stuck to the marble like glue, and required a great deal of scrubbing to remove completely. Eli would never dream of leaving even a trace behind, and always put in plenty of elbow grease. People tended to underestimate his strength and determination – in part, thanks to his thin frame, mild manners and quiet voice – but he was surprisingly strong.

For over an hour, he worked diligently, bit by bit over the marble tiles, until everything was spotless. Humphrey's light was no longer required by then because the sun had risen outside and was flooding in through the many windows. The pillars and balcony were drenched in white and gold, and the Long Room was airy and pristine. Sometimes it really felt to Eli that the air was purer here, lighter, easier to breathe. He was never happier than when he was at the library. Apart from seeing Nana, Humphrey and Jeremiah, he would have been quite content if he never needed to leave and interact with the outside world at all.

He whistled to himself as he dragged the stained leather sheets out to the courtyard to be hosed down. Once he'd finished, he made his way through the rest of the library, unlocking doors and making sure that everything was in order. Thankfully, the bats only had access to the Long Room. Eli shuddered to think how many hours it would take him to clean if they could get into the other areas too.

The next largest space was the polished wooden Philosophers' Hall, with its globes and rarity cabinets and marble busts of the world's greatest thinkers. Also contained within the library building was a manuscript restoration chamber, a planetarium, a music library and multiple cosy reading rooms.

Once he'd opened them all up, Eli returned his cleaning clothes to his briefcase and tracked down Humphrey in the ancient poetry corner. He groaned aloud to find him on his back, his stumpy legs kicking as he unsuccessfully tried to right himself.

'You tried to climb the shelves again, didn't you?' he said.

'I can't understand it,' Humphrey said. 'Usually, I'm an excellent climber. Why doesn't this place have a tortoise ramp anyway?'

Tortoises had been around, in one shape or form, for millions of years. They were one of the oldest surviving species on the planet. This fact never ceased to amaze Eli because it seemed like they had very little in the way of survival instincts. They were wise about things like poetry, but less so when it came to practical matters. Not only that, but once a tortoise was on its back, it was quite difficult for it to right itself without help. Tortoises could die that way. Plus, they couldn't swim, or regulate their own body temperature, or tell which plants were poisonous. They didn't realise that they weren't designed for climbing, or swimming, or jumping. And they had terrible memories too.

Eli scooped Humphrey up and headed to the library staffroom. As they walked down the corridor, Humphrey told him excitedly about a poem he'd read that morning.

'It's called *The Epic Song of Theodora*,' he said. 'And it's perfect for you or Jeremiah to read at my party.'

Eli gave a splutter that he turned into a cough. 'I know that poem,' he said. 'It's very fine, but ... well, it's a bit on the long side. In fact, it's one of the longest poems in existence. It takes more than two hours to read it out loud.'

'What does that matter?' Humphrey replied. 'You

think Jeremiah won't like it?'

Eli said nothing. He was supposed to have had a planning meeting with Jeremiah about Humphrey's party last week, but his friend hadn't shown up. Jeremiah detested poetry and probably thought the entire notion of having a party for a tortoise was a bit foolish anyway, but Eli had still been hurt that he hadn't bothered to come at all. And Humphrey was very fond of Jeremiah, so it was important he was there.

'I just thought you might prefer to have a bit more variety,' he said. 'Rather than using up the whole time with one poem.'

'That's a good point,' Humphrey mused. 'A very good point.'

They settled themselves in the staffroom for a quick breakfast – a peanut butter sandwich, which Eli's grandmother had made the night before. No one made sandwiches like Nana. Not only did she carefully remove the crusts, and put in just the right amount of filling, she cut the sandwich into shapes too. One day it might be a dolphin, the next a train, or a sheep, or a monkey. She had her own restaurant in the Floating Quarter, and also organised children's picnic parties. It seemed like she was always coming up with new and imaginative ways to make food fun.

Today, Eli's sandwich was violin shaped, and when he took his first bite, it began to play a lullaby from his childhood. Hearing it immediately transported him back to being five years old, bewildered and frightened in his grandmother's lap, her arms holding him so very tightly as she tried to explain things in a way that he would understand. Something dreadful had happened and his parents were gone. It was the only time in Eli's life that he had ever seen her cry. And for a while, his bright, happy world became dark and hopeless, but each night there was always that soothing lullaby that Nana sang as she tucked him up in bed. Bit by bit, her love chipped away at the terror and grief and brought Eli back into the light. Even now, after all these years, that simple tune brought a lump to his throat and made a great burst of love for Nana fill up his chest.

He shared the sandwich with Humphrey and then reached into his bag and brought out a little woolly tortoise jumper. When he'd first started looking, Eli had discovered that tortoise jumpers weren't easily obtainable in local pet shops – ordinary tortoises had no need of them, after all – so he had made this one himself. His grandmother had taught him to knit, and he found he very much enjoyed it – and was pretty good at it too.

Strictly speaking, people weren't supposed to bring pets into the library, so Eli always brought a little jumper for Humphrey to disguise his light and make him less conspicuous when Eli put him out in the courtyard. Members of the public weren't permitted back there anyway, and if any of the other librarians had ever noticed Humphrey contentedly munching on a patch of grass, or snoozing under a bench, then they turned a blind eye. Librarians were good eggs like that.

Eli put Humphrey out there now and then dashed to the toilets to check that his appearance was in order. He carefully combed his light brown hair, straightened his tie and fastened it with his favourite tortoise tiepin – the one with the shining opal shell. It had once been a hair clip belonging to his mother. He spent the rest of the day attending to his librarian duties – cataloguing books, stacking the shelves, dusting the stacks and answering queries from members of the public.

These were all things that Eli enjoyed very much, and his day passed quietly and pleasantly, as it always did at work. Soon enough, it was time to lock up the doors, drape the leather sheets over the furniture and say goodbye to the library for the night. He put Humphrey back in his tortoise bag and drew the curtain aside so that Humphrey could see out. As usual, Eli paused beside the library front doors for a moment and watched the bats swooping about up near the domed ceiling. The books, and the bats, and the quiet, and the dark were all like a balm to Eli's soul. He breathed in the hush and the peace, savouring it, trying to fill himself up with as much of it as he could. Because enjoyable as his day had been, Eli knew that the evening was going to be difficult. What he didn't know was that it was going to be even more difficult than he could have possibly imagined.

CHAPTER TWO

The Royal Library steps were bathed in sunlight during the early evening, which made them a popular spot for people to hang out and relax, chat and eat pizza slices from the nearby cart. All Eli could hear from every direction was excited talk about the Glorious Race of Magical Beasts. The race took place every year, and each time the buzz around it got louder and louder. It seemed that the entire country got swept away in racing mania. Everyone except Eli and his nana, that is. The Glorious Race of Magical Beasts had cost them too dearly. Eli's parents would still both be here if it wasn't for the race.

But there was no avoiding it in Harmonia, especially as the event started there. The route varied every year, but it traditionally began in Harmonia, and there were always three checkpoints and three rounds. Spectators could watch footage of the race on the big screens that were currently being erected in the square, across from the fountains. Some of the busier cafes and restaurants had them too.

As he made his way down the steps, Eli tried not to listen to the racing talk and to think instead of happy things, like books and stamps and tortoises. He was tired from his early start, and from being on his feet all day, but there was no time to rest because in the evenings he waited tables at his nana's restaurant.

Eli didn't mind the work, normally – he was proud of the restaurant and glad to be a part of it – but tonight he would have preferred a different job, one that didn't involve being around a lot of people talking about the race. It was even worse when customers realised or remembered that he and his grandmother were Fleets – related to the famous Lara and Theo Fleet, who had won so many races in their time. Before it all went wrong. Then they wanted to speak to Eli about them, asking questions and reminiscing about their best racing moments and asking Eli if he'd ever had any ambitions to enter the race himself. People always seemed disappointed when he said no. Of course the race had seemed thrilling and exciting to him once when he'd been very small, and perhaps for the briefest time he'd had dreams of entering, but when his parents died he vowed he'd never go anywhere near it. Far better to live a life that was safe and sensible.

Eli straightened his shoulders and was hurrying across the square when Humphrey said, 'Eli! It's that boy. He's watching you again.'

The tortoise's voice appeared inside Eli's head, and of course, no one else would have been able to hear him speak, even if they were nearby.

'What? Where?' Eli stopped and turned around, his eyes scanning the crowds. About a week ago, he'd noticed a boy, perhaps sixteen or seventeen years old, with a mane of blond hair and a rainbow panther prowling around his feet. He was obviously a racer, with his big leather cuffs and an ostentatious studded belt and a holster carrying a pair of pistols. It wasn't unusual for racers to arrive in Harmonia a week or two before the race began, but Eli had noticed the same boy several times now, and he always seemed to be watching him. He'd even popped up in the library. Eli had seen him hunched in a chair, pretending to read a book. It was obvious he was pretending because he barely glanced at the pages and once the book was even upside down. The volumes he selected didn't seem likely to be ones he could possibly be interested in either. Certainly, Eli had never seen anyone absorbed by *The Pampering and Perming of Pretty Pink Poodles* for more than a few minutes, yet this boy sat with it for almost two hours. He made Eli uneasy, especially as there was something hard and cold in his gaze.

'He's gone now,' Humphrey said. 'But he was there. By the fountain.'

Eli didn't doubt what Humphrey had seen, but there wasn't much he could do about someone looking at him, even if the boy had still been there. He pushed the racer out of his mind and walked over to where the hot-air balloons were transporting people up to the Floating Quarter. There were three balloons today and they were beautiful, with their pale blue and cream stripes and smart wooden baskets.

The Floating Quarter was a popular spot at night, offering restaurants and spectacular sea and city views. It was already getting busy as Eli joined the queue. Fortunately, the balloons could carry fifty people at a time, so it wasn't long before he was ushered on to one. The journey only took a few minutes and Eli always enjoyed standing by the side of the basket and looking down at the square as it dropped away. If he looked up he could see the underside of the Floating Quarter, a collection of floating wooden planks that formed the boardwalks. It had been his home since his parents died seven years ago, and sometimes it was almost hard to remember the cottage where he'd lived with them on the outskirts of Harmonia.

It had been a hot day, and the evening still felt warm, so a couple of balloon staff were walking around the basket handing out chilled towels for people to freshen up. The balloon was filled with guests dressed for dinner, all talking about the race and who they thought was going to enter and who might drop out at the first hurdle – and who might die.

People always seemed keen to speculate about who was going to die. Nobody had been killed last time, but it had been the first race in many years that had not had any fatalities. Eli got the sense that people were a bit disappointed by this – that it somehow made the race less thrilling if everyone survived and returned home safe to their families.

It was this sort of thing that made him want to disappear back into the library and not come out until the race was over. But it would go on for several weeks and Nana always said that it did no good, in the long run, to try to hide from difficult things. She was always so strong, and matter-of-fact, and no-nonsense, and this made Eli feel a tiny bit better and a tiny bit stronger himself. They would get through this year's race, like they had all the others, and then everything could go back to normal.

The balloon soon arrived at the quarter, and suddenly the view switched to picturesque restaurants, splashing fountains and a network of wooden skywalk bridges. People began filing out of the basket, and Eli thrust away unhappy thoughts and unwelcome memories, deliberately straightening his shoulders the same way he'd seen Nana do.

'Sometimes,' she would say, 'you just have to give yourself a stern talking-to and get on with things, whether you feel like it or not.'

Eli followed everyone on to the bridge, the wooden planks glowing golden as spilled honey in the evening sun. The most luxurious and prestigious restaurants formed a crescent around the hot-air balloons. Leading away from these were more skywalk bridges winding their way higher and higher into the sky. The further up you went, the quieter everything became.

Eli was glad to leave the hustle and bustle of the lower levels behind and climb the bridges to the top of the Floating Quarter. There were no fancy restaurants here, only cosy cafes and family-style food. Nana's house – which was also her restaurant – was at the top of the sky street, surrounded by fireflies and stars. There wasn't room for any tables inside, so they were placed on the decking outside, beneath strings of glowing lights.

An illuminated sign over the door read *Nana's Kitchen*. The checked tablecloths were all slightly different sizes, and none of the cutlery matched, but people didn't seem to mind that the restaurant was humble, or that it only served desserts day and night – in fact, that was part of the appeal. Customers often came to Nana's for their pudding after eating their main meal in one of the other restaurants below.

Eli quickly removed Humphrey's jumper and set him down to stump about on the decking. Then he went into the kitchen, where Nana was already hard at work, alongside two other chefs. She paused for a moment to greet Eli, pulling him in for a quick hug. As always, she smelled of milk chocolate and pancake mix. Eli still couldn't quite get used to being almost as tall as her. He'd shot up during the last year and could now look Nana in the eye. Today, her grey hair was tucked neatly away beneath a chef's hat, and she wore her usual red lipstick, which always matched her nails.

'The penguins have just gone outside,' she said, handing him a bunch of tiny aprons. 'Take a cookie before you go, too,' she added, thrusting one at him.

It was still warm from the oven and Eli took it with a grin. He was always rather proud of the fact that tragedy hadn't left too much of a mark on his nana. She smiled often, laughed loudly and seemed to enjoy life about twice as much as the average person. People flocked to her restaurant because she made the best desserts in Harmonia, but also because Nana's Kitchen was the only place in town with chocolate penguins for waiters.

They rushed up to him as soon as he went outside, honking, and flapping their stubby wings, and hopping up and down on their webbed feet in excitement. The penguins each had their own name and distinct personality, and Eli was fond of all of them, although Barnaby was his favourite. He was the smallest penguin, but also the most determined and the most tireless, still working hard long after the other penguins had gone on their fish break. They were all excellent waiters, never getting an order wrong or spilling a single drop of pudding.

Eli tied a small white apron with red frilly bits around the edges of it on to each of them and then handed out some notepads. After that, he set the tables and lit the candles in their glass jars, finishing off just as the first customers started to arrive. Eli and his nana worked together to welcome guests, and before long, the restaurant was full. From his position at the meet-and-greet podium, Eli saw that several diners had magical beasts with them. Pegasi and dragons weren't permitted, of course – the dragons tended to set fire to things and both creatures were too big for such a small space, and prone to knocking over furniture and generally causing a ruckus.

But Eli spotted a ninja starfish on one of the tables, occasionally breaking into an energetic spin. And there was a hurricane ostrich at another, batting a puff of wind across the restaurant every time it blinked its incredibly long and pretty eyelashes. And there, right on the edge of the decking, stood a graceful star gazelle, silver and sparkling, just like the type Eli's parents used to have.

It made his heart ache to look at the gazelle. He thought of Hero and Hera, his parents' gentle pets, and how he used to love watching them walk around the garden at their old cottage, mesmerised by their sparkling light. You could immediately tell who the racing humans were too. They all wore clothing designed in some way for physical activity. Or else made to withstand a particular weather element. There were windproof jackets, and snowshoes, and leather riding trousers, and cowboy boots with spurs.

He was glad that the restaurant was busy, because being rushed off his feet gave him less time for thinking melancholy thoughts. He put a sign on the podium saying the tables were fully booked, and then went back to the kitchen to help with the washing-up. All evening the penguins hurried back and forth, carrying out platters of pancakes and waffles, along with tall glasses of ice-cream sundae, and generous slices of gooey chocolate cake dripping with hot fudge sauce.

None of the desserts themselves were magical – not like the ones Eli's nana sometimes made for him at home. She said the chocolate penguins were more than enough to draw people in. Magic was as strong as it had ever been in the animal world, but everyone knew that it was dying out in the human one for some reason. There might be the odd person, like Nana, with a bit of picnic magic, but all the powerful wizards and mages and witches had long since gone. At least, that was what most people believed – despite Eli almost giving the game away at school back when there was that business with Tom Penman ...

Eli's hands were pink and wrinkly from the constant washing-up, so he was quite glad when Nana appeared and told him to take a break outside. It was hot and noisy and bright in the kitchen and the decking was always pleasant in comparison, with cool breezes and sleepy fireflies. Plus, his little free library was out there too. Eli dried his hands and was about to head to the door when his eyes fell on Nana and he paused.

'Are you okay, Nana?' he asked, thinking she looked tired.

She seemed startled by his question. 'My dear boy, of course.'

He hesitated, not entirely believing her. It would make sense if she was feeling a bit blue, what with all the chatter about the race, but there had been odd moments like this – when she seemed sadder, or more tired, or just not quite herself – for several weeks now. Before he could say anything else, Humphrey's voice suddenly appeared faintly inside his head from the decking.

'Eli! It's that boy again ...'

'I'll just take a quick break,' Eli said to his nana before hurrying outside.

He gazed around the decking. He couldn't see

Humphrey but his eyes soon landed on the blond boy who'd been following him around Harmonia. He sat alone at one of the tables, his rainbow panther wedged awkwardly underneath. Eli hadn't noticed him earlier, so it must have been Nana who'd shown him to his table. For a moment, Eli considered ignoring the boy and slipping back into the kitchen, but he was getting a little tired of looking over his shoulder all the time and this seemed like a good opportunity to find out what was going on. The racer probably wanted to talk to him about his famous parents. Feeling a bit nervous, he forced himself to walk over to the table. The boy didn't look up, so Eli cleared his throat and said, 'Can I get you anything else?'

The racer glanced up and immediately narrowed his eyes at the sight of Eli. Then he scowled and said, 'About time someone came out. I've been trying to get one of those penguins to bring me a coffee for the last half hour.'

'I'll fetch you one,' Eli said pleasantly. He paused. 'How many pink poodles do you have, then?'

The boy gave him an offended look. 'I *beg* your pardon?'

'Poodles,' Eli said, pronouncing the word very clearly. 'I thought you must have at least one as you spent quite a long time reading that book in the Royal Library the other day.'

A flush crept over the boy's face, but he seemed irritated rather than guilt-stricken.

'Why are you following me?' Eli asked quietly.

The boy snorted. 'I'm not.'

Eli opened his mouth, but there was the sound of breaking glass from behind him, followed by a shout and a commotion.

CHAPTER THREE

Eli's first thought was that one of the magical beasts must have knocked over a table. It happened sometimes. After all, they were often large creatures, and although the beasts were supposed to be well trained if they came to the Floating Quarter's restaurants, the reality was that they were often less obedient than their human owners claimed.

But, instead, the wreaker of the havoc turned out to be one of the penguin waiters. It had flapped up on to the table and was slurping a customer's ice-cream sundae. Drops of chocolate ice cream flew all over the place, staining the fine clothes of the guests at the table, who leapt back, shrieking. Eli saw that the same thing was already happening at the neighbouring table, where a penguin waiter was knocking half the plates to the floor in its attempt to gobble up every last shred of pancake.

All around, people were exclaiming, and staring, and complaining, and Eli could hardly take it in. The penguins never acted like this, never. They were all remarkably good at their jobs – they never got an order wrong, they never dropped a plate and they certainly never pinched any of the dessert for themselves, let alone flew up on to the tables to generally be a penguin nuisance. It was beyond belief, yet here it was, happening in front of Eli's eyes.

And it got worse. The next moment, all the remaining penguins had abandoned their tasks to flap up on to the tables and gobble up the puddings. One penguin got his head stuck inside an ice-cream sundae glass and then ran about the decking, honking loudly. Caramel sauce and strawberry sprinkles and maple syrup went everywhere, and customers scrambled to get out of the way.

Eli saw one of the penguins snatch up a jug of fudge sauce and deliberately tip it over a woman's head. Another penguin was trying to get into the telephone box that contained Eli's little free library – all his favourite books neatly lined up upon the makeshift shelves for people to borrow and return as they liked. Fortunately, the penguin wasn't tall enough to reach the door handle, or Eli shuddered to think of the sticky damage it might have done to the books. He wore the key to the library on a chain around his neck, like always, and ran over to lock the door, just in case.

Behind him, Nana was yelling at the penguins to stop, though they didn't seem to hear her. Eli wanted to help, but had no idea where to start or what to do. Nothing like this had ever happened at the restaurant, and they didn't have many emergency situations at the library.

His mind seemed to freeze. There were too many penguins on the run, too many customers and magical beasts scrambling around, tables turning over, plates breaking. Eli heard Humphrey calling for help and spotted him wedged beneath a chair. He hurried across the decking to pick him up before he could be kicked or squashed, glad to find something useful to do.

And then, all of a sudden, the penguin waiters melted. Every single one of them. They'd been right there, honking and flapping and creating a scene, and then they were just … sad little puddles of warm chocolate. Eli stared, appalled, a sinking feeling in his stomach. Were they *gone* gone? Surely not. It didn't make sense – they were supposed to be made of unmeltable chocolate. But before he had the chance to ask, all the customers had crowded around to complain.

Eli could hardly see Nana at one point for the number of people there were.

He could hear her, though. Her voice was calm and steady as she promised everyone a full refund and asked them to send her the bill for any ruined clothes. Most of the customers seemed placated by this, and went off to collect their bags, albeit still grumbling beneath their breaths. But there was one person who seemed absolutely livid and refused to let it go – the boy who'd been following Eli. He was actually shouting at Nana in a booming voice, whilst his rainbow panther slunk about his feet, occasionally drawing back its lips in a snarl.

'—such rubbish service!' he was yelling. 'What kind of place is this? You ought to be closed down!'

Eli clutched Humphrey, feeling a horrible, prickly combination of helplessness and anger building inside his chest. Startled by all the commotion, the moon tortoise had withdrawn right into his shell.

'I don't like it out here, Eli,' Humphrey whispered. 'Please, let's go inside.'

Eli was quiet by nature and disliked confrontation as much as Humphrey did, but he couldn't stand seeing someone be rude to his grandmother. He longed to march over there and tell the boy to leave, but he knew that Nana was perfectly capable of dealing with this customer on her own. In fact, she was quite adept at giving rude people a stern telling off and sending them on their way. Plus, she could turn someone's hair into candyfloss with a twitch of her finger if she wanted to and that always seemed to get people to cooperate pretty quickly. At least ... normally that was the case. But tonight, something was different. Something was wrong.

Nana wasn't telling the customer off. She wasn't sending him on his way, or turning his hair into candyfloss. She was just standing there, and her face was grey and she wobbled a little on her feet. Eli tucked Humphrey under one arm and hurried to her side, reaching out to clasp her by the elbow.

'Nana,' he said in an urgent tone. 'What's wrong?'

'I'm fine, dear. Go back into the kitchen.'

But Eli knew she was lying, and he wasn't leaving her. He turned to face the racer. 'What do you want?' He'd meant for his voice to come out stern and calm, but instead it trembled, and he hated himself for that. Why couldn't he be fearless and useful just once? 'She's already offered you a refund,' he struggled on. 'What else is there?'

The racer's lip curled up, rather like his panther's.

'Don't get cheeky with me, kid. I want compensation. And I'm not leaving until I get it.'

Eli frowned. 'How much compensation?'

As soon as he spoke the words, he knew he shouldn't have. It made it seem as if he accepted the demand, when he should have refused to consider it at all. Eli looked around, a little desperately, but there was no one to help, no one more capable to take control of the situation. The last few remaining guests were leaving in a disgruntled fashion and the other chefs had finished their shift an hour ago. He was suddenly very aware that he was thin, and not very tough, and a bit scared. He was holding Nana's elbow with one hand and his moon tortoise with the other, and he'd never felt more useless in his life.

The racer cocked his head and said, 'Three hundred dollars ought to do it.'

'Three *hundred*?' Eli was aghast. Nana's Kitchen wasn't a fancy restaurant and their menu items weren't expensive. They never made that much money in a single night, and most of today's guests had left before paying their bills anyway. He could feel his face getting hot and a growing sense of desperation, like a fist closing around his throat. But he swallowed down his panic and turned to Nana.

'I'll take care of this,' he said, giving her a little nudge. 'Go inside and have a sit down.'

Part of him still expected – and hoped – that she would suddenly be back to normal. That she'd give herself a shake and then she'd square up to the racer, and say all the right things to send him on his way. But she didn't. Instead, she gave Eli's hand a brief squeeze and then turned and walked, slightly unsteadily, inside. Now it was just Eli and the racer standing amidst the overturned furniture on the decking.

'We don't have three hundred dollars here,' Eli said quietly.

The boy folded his arms over his chest. 'How much *do* you have?'

Eli's palms were sweating and he clenched them into fists at his sides. 'What's the compensation even for? There're no stains on your clothes and—'

The racer grabbed a fistful of Eli's shirt and dragged him up so that they were face to face and his toes barely touched the ground. 'All that ruckus upset my panther.' He gestured at the beast lying by his feet. She didn't look particularly upset to Eli. 'You can't put a price on that.'

'But ... but the race doesn't start for days,' Eli attempted to point out. 'Surely, by then your panther will have forgotten all about—'

'Don't tell me about my own panther, you little twerp! I think I know her better than you do!'

'All right, but listen,' Eli gasped. 'We don't have that kind of money here.'

But the boy wasn't paying attention. He'd noticed Humphrey tucked beneath Eli's arm. 'I'll take the tortoise,' he said, setting Eli back down on the floor. 'It'll fetch something at the Night Market. At least then I'll get something out of this stupid job.'

Eli looked down at Humphrey, still tucked up tight inside his glowing shell. He took a step back, shaking his head. Panic swirled in his stomach, making him feel sick. His thoughts were in a whirl.

'What job?' he asked. 'Is this . . . is this something to do with why you've been following me?'

'I have *not* been following you, you puffed-up little pipsqueak! Don't you think I've got better things to do with my time than trail around after you? Now, hand over the tortoise.'

'Don't let him take me,' Humphrey whimpered from inside his shell. 'I'll be turned into soup for sure.'

Eli didn't think this was too likely, given how much moon tortoises were worth, but Humphrey had a bit of a phobia about being turned into soup. He could be sold and smuggled out of the city, though.

'You can't have Humphrey. He's my pet.'

But the racer leaned forwards and easily wrestled him from Eli's hands. The next moment, he was stalking towards the exit, his rainbow panther prowling along behind.

'Eli!' Humphrey called in a panicky voice. 'Eli, help!'

Eli's eyes went to his little free library. For a moment, he considered running to get a book, but he couldn't do anything to the racer without knowing his name, and he didn't want to risk losing sight of him either.

'Sir, please!' Eli ran after him. 'Please don't take Humphrey. He's— Oh!'

He broke off, spluttering in shock, as the racer snatched up a jug of lemonade from a nearby table and dumped the whole lot over Eli's head. The jug had been full of ice cubes and the liquid was cold and sticky on his clothes and skin. His hair was soaked.

'Clear off!' the boy snapped. His lip curled in a smirk as he added, 'Go on back to your granny.'

He gave Eli a push, knocking him into the table, which fell over with a crash. Plates of dessert and unfinished drinks tumbled down on top of him and he could hear the racer laughing as he walked away. By the time Eli had struggled free of the tablecloth, the boy was gone – and so was Humphrey.

CHAPTER FOUR

Eli looked around at the mess spread across the decking. There were tables and chairs knocked over, smashed plates and broken glasses, crumpled tablecloths and melted penguins. He took a deep breath. The clean-up would have to wait. He had other things to worry about. For a start, he needed to get Humphrey back. Eli was pretty sure this was doable, although it would involve a trip to the Night Market, and bending his moral rules slightly. First, though, he needed to make sure Nana was okay. He hurried into the house and found her at the kitchen table, still looking pale and a bit shaky.

'Has he gone?' she asked. Then she did a double take at Eli's stained and rumpled clothes. 'And are you all right?'

'Yes, he's gone, and yes, I'm fine,' Eli said. 'I'm worried about you, though.'

Eli had intended to start firing questions at Nana immediately, but she looked old and frail and tired sitting there, so he made them both a cup of tea instead. Here, at last, was something he could actually do, although his hands still trembled as he poured an extra spoonful of sugar into Nana's mug. He set it down in front of her, along with a chocolate brownie. By the time she'd finished, he was pleased to see some colour had come back into her cheeks.

'Thank you, Eli,' she said, finally looking up at him and managing a small smile. 'It's not been a very good night, has it?'

Eli scooted his chair closer to her and reached for her hand, giving it what he hoped was a reassuring squeeze. 'I know something's wrong,' he said. 'Please, Nana, I'm not a little kid any more. Tell me what's going on.'

She slowly lifted her gaze to his. 'Well, all right,' she said. 'I suppose I've put it off for too long as it is. I'm afraid I have some bad news, Eli. It will be difficult for you to hear, but it's time to face facts.'

A feeling of unease prickled over Eli's skin. 'Facing facts' was one of Nana's phrases that only ever got brought out for the bad times. When Eli's parents died. When he was being bullied at school. When money was tight and they struggled to make ends meet. Eli had a great deal of common sense himself, and agreed that facing facts was an essential thing, generally. He just wished that they didn't have to face quite so many unpleasant facts in such quick succession.

'I'm not very well,' Nana said.

'I've noticed that you've been more tired recently,' Eli hurried to say. 'But couldn't we hire some more staff for the restaurant? Or I could take on extra shifts. Once you have a chance to rest and—'

'No, Eli. I mean, I'm really not well. And I'm sorry to have to tell you this, but I'm not going to get better. My magic is leaving. You saw what happened with the penguins.'

Eli stared at her. People like them – people with magic – generally had longer lifespans than ordinary humans. But if the magic ever started to drain away, that could only mean one thing – that they didn't have much time left. Magical people needed their magic to survive.

'I'm truly sorry,' Nana went on. 'This is so dreadfully unfair, with everything you've already suffered. My dear boy, I would do anything to change things – to stay with you a little longer – but we must be realistic. I imagine I have a few months, maybe a year.'

Eli shook his head. Nana was the only family he had

left in the world and he loved her fiercely. The thought of losing her was unbearable.

'No. No, there must be something we can do.' His mind cast about desperately for a solution. 'How about a . . . a magic ruby?'

He'd never seen one himself, but he'd read about them in the library and knew that they could be used to store magic. For someone in Nana's position, if she put the last of her powers into a ruby and kept it with her always, then she could have years and years of extra time.

But Nana was already shaking her head. 'We would never be able to afford one, Eli. Even if I sold the restaurant, and everything we own, it wouldn't be enough.'

Eli knew she was right. Magic rubies were extremely expensive, and yet he couldn't give up just like that. He felt a sudden burst of irritation towards his parents. They had been famous for winning the Glorious Race of Magical Beasts in a noble way, never harming any other contestants or animals in the process. Not only that, but they always gave the magic prize away at the end. They said that they raced for the thrill of it, not the prize, and that there were people out there more in need of magic than they were. But now Eli wished they had kept at least some of the magic for their own family. Without that, he wasn't sure what to do, but there had to be *something*, some way of fixing this . . .

'Eli,' Nana said gently. 'Please don't torture yourself trying to come up with a solution. This is why I've been putting off telling you. I knew that you'd want to fix it. That you'd set yourself to finding an answer in one of your books. Don't waste precious time looking for something that doesn't exist. This isn't something you can change. It is what it is, and we'll just have to get on with it. I'd like us to make the most of whatever time we have left together.' She glanced towards the kitchen door and said, 'I clearly can't maintain chocolate penguin waiters any more, so we'll have to hire human staff. It'll be an additional expense, but hopefully people will still come for the pancakes.' She gave him a small smile and stood up. 'Now, I know we have a lot of tidying up to do, but I don't think that's a job for tonight. You must be tired, and I am too. The mess will still be there in the morning. We'll stay closed for the breakfast service and see to it then. I'd like to get some sleep before tackling anything. Goodnight, dear.'

She got up, gave him a quick squeeze around the shoulders, and then went towards the door. Eli remained seated for a moment, trying to process it all. He was furious with himself for not realising there was something seriously wrong sooner. As ever, he supposed his mind had been on books and he'd failed to pay proper attention to the warning signs right in front of him. His mind was racing for a solution but coming up with nothing, making him feel hot and panicky. Finally, he took a deep breath and forced himself to slow down. He couldn't do anything about Nana right this second, but he could do something about Humphrey.

He slipped out of the back door and ran down the sky streets to the hot-air balloon depot. Most of the visitors had already finished their meals and returned to the city below, so Eli didn't have to queue this time. He walked straight on to a balloon, and moments later he was back in the floodlit square, the fountains splishing and splashing around him, the stone lions watching him calmly as he ran past.

Eli knew he wasn't very good at running. His arms always seemed too long for his body and flapped about in an ungainly sort of way. He got out of breath really fast, and red in the face, and usually felt a bit sick too. His smart shoes rubbed at his little toes and the back of his heels. But he had to run now because he was frantic to get to the Night Market and find Jeremiah. Without him, he had no hope of getting Humphrey back. And every moment that Humphrey was in that horrible boy's possession was a moment too long. You had to be gentle with tortoises, and the racer didn't look like he'd care about Humphrey's well-being one way or the other. He certainly wouldn't care that it was Humphrey's one hundredth birthday in a few months. He wouldn't care that Humphrey had been planning his party for ages and had his heart set on pointy hats and macarons. In fact, if Humphrey wasn't with Eli, then there would be no party at all.

This awful thought gave Eli the final push he needed to carry on running down the cobbled streets. Before long, the briny scent of seaweed and fish told him he was approaching the Night Market, which took place every night on and around the docks. There were stalls set up on stilts directly over the dark water, which glittered in the moonlight. Eli could make out the silhouette of several large galleons moored nearby. All around there was the hustle and bustle of people buying and selling, chatting and hustling, drinking and eating. The air was full of the smoke and sizzle of various grilled meats and fish fried on open flames, along with the raucous cry of seabirds scuffling for scraps.

Eli had always been a little scared of the Night Market. It was too busy, and noisy, and while most of it was above board, there were also a fair number of somewhat dodgy stalls selling anything from fake documents to stolen goods. Some of the market was located above ground, but the majority of it was found in the old smugglers' caves below the waterline.

Eli weaved his way past burly fishermen and one or two badly disguised pirates until he reached the entrance to the caves. The steps were cut straight into rock and Eli slipped and slid on the damp stone as he tumbled his way down the uneven staircase.

Ever since the huge glass windows had been fitted, the caves no longer filled with water. Now you could look out and see colourful shoals of fish gliding past, along with sleek sharks and graceful rays. There were entire underground streets down there, complete with crooked houses, and shops, and eating establishments. They formed a labyrinth that a person could easily get lost in if they didn't know the way. Eli was mildly claustrophobic and avoided the place when he could. It made him shiver to think that so many criminals had passed this way – and probably still did – sneaking about in the dead of night, committing various unsavoury and nefarious deeds.

He was suddenly very aware of the fact that he was wearing a tweed suit, and wished that he wasn't. Even though it was stained with dessert and lemonade, and not at all up to his usual standards of neatness, it was still making people give him funny looks, and drawing attention when he would rather have been invisible.

He dashed through the caves, searching for Jeremiah. The place was busy – both with people and with their magical beasts. Fortunately, Eli had a pretty good idea where his friend was likely to be. The last cave in the chain was home to a pub called the Albatross. It got its name from the fact that it had an excellent view of the *Albatross* shipwreck on the seabed beyond. The old galleon was a hundred years old at least, and there was nothing left of its sails, but the hull remained, tilted at an angle, covered in barnacles and seaweed.

Eli had always thought the wreck was sad and a bit creepy. He'd read about the ship in the library and knew it had been involved in several famous sea battles, as well as exploits in smuggling and piracy.

The Albatross pub was crowded at this time of night, which made Eli even more claustrophobic. Everywhere he looked, there seemed to be big customers sloshing beer, or talking loudly, or throwing darts. The pub itself was quite basic – there were a few rickety wooden tables and chairs scattered about the place; otherwise people sat on overturned kegs that, from the smell of them, had once contained fish.

The most striking thing about the pub, though, was its walls. They were adorned with shark heads. Everywhere Eli looked, there were cold, dead eyes staring at him, and rows of glisteningly sharp teeth. He shuddered and wondered for the hundredth time why Jeremiah would voluntarily spend his evenings in a place like this when he could be tucked up at home with a good book. When it came down to it, Eli really didn't understand why any of these people were here when they could be at home reading.

His eyes scanned through the crowds and over to the bar, which was actually a large, overturned lifeboat propped up on wooden legs. A stuffed albatross perched on one end, and a ship's bell hung from a hook in the cave ceiling beside it. But Eli couldn't see Jeremiah anywhere. A sense of dread began to churn up his insides. What if he didn't find him in time and Humphrey was sold and lost for good? Nervously, he tried clearing his throat and tapping the nearest person on the elbow. 'Um, excuse me, my good woman, have you seen a boy around here? He's about my age and—'

But the customer swatted him away as if he were an annoying fly, and continued her conversation. Eli began to feel desperate. He'd counted on being able to find Jeremiah fairly easily. After all, wherever Jeremiah went, there was usually some sort of commotion following close behind and he was always getting up to some sort of mischief in the smuggling streets . . .

He'd barely finished the thought before he heard a startled shout from the other side of the pub. Then more and more people were yelling and pointing, and jostling each other to reach the large glass window facing out towards the ocean. Eli groaned, suddenly having a pretty good idea of what he was going to see. He hurried across the room and managed to find a gap near the window. Sure enough, Jeremiah was submerged in the sea beyond – and he was fighting with a shark.

CHAPTER FIVE

Jeremiah Jones was the same age as Eli, as far as they knew – but the two boys couldn't have been more different. Jeremiah wasn't at all interested in books, for a start. In fact, Eli didn't think he'd ever read one in his life. Jeremiah hungered for adventure – the more daring and dangerous the better. Eli had thought that his friend had given up shark wrestling, but he wasn't all that surprised to discover that this wasn't the case. He'd heard the rumours about a mysterious masked shark fighter who sometimes appeared in the sea near the *Albatross*, and he knew the pub was busier than it had ever been as a result, with people hoping to catch a glimpse of this thrilling spectacle.

'He'll be eaten alive!' one of the customers exclaimed,

sounding quite delighted by the prospect. 'That's a tiger shark! Absolutely ferocious! A man eater!'

'Don't be so sure,' another customer said. 'I've seen that boy fight before. He always gets away. Devil knows how he does it.'

'How is he managing to hold his breath for that long?' someone else demanded. 'Surely he should have drowned by now?'

Jeremiah had gone into the sea fully clothed in his usual outfit – a long captain's coat, dark trousers and pirate boots. His black hair reached almost to his shoulders, and even without the mask it would have been difficult to make out his features when he was tussling with a shark the same size as him. Eli knew that his friend would probably be fine – he'd done this before, after all, many times – but it was hard not to feel worried. The shipwreck loomed in the distance, and Jeremiah thrashed and grappled with the shark, which seemed to be doing its very best to tear him to shreds.

And for a moment, Eli was a six-year-old boy again, clutching his battered copy of *The Seafaring Adventures and Exploits of Jeremiah Jones*, marvelling at all the amazing things Jeremiah could do, and internally cheering whenever he saved the day, or battled a sea monster, or outsmarted a pirate captain and lived to tell the tale. Jeremiah didn't have parents either, but he wasn't heartbroken about it. He was larger than life, and he looked cool with his captain's coat, dark eyes and bronze skin. He always knew just what to do and what to say and how to be. Eli thought he was the most extraordinary person he had ever read about – and that was why, one day when Eli was nine years old, for better or worse, he took him right out of the book.

Nana had been horrified when she found out. She'd known that Eli had book magic, of course – library keys from all over the world were drawn to him like a magnet – but they'd assumed he just had a sprinkling, the same as Nana. Eli's father had had hardly any magic of his own, but sometimes the magic skipped a generation and ended up being stronger than anyone had expected. Taking a character out of a book was big, powerful magic – the type that Eli shouldn't have been able to do, the type that only a mage could perform.

'Do you understand what this means, Eli?' Nana had said, all those years ago. 'It means you're ... you're different from the other magical people in our family. Special. In fact, it means that you must be a mage. I suspected as much when you said Humphrey talks to you. Only mages can hear moon tortoises.'

Apart from the perk of hearing his tortoise speak,

Eli didn't care about being a mage. All he cared about was meeting Jeremiah, his idol. They hit it off immediately, despite being so different. Nana told Eli that he must put Jeremiah back in the pages where he belonged at once. She said that fictional characters weren't supposed to be permanently removed from the pages of their books, and that they didn't know what the consequences might be if Jeremiah stayed in their world. But Eli couldn't bear to give him up. It was the only time in his life that he'd ever defied his grandmother, and even now, he wasn't sorry. The two boys were more than friends – Eli loved Jeremiah like a brother.

He no longer worshipped him the way he had when he'd been small. He'd found out for himself that things change when you meet your idol for real. No one could quite live up to that expectation, and Jeremiah could be difficult sometimes, and temperamental, and stubborn, and a bit rude. There was a dark side to him too that worried Eli occasionally, but, still . . . they had become very close friends, and it was quite amazing to see Jeremiah fight a shark with his bare hands, just like he did in the book. It wasn't something an ordinary person should have been able to do, and yet there Jeremiah was, doing it, and excelling at it, and winning.

Eli watched as his remarkable friend lifted his arm and brought his fist down with maximum force right on the shark's snout. The creature recoiled in a burst of bubbles, but Jeremiah pursued him through the water, landing blow after blow. The next moment, the shark turned and swam away into the depths of the ocean, admitting defeat. Everyone in the pub gave a cheer, although Eli suspected that some of them were disappointed not to have seen Jeremiah gobbled up, or at least lose a hand. Jeremiah always defeated his foes and came away 'without a scratch'. That's what it said in the book, anyway, but it wasn't quite like that in the real world. Eli knew that his friend could fall ill and bleed here. He could grow older too. It worried Eli sometimes – the implications of it all. Just last month, he'd come across an interview with Lionel Gaskins – the author of Jeremiah's book. He'd been discussing his terrible case of writer's block and the fact that he'd not been able to write a sequel, despite trying for the last three years.

Eli had felt such a hot flush of guilt and shame at this that – after much soul-searching – he had done something that had felt wise and right at the time, but he'd since realised had actually been a dreadful mistake. In fact, he'd only made things worse. But there was nothing much he could do about it now, so he tried his best to get on with his life and not think about it.

There was a great stream of bubbles as Jeremiah kicked ferociously to reach the surface. Eli knew he must be desperate for air, or else he would have acknowledged the audience in some way. Waved, or given a bow, or something like that. Something with a bit of flourish. But today he was kicking and splashing to the surface as if his life depended on it – which it probably did.

'Must have made a deal with the devil,' one of the customers muttered.

'Too right,' another customer replied. 'I heard he disappeared in the middle of a shark fight the other day.' He snapped his fingers. 'Gone, just like that. Into thin air.'

Eli turned and began to hurry towards the door. He knew where Jeremiah would be heading next, but before he could reach the exit, a hand dropped heavily on to his shoulder. He looked up into the face of Lana Gold, the owner of the Albatross. She was petite, with a long blonde plait hanging down her back. Rumour had it that she had once been a pirate herself, and Eli knew no one ever messed with her.

'You're the librarian, aren't you?' she said.

Eli nodded. 'Apprentice librarian, yes.'

'Thought so.' She smiled. 'We don't get too many librarians around here. I suppose you're going to see him?'

Eli didn't need to ask who. He just nodded.

'Here.' She dropped a bag of money into his hand. 'You can pass this on. Save me a trip.'

Eli had long suspected that Jeremiah had an arrangement with Lana to shark fight in view of the window – that sort of display was good for business, after all. He stuffed the money into his pocket and hurried from the pub, feeling frazzled and annoyed by how much time he had wasted chasing Jeremiah about. The racer could already have sold Humphrey by now, and the new owner might at this very moment be on their way out of Harmonia ...

Eli retraced his steps through the smuggling streets and went back up to the seafront. From there, he skirted around the edge of the Night Market and over to the Beach of Bones. It was named for the fact that dozens of bones had washed up there over the years – something to do with the currents. They brought everything from tiny terrapin bones to huge whale ribs. There were even gigantic bones from mysterious sea monsters that no living person had ever laid eyes upon. It was a strange, melancholy place to make a home, but Jeremiah liked the solitude.

The beach glowed white in the moonlight and Eli had to pick his way carefully, scrambling over the larger bones to get to the small, secret cave tucked away by itself on the other side of the beach. When Eli first brought Jeremiah out of the book, and it had been accepted that he wasn't going back, Nana had wanted him to live with them. The boys were only nine years old back then, and Nana said that a boy that age needed a home and support. But living in a normal house with a normal family just didn't suit Jeremiah.

'I'll suffocate here,' he'd told Eli. 'I need to be free.'

Eli knew that Jeremiah lived in several different places around the city, but the one he was likely to come to tonight was his cave on the Beach of Bones. It was the nearest one to the Albatross and he'd need to dry off and change his clothes after his shark battle. Fortunately, no one else ever came to the beach – it wasn't exactly the most picturesque spot and the monster bones made people nervous.

Eli ran along the beach as quickly as the bones and his shiny shoes would allow. He was soon out of breath, wincing at his sore feet and thinking that the last time he'd done this much running had been when he'd still been at school and they'd had a sports day. Eli had come last in every single race. He'd been sick in a bush at one point too. Everyone thought it was hilarious that the son of the famous Fleets was so very bad at racing. But Eli had never been good at physical pursuits, and he didn't especially want to be. Running and racing and glory were for other people. Eli only wanted a quiet life of books and tortoises.

He finally arrived at the cave, where he found Jeremiah with his clothes and hair still dripping wet and dusted with salt crystals. Eli knew Jeremiah didn't mind getting wet, and he also knew that fighting with sharks made him hungry. So he wasn't surprised to find his friend sitting in the entrance to the cave, his legs stretched out in front of him, one ankle crossed over the other, tearing ravenously into a loaf of crusty bread.

When Eli staggered up, he was so out of breath that he had to lean over and put his hands on his knees, gasping out his words. 'You've got ... to help! This racer ... came to ... the restaurant. Took Humphrey. Snatched him ... right out of ... my hands ...'

Jeremiah was on his feet at once, taking Eli by the shoulders and peering into his face. 'Are you hurt?'

Eli shook his head so hard that the beach seemed to spin around him. They didn't have time for Jeremiah to waste being worried about him.

'I'm fine,' he gasped. 'But ... but ... my tortoise ...'

'Take a breath,' Jeremiah said. 'There's nothing to flap about. I've already got your tortoise.'

Eli stared. 'Wh-what—?'

Jeremiah sat down and jerked his thumb over his shoulder. 'He's in there, having a salad.'

Eli looked around and, sure enough, Humphrey was munching happily on a little pile of leaves, his moonlight filling the cave with a silver glow.

'Oh!' Eli gasped. 'Oh, Humphrey! Are you okay?'

'Perfectly fine,' Humphrey replied, still focused on the salad. 'Mmm, these leaves are crunchy fresh! My compliments to the chef.'

Eli knew that tortoises lived in the moment, never lingering much in the past or the future. Humphrey had probably already half-forgotten the incident, and it was almost impossible to get him to focus on any sort of conversation whilst he was enjoying a salad anyway. Eli took a breath to steady himself. He didn't often come into Jeremiah's cave – normally they hung out on the beach outside. Jeremiah was quite private about his personal space. Even during the many times that Eli had visited the *Nepo* – Jeremiah's ship – he'd never set foot in his friend's private cabin. And so Eli couldn't resist having a quick glance around the cave now.

When Jeremiah came out of the book, his sea phoenix, Luther, came with him, and Eli wasn't surprised because Luther always went everywhere with Jeremiah. The same went for his ship. But there was a sea chest too – one that shouldn't have been there. Now Eli saw it in the cave: large and solid, fashioned from shining black wood, with tarnished silver clasps and a brass plate stamped with Jeremiah's name. Like always, it was fashioned with a big, heavy padlock. The sea chest went everywhere with Jeremiah, and no one knew what was inside it – not even Eli. He'd asked once, but his friend had just gone very still and said, 'What do *you* think is in there?'

The look on his face and the icy edge to his voice had made Eli hesitate, but he was burning with curiosity, not least because he found himself a bit nervous around the chest. Maybe it was something to do with the fact that it wouldn't stay locked. No matter how many times Jeremiah attached a padlock, sooner or later it would click open, all by itself.

'It's just that ... I mean, it was never mentioned in the book, not once,' he'd said.

'Believe me, there were plenty of things not mentioned in the book,' Jeremiah had replied. 'Think about it. It wouldn't be possible to write down every single object in every room, or mention every cobblestone or passing stranger. I've read the book.' His eyes gleamed slightly as he looked at Eli. 'There's no need to look so surprised. I *can* read, you know. And, yes, every word in those pages is true, but it's not the *whole* truth; it's not the whole picture. There are bits you don't see. Like in the chapter when I was escaping the clutches of Captain Dread. The author wrote: "It was cold on the raft, and Jeremiah shivered beneath his scraps of rag." He didn't say the cold was sharp as knives that would peel your skin off. He didn't say that the salt spray stung my eyes so badly I could hardly keep them open, and dried out my lips so much that I couldn't stop licking them, but licking only made it worse. He didn't say I was scared I might actually drown. He didn't say that huddling under the rags on those rough wooden boards was so uncomfortable that at one point I got the most awful cramp in my right foot, so bad I thought I'd broken a toe. He didn't say—'

Eli had held up a hand and tried, gently, to interrupt. 'I understand how novels work,' he said. 'Of course it's not possible to mention everything on the page.

Otherwise our books would be so long they wouldn't fit on the shelf, and no one would want to read them. But all the important stuff gets mentioned, doesn't it? That's kind of the point.'

'There you are, then,' Jeremiah replied. 'The sea chest was never mentioned. Therefore, it must not be important.'

'But ... but then why did it come out of the book with you?' Eli had asked. 'Why do you carry it about with you everywhere?'

'Why do you choose to be an apprentice librarian when you could be a powerful practising mage?' Jeremiah had snapped. 'People make weird choices sometimes, Eli, and it's no one's business but their own. I don't want to talk about this any more.'

Eli knew the sea chest was strictly off topic, but he couldn't help staring at it now. It was right there in the cave, close enough to touch. He half-expected the padlock to click open, as he'd heard it do before, but it stayed closed. Luther was perched on the lid, casually grooming his blue feathers.

'Are you staying in there all night?' Jeremiah asked. 'Why don't you let Humphrey finish his salad and come out here with me?'

Eli had expected to be summoned back outside.

Jeremiah didn't like anyone to be near the sea chest for long. He went out to join his friend.

'Thank you so much for saving Humphrey!' he said, sitting down. 'How did you find him, or even know that he'd been stolen?'

'Have some bread and I'll tell you,' Jeremiah replied. 'You still look peaky and I don't want you passing out. Or being sick in my cave. Remember that sports day?'

Eli took the bread Jeremiah offered him. It was a piece of crusty baguette, slathered thickly with salted butter, and Eli thought it might well be the most delicious thing he'd ever tasted. His whole body seemed to sing with happiness at the sight of Humphrey contentedly munching his greens, safe and sound in Jeremiah's cave.

'I noticed some sleazy racer called Vincent Tweak trying to flog him at one of the stalls earlier,' Jeremiah said. 'And I don't need to be able to hear Humphrey to know that you'd never give him up and that something fishy must be going on. So I swiped him back for you.'

Jeremiah could move as silently and gracefully as a cat, which made him an accomplished thief when the occasion called for it.

'He's been following me,' Eli said.

Jeremiah gave him a sharp look. 'What do you mean?'

'I've seen him around the city, watching me. I thought he wanted to talk about my parents, but maybe he was after Humphrey all along.'

Eli told him about what had happened at the restaurant, and how Vincent had behaved.

'You should have told me someone was following you,' Jeremiah said. 'I would have warned him off.'

'I *was* going to tell you,' Eli replied pointedly. 'Last week.'

Eli had been at their meeting spot at the agreed time, but Jeremiah had never arrived. This had happened a couple of times recently. Something was changing between them. Eli wasn't sure how or why, but things had seemed off ever since he'd started working at the library. He knew Jeremiah was wary of books, but Eli's love of them had never been a problem before.

He half-hoped that Jeremiah might offer some explanation now for why he hadn't appeared last week, but his friend just shrugged and said, 'Well, Vincent will be off on the race soon and then you won't need to worry about him. Snatching your tortoise back almost made me late for the shark fight, by the way. A few more minutes and the tiger shark would have finished the bait I left to lure him out and gone on its way.'

'I wish you wouldn't shark fight,' Eli said. 'You might get hurt.'

'I won't.'

'People might guess the truth about where you came from,' Eli went on. 'Ordinary people can't fight sharks with their bare hands. It's quite a unique skill.'

Jeremiah shrugged. His brown eyes gleamed in the darkness. 'So what if people work out where I'm from? It's not like they can send me back, is it?'

This was true – but Eli still worried about what people's reactions would be if they found out that Jeremiah was a fictional character. And he didn't want anyone to know he was a mage either. If that got out then there was bound to be a stream of people queuing outside his door for magic spells and enchantments and astonishing spectacles, and it would make it very difficult to carry out his librarian duties. Besides which, mages tended to find themselves tangled up with kings and quests, which was the last thing Eli wanted. There'd be no peace and quiet on a quest.

'Anyway, I've got to make money somehow,' Jeremiah went on. 'You said you didn't want me to steal any more. Although, now that you mention it, I don't hear you complaining about me stealing Humphrey earlier.'

Eli sighed. 'It's not really stealing when he belonged

to me in the first place. Let's not argue about it. Lana said to give you this.' He took the bag of money from his pocket and handed it over.

'Thanks.' Jeremiah tucked it into his coat. 'And don't look so glum. We got Humphrey back, didn't we?'

'Yes, but there's something else.'

All Eli's fear and worry about Nana came crashing back over him as he told Jeremiah what she'd said about her magic fading.

Jeremiah went very still as he listened. He may not have wanted to live with them, but he'd spent a great deal of time at Eli's house over the last three years and Eli knew that he was fond of Nana. Hearing what was being said, Humphrey stumped out of the cave too, and Eli could see the sadness on his wise old face. When Eli told Jeremiah about the ruby, though, his friend said, 'Well, that's the answer, then. For a moment you had me worried.'

Eli frowned. 'But I can't get a ruby. I just told you – they're really expensive.'

'So what?' Jeremiah replied. 'That's not a problem, is it? Not to you. Not if you don't want it to be.'

There was a breeze on the beach, but Eli suddenly felt a bit clammy. He forced himself to meet Jeremiah's eyes and said quietly, 'Please don't.'

Jeremiah stared at him. 'What? Are you really not going to steal a book? Even now, when it could save your nana's life?'

'It's not that simple,' Eli insisted. 'Stealing is wrong. And stealing books is especially wrong. They're put in libraries to be read and shared. I can't ruin that. I won't. What kind of librarian would that make me?'

Jeremiah crossed his arms over his chest. 'You've always been stupid about this, Eli. They're only books.'

Eli shook his head. He shouldn't have expected Jeremiah to understand. It wasn't just that books were special and magical and wondrous, it was also that it was his sacred duty as a librarian to protect and look after them.

'Take heart,' Humphrey said in Eli's head. 'We'll think of something.'

Eli hoped his tortoise was right. Much as he hated to admit it, his calm, peaceful life suddenly seemed to be disappearing, like sand shifting beneath his feet. The wind was changing and, already, Eli could feel it tugging him down a path he had no wish to travel.

CHAPTER SIX

'I should go home,' Eli said, standing up and brushing himself off. 'The restaurant's a mess and I want to clean it before Nana gets up in the morning.'

Jeremiah groaned. 'Are you really going to do it all by yourself? Why don't you wait till tomorrow – the other chefs would help, wouldn't they?'

'I don't want Nana to see it,' Eli replied. 'It will upset her.'

Eli knew that some small part of Jeremiah would like to help, but that he also wanted to snuggle down in his cave and go to sleep listening to the roar of the waves outside.

'I'll come and lend a hand if you wait until the morning,' he finally offered. 'But don't expect me to do anything tonight. I'm tired. I *have* just been shark fighting and tortoise rescuing, in case you'd forgotten, and now I'd like to have a bit of a rest, if that's not too much to ask.'

'Don't worry,' Eli replied, picking up Humphrey and tucking him under his arm. 'I never expected you to help with the restaurant. You've already done enough saving Humphrey. Thanks again. I'll see you later.'

He left Jeremiah getting comfortable in the hammock he'd strung up in the cave, and made his way back to the Night Market. Humphrey remained quiet in his shell, and Eli guessed he was still processing everything from earlier – either that or he'd already forgotten about it. Eli quickly found a locked door to a shut-up shop, and after a quick glance around to check that no one was watching, he slipped the key to his free library from beneath his shirt and inserted it into the door. There was a soft click as the lock slid back, and then he opened the door – only it didn't open into a dark shop, but into Eli's little free library at Nana's Kitchen. The neat rows of all his favourite books immediately soothed him, and Eli quickly stepped through and closed the door behind him. The Night Market disappeared, and Eli was home. It came in handy having magic keys sometimes, but his heart sank when he looked through the glass panel at how much there was to do. It hadn't been quite as bad as this in his head, but now he realised that it would probably take him hours to get everything straight. There was melted chocolate everywhere, and dirtied tablecloths, and broken furniture, and smashed-up crockery.

For a paralysing moment, he didn't know where to start. But then he unlocked the library door, set Humphrey down on the decking and made himself pick up a nearby tablecloth. Then another and another. He tried to pretend he was in the library, removing the leather sheets, clearing up after the bats, surrounded by the hush of books and the comfort of words. The thought calmed him a little, and he was soon in the swing of it.

It had been a long, hard day. Eli's legs and feet were sore from running, and his back hurt from bending. He ached for his bed and yet there was so much to do. He was on his hands and knees, scrubbing at some melted chocolate that had stuck to the decking like glue, when a pair of sea boots suddenly planted themselves before him. Eli felt tears of gratitude prickle his eyes as he looked up to see Jeremiah standing there, holding a mop.

His friend whistled through his teeth and said, 'Well, you weren't exaggerating. This would take you half the night on your own.'

'Thank y—' Eli began, but Jeremiah held up his hand to stop him.

'I couldn't sleep,' he said. 'So I thought I might as well give you a hand.'

The boys set to work. It went much faster with two, and they finally got everything straight just as the sky was beginning to lighten. In another hour or so, Nana would be up, and the rest of the Floating Quarter would start to come to life, setting up to serve breakfasts. Eli felt a small burst of pride that he'd managed to get everything in a fit state for Nana's Kitchen to serve its usual waffles and pancakes. The chefs would be here soon, and they'd be able to open their doors, although he guessed it would need to be a reduced service without the penguin waiters there to help.

'Would you like to stay?' Eli said to Jeremiah. 'You could get an hour of sleep on my floor and then have some breakfast?'

'No, thanks. I don't need you to sing me a lullaby.'

Suddenly, it felt as if lots of little sparks were flaring into life inside Eli's head as Jeremiah's words made him think of a book – a very special book, one that could help, one that might actually be able to solve everything…

'I'm going to head back before the balloons get busy,' Jeremiah was saying. '*You* should definitely have some pancakes or something, though. You look a bit ... wired.'

'I'm fine,' Eli said, although his fingertips were tingling and he suddenly felt wide awake and as if he had too much energy to fit inside his body. This was something that happened to him sometimes, when unusual things occurred and he got a bit excited or stressed. These were the moments when he could feel the magic fizzing in his blood, when he felt less like a librarian and more like something else, something secret, something powerful.

He waved goodbye to Jeremiah. Humphrey had tucked himself into his shell and gone to sleep under one of the tables, so Eli left him where he was and then hurried into the house and up to his room.

An hour ago he had been desperate for his bed, but now sleep seemed out of the question. He was too eager to test his idea – to see whether a book might be able to save the day. He knelt on the floor and pulled out a box from beneath his bed. It was a plain, wooden, ordinary sort of container, but when Eli pushed back the lid, a blast of magic came out so strongly that it blew his hair back from his face. He reached inside and drew out a large bunch of keys. They clinked and jangled in his hands, the metal felt cold and inviting, and he could practically hear the keys begging to be used.

When Eli first discovered that not only did he have a bit of magic, but a *lot*, and that he was, in fact, an actual mage, he'd been a bit annoyed. He didn't want magic. He only wanted books and the quiet life of a librarian. It was a side of himself that he normally tried to ignore. But Jeremiah's words had been going round and round his head, and perhaps, after all, he was right. He'd used the magic keys before, of course, to visit the other libraries, but maybe it was time to do more than visit. Maybe it was time to do something useful with the keys, something that could help his nana. She was the person who had done so much for him and who he loved more than anyone else in the world. If his magic couldn't save her, then what was it good for?

He stared down at the keys in his hands. They were a large, heavy, jangling bunch. There were big keys and small keys, made of iron, and brass, and silver. They opened doors to libraries all over the world. The keys on the ring changed constantly, so Eli never quite knew what he would find. Today they included one to unlock the underwater library in the Lost City of Poot. And a floating library in the cloud city of Gala. Another opened the law library of Ponton University. And still another was for the world's smallest library in the caves of Jalla, which consisted of a single bookshelf with just three priceless books stacked carefully upon it.

Eli was still getting to know the keys. Often they turned up by themselves, in his pockets or in his bedroom, or attached to the key ring with the others. Sometimes he could tell what door they opened just by looking at or touching them. Other times it was a mystery until he stepped through the door – which was how he'd inadvertently flooded his bedroom that one time whilst attempting to open the door to the mermaid library of Medea. Usually, Eli was content to visit the libraries of whatever keys happened to be on his ring at the time, but occasionally he had a particular place in mind, and then he had to try to summon the key. It was still something of a work in progress, but it was a skill that he would need to practise today, because the key he was after wasn't there.

Eli sat down cross-legged in the middle of his bedroom, with the bunch of keys clasped tight in his hands. He took a couple of deep, steadying breaths, then closed his eyes and concentrated hard on the Night Library. He needed to put all his mental focus into seeing it as clearly as possible, but this was a difficult thing to do when he'd never been there before. He'd never dared.

Some library keys were hard to summon, but not this one. Eli could sense it the moment he looked for it – shining in his mind, like a dark, forbidden star. The air around him filled with the usual ringing, but it sounded deeper and more melancholy than normal, like funeral bells echoing in a cold steeple. Eli still wasn't skilled enough at summoning to pick out a particular key, and so several others were drawn to him too. When he opened his eyes he saw dozens of keys suspended in the air around him – almost but not quite there, fading in and out like ghost keys. They jingled softly as they became more and more solid until, finally, they tumbled to the floor one by one and were silent.

He got up and gathered the keys, looking for the one he was after. At last, he spotted it, on the floor beside his bed – it was bone white and topped with a grinning skull. The empty eye sockets gazed at Eli, almost daring him to touch it. When he plucked the key from the floor, it was icy cold.

Eli picked it up, grabbed his bag and walked over to the wardrobe. Then he took a deep breath and inserted it into the keyhole of the door. When he opened it, instead of the usual rack of pressed tweed suits and neat row of polished shoes, there was an entire library within.

CHAPTER SEVEN

It was the one library he'd never imagined he'd ever set foot in, never even thought that he might peer through its windows. Steeped in mystery as it was, Eli didn't know too much about the Night Library, but he knew enough. He knew this library was a place for the undead, a vampire domain, a twilight realm. It wasn't for boys – even if they were apprentice librarians and book mages.

But the Night Library contained a very special book, a book not found anywhere else in the world – the Book of Lullabies. Within its pages were songs for all the different species on the planet, from humans and faeries to elephants and mice. For each type of creature, there was a special song that would send them to sleep. In addition, there were rumours of a few very special lullabies in there that could do things like make a person fall in love, recall lost memories or – most importantly – heal sickness.

Eli stepped over the threshold of his wardrobe and into a dark, vaulted room. Dozens of candles flickered within, reminding Eli of a cathedral – or perhaps a crypt. The Night Library was so cold that Eli shivered as he closed the door behind him. When he glanced back, it no longer resembled his wardrobe door at all – in fact it was twice the size and decorated in skulls, just like every other door in this building.

The library was located in a part of the world where it was always night, and darkness pressed in against the tall windows. Eli could see snowflakes coming down in flurries, pale and bright in the darkness, and the dim outline of ghostly mountains beyond. The room itself was illuminated only by the soft glow of candlelight. The small flames flickered from sconces on the walls and from graceful chandeliers suspended from the ceiling. The library smelled of cold velvet and warm wax. Ebony-black bookcases lined the room, filled with handsome books bound in red leather.

There were no chairs anywhere, but a scattering of chaises longues, upholstered in deep, ruby red velvet. One side of the room was dominated by a gigantic fireplace, filled with dozens more candles, and a massive white bearskin rug was spread on the floor before it. It was certainly one of the most elegant libraries Eli had ever seen. But the most peculiar thing was the trees. They were white and skeletal, their leafless branches twisting up into the air. When Eli peered closer he saw that there were tiny swings suspended from them, with plush red cushions the same shade as the chaises longues.

'The trees were there for the night sprites and the bad faeries,' said a voice behind him. 'But they hardly visit any more. In fact, you're the first visitor we've had in a very long time, and you shouldn't even be here. Humans have a tendency to get eaten in the Night Library.'

Eli swallowed hard and turned around. He'd heard that the librarian of the Night Library was a vampire, and he'd expected a tall man in a velvet suit, perhaps even a top hat. But the vampire before him was a woman, pale-skinned and dark-haired. He'd got the velvet part right, though. She wore a lavish velvet red gown, the skirts cascading out on the dark, marble floor. Her glossy hair was piled on top of her head and she wore a pair of long white gloves. She looked as if she was on her way to a ball rather than a library, but Eli had heard that vampires were the most stylish of all the librarians.

'H-hello,' he stammered. 'I'm Elijah Cassius Dewey

Fleet. I'm . . . I've come to look at a book. I know human visitors aren't usually permitted, but I'm a librarian too.' He rummaged in his bag and held up his badge. 'So I hoped you might make an exception.'

The woman raised a perfect eyebrow. 'It says apprentice librarian.'

'Well, yes,' Eli conceded. 'But I hope to qualify very soon.'

There was a cold, still moment where Eli couldn't tell whether the vampire librarian was about to order him to leave, or try to bite him, but thankfully she did neither of these things. Instead she said, 'I'm Giselle. What book are you looking for?'

'The Book of Lullabies.'

'One of my favourites.' She cocked her head slightly, and Eli saw that diamond earrings glittered in her ears. 'Which library are you from?'

'The Royal Library of Harmonia,' Eli said proudly.

'Ah, yes, the one with all the bats. I should like to see them someday. It seems like bad form to feast on a fellow librarian, even if you are an apprentice. You really can't stay, though. I haven't had dinner yet and I'm . . . quite peckish.'

Eli swallowed hard and forced himself to meet her eyes. 'I can't leave without the book.'

'I'm afraid you'll have to. The book isn't here. It's out on loan.'

'Oh.' Eli's face fell. 'When is it due back?'

'It's overdue, actually. I shall have to chase it up.'

Eli felt his hopes rapidly draining away. 'Could you please put it on order for me?'

The vampire gave him an appraising look. 'Why do you want it so badly? Who are you hoping to send to sleep?'

'My nana. She's not very well and I heard that the book has a lullaby to heal sickness.'

Giselle shook her head. 'If you're a librarian then you ought to know better than to listen to rumours,' she said. 'To the best of my recollection, the book contains no such lullaby.'

'Oh.'

Now Eli was thoroughly deflated. The worst part of it was that the librarian was right – he *should* know better than to listen to rumours.

'I can put it on order for you, though,' the vampire went on. 'Although I wouldn't expect it back any time soon.'

There wasn't much point if it didn't contain a healing lullaby, but Eli didn't want to appear rude, so he just thanked Giselle as politely as he could and tried not to look too glum.

'Let me fetch you a ticket.' She walked over to a nearby desk, took a piece of card from one of the drawers, scribbled something on it and then walked back to hand it to Eli. 'If you keep this in your bag then the book will appear as soon as it's available. Now, you must go or I really shall bite you.'

Eli thanked her and slipped the ticket into his bag.

'How did you get here anyway? Harmonia is on the other side of the planet. Don't tell me you spent three weeks travelling around the world just for the Book of Lullabies?'

'Oh, no, I'm ...'

Eli trailed off, staring at her.

Travelling around the world ...

A bright, shining bubble of an idea had suddenly formed in his mind. It was delicate and fragile, and Eli worried it might pop if he prodded it too hard, so he said nothing out loud. Instead, he wished the other librarian a hasty goodnight and then used the key to his little free library to unlock the nearest door. When he pushed it open, the corridor beyond had vanished, and he looked into the telephone booth that made up his little free library in Harmonia.

He stepped through, closing the door behind him. It was disorientating to find himself swept away from the Night Library's chilly halls, but Eli's heart beat fast as hope bloomed in his chest once more. There was one more thing he could try. Perhaps everything was not quite lost, after all.

CHAPTER EIGHT

Eli realised there was no point going to bed when he was never going to be able to sleep. He went back downstairs, left a note for Nana saying he'd gone to the library, then scooped Humphrey up and put him in his tortoise bag. He thought of using a magic key to travel straight there, but decided the walk might help to clear his head.

He took a balloon down to the square and soon arrived at the Royal Library. It was his day off, so he left the bat droppings to the janitor and made his way to the one part of the building that he never voluntarily entered – the Chamber of Glorious Races. It held written accounts of every single race that had been run since the event began, over a hundred years ago. There were books for each year, detailing the names and skills of each human racer, along with stats about their magical beast. There were atlases containing maps of the various routes that had been taken. Travel guides for the destinations passed through. Record books for the fastest entrant, and the slowest; the largest magical beast and the smallest; the shortest race and the longest.

Dotted around the chamber were marble statues of various beasts that had triumphed in the past – ice hares and star gazelles, hurricane ostriches and ghost stingrays. Upon the wall hung paintings of famous racers – including Eli's own parents. Theo and Lara Fleet smiled down from their portrait, flanked by their sparkling gazelles.

'Are we in the Chamber of Glorious Races?' Humphrey asked, peering out through the vent of his bag. 'What are we doing here? You hate this room.'

'Hang on,' Eli said. 'I'll explain in a minute.'

He grabbed a stack of books and went to sit at a table directly beneath his parents' portrait. It took a while to find the right volume, but eventually the rules were there in black and white before him:

Rules for the Glorious Race
of Magical Beasts

Each entrant must sign up with
a living magical beast.

Entrants must travel with their beast at all times.

Entrants must wear their racing
medallion at all times.

Entrants must collect a map from each checkpoint.

Eli looked at the rules for a moment before turning to another one of the books in the pile. It contained a complete list of all the bottles of magic that had been awarded to first place. The bottles sometimes varied a little in size – and people said the race would end one day because they wouldn't be able to find any more magic to offer as a prize. The magic wouldn't be enough to help Nana on its own, but it would be valuable enough for him to sell, and to buy a magic ruby with the proceeds. In the same book, Eli found a list of all the magical beasts that had ever raced. There wasn't a single moon tortoise named there. Yet a moon tortoise certainly was a magical beast because of its moonlight shell, and ability to sniff up words, and speak to mages.

Eli felt like there were cogs turning and shifting inside his head as he worked it all through. There was nothing in the rules to stop him from entering the race with Humphrey, nothing at all. He would be allowed to enter. All he had to do after that was work out how to win.

He looked up at his parents' portrait, excitement and fear battling for first place inside him. Entering any kind of race – let alone *this* race – was really the last thing Eli wanted to do. He wanted a safe, quiet, comfortable life. He didn't want danger, or adventure, or glory. And it was ludicrous, anyway. Preposterous to even think of entering a race with a tortoise – one of the slowest known creatures in the world. People would laugh at him, probably, but then Eli had been laughed at before for being too bookish, or too tidy, or too uptight. People would always find something. Eli knew that he would quickly be assigned the role of joke contestant, the one no one expected to cross the finish line, let alone win.

But Eli was, after all, a mage. That meant he had a trick or two up his sleeve. He didn't believe anyone could possibly want to win the race more than he did, and that counted for something. Plus, Eli's love of books and time in the library meant that he had a much vaster general knowledge than most people. He knew a lot of things about a lot of things, and that would help him too.

Eli was scared of the race, of course. His parents had died participating in it. For many years, the Glorious

Race of Magical Beasts had been the ogre of his family, the shadow that could darken the happiest of moments. And Humphrey was an old tortoise, who deserved a safe, peaceful life. But even worse than all that, the thing that really made Eli hesitate was that he had made a promise to Nana that he would never enter the race. And now he would have to break that promise. It was a thought that made him shudder, but some things were even more important than keeping promises.

'Humphrey,' he said – quietly, so as not to disturb the hush of the library. 'Do you remember what I told you last night about Nana? That she's ill?'

It was always best to check because – with the exception of his birthday – you could never be completely sure what Humphrey would or would not remember. But this time the tortoise said, 'Yes, of course I do! There's nothing wrong with my memory, you know. Tortoises have excellent memories.'

'Well, I have an idea – a way to save Nana. You know which room we're in, so I'm guessing you already know what it is. But I'll only enter if you agree to it too. I won't take you without your permission.'

Humphrey knew how Eli felt about the race and so it was a subject they normally avoided. Eli realised now that he had absolutely no idea how his tortoise would feel about being asked to participate. But to his relief, Humphrey said, 'Oh! I would *love* to follow in the footsteps of my favourite adventurers and poets! Only ... will we be back in time for my party, do you think?'

Eli grinned. 'We should be. The race is usually finished in a couple of weeks. Thanks, Humphrey. You're the best tortoise a boy could ask for.'

He tried not to think about how furious Nana would be. Furious and upset. He hated the thought of her worrying at home alone, but what choice did he have? She would forbid him to go, but she wouldn't be able to stop him. Eli was generally very obedient, but this time he had to be true to himself. He had to try. Even if it was hard, even if Nana didn't want him to and everyone laughed at him. None of that mattered.

His mind made up, Eli felt a new peace settle over his shoulders as he gathered up the books and returned them to their rightful places on the shelves. He gave a final glance to his parents' portrait, wondering what they would make of his decision. Maybe they wouldn't approve, given that they'd both lost their lives to the race? And yet, they had both loved the race the way Eli loved the library. He thought they would have been pleased for him and excited, maybe even a little bit proud.

He left the library, which was just starting to fill with visitors, and made his way to Paradise Pier. This was a very different place from the docks. There was no Night Market, no shipwrecks, no beaches full of bones. Instead there were Ferris wheels, and stalls selling candyfloss, and pleasure boats that took people out on to the water for dinner, and drinks, and fireworks.

Registration booths had taken over a large part of the space, and the crowds milling about the pier all lingered to peer curiously at the racers lining up to enter. It was only the second day that registration had been open, so there were long lines full of the usual racer types. Eli saw lots of athletic builds and impressive beasts. Some people were his age, although many were teenagers or adults. The race appealed more to younger people in general, probably because of how physically taxing it was, although Eli saw one grey-haired man in the queue next to him, with what looked like a lightning parrot on his shoulder. He very much hoped he wouldn't see Vincent Tweak among the crowds. He could hear people around him gossiping about the rumour that a princess was entering the race this year, but there was always wild speculation about the contestants.

Eli had to queue for some time, and the straps of

his tortoise bag were digging into his shoulders and making him sweat by the time he reached the front of the line. Finally, it was his turn, but before he could even open his mouth, the man behind the desk said, 'Ah, you must be the clerk. Here's the paperwork for the entrants. We expected you an hour ago, by the way. You've got quite a stack to carry now.' He eyed Eli's skinny frame dubiously. 'Do you think you can manage it?'

'I've carried piles of hardbacks much heavier than that,' Eli replied. 'But I'm not a clerk actually, I'm a librarian.'

'Oh.' The man looked confused. 'Well, what do you want?'

'I've come to join the race.'

The man squinted at him. 'Is this some kind of dare?'

Eli frowned. 'Why would you think it was a dare?'

'Well, I've never had anyone sign up for the race wearing a suit before,' the man replied. 'Is that tweed?'

'Certainly,' Eli replied, automatically straightening his already straight cuffs. The movement caused his cufflinks – which were shaped like dictionaries – to flash in the sun. 'It makes for the best kind of suit.'

The man stared. 'If you say so. All right, mode of travel?'

'Library.'

This time the man set down his pen. 'Now, look, boy. I have a lot of entrants to get through and I don't have time for practical jokers. Get out of here.'

'But I *am* travelling by library,' Eli said, in a firmer voice.

'It's not possible to travel by library.'

'This fellow is very rude, Eli,' Humphrey said. 'Why don't we just go home?'

Eli took a deep breath. This was it – his last opportunity to turn back, to pretend it had all been a joke. If Eli revealed his secret, then it would disrupt his life in ways he couldn't even imagine. People would want to see what he could do, everyone would want a piece of magic for themselves, he might find himself tangled up with kings and generals, helping them to win wars and defeat enemies and such. But it was the only option he had and Eli wasn't about to turn back.

'It's possible if you're a mage,' he said.

The man laughed. 'You're not a mage.'

Eli lifted his chin. 'I am.'

'You must think I was born yesterday,' the man sneered. 'Mages don't look like you. And everyone knows there are none left in the world any more anyway.'

'I'm the last one.'

'Prove it.'

Eli reached into his pocket and dropped his large bunch of keys on the clerk's desk. 'These are my Keys of Knowledge,' he said. 'I intend to race with a moon tortoise. I also have some magical candles. One smells like an old bookshop, and another smells like a rainy day reading nook, and another—'

'I don't know what scented candles have got to do with anything,' the man interrupted.

Eli heard a smattering of chuckles and realised that a few passers-by had paused to watch, probably drawn by the fact that there was an argument going on.

'And these keys could be something you picked up in a junk shop.'

'A *junk* shop?' Eli was aghast.

'Let me speak with him,' Humphrey said. 'Tortoises are very persuasive.'

'He won't be able to hear you, remember?' Eli groaned.

'I can hear you perfectly,' the man replied.

'For goodness' sake!' a voice behind him exclaimed. 'What does it matter where his keys came from or how many scented candles he's got? He's got as much right to enter as the rest of us. Just sign him up.'

Eli looked over his shoulder at the girl behind him.

She was about his age, with a long curtain of shiny black hair hanging loose down her back and a gold circlet on her head. She had dark eyes and brown skin and wore a pair of glasses with bright red frames. An arrow quiver hung from her belt and a large bow was slung across her back. A sparkling white ice hare hopped around by her booted feet. Eli was surprised to see the creature and wondered how the girl was planning to race with it. Ice hares had once been quite common competitors since they were the perfect animal for a faery to ride, but rather like the great witches and wizards, it seemed that faeries were dying out and were now quite rare.

Eli wondered whether the girl had bought the hare from a faery, though, since it was fitted with a saddle, bridle and reins. The girl was dressed for riding, with a sleeveless white top tucked into a belted pair of white high-waisted breeches. Her black riding boots reached to her knees and gold flashed at her buttons and belt buckle. She looked every inch a professional rider, yet her ice hare was clearly far too small. Eli briefly considered pointing this out, but then realised that a boy racing with a tortoise was probably not best placed to be offering advice. Besides which, the girl had her arms crossed over her chest and was tapping one foot impatiently, with an annoyed expression on her face.

'No one signs up without a magical beast,' the man said, sticking out his chin stubbornly.

The girl looked at Eli. 'Have you got the tortoise with you or haven't you?'

'I have,' Eli replied. 'He's in my tortoise bag. He's—'

'Well, get him out, then!' the girl said. 'You should have done that to begin with, instead of going on about your candle collection.'

'It's not a collection,' Eli said. 'I've got a stamp collection, with more than two hundred stamps, but I've only got four candles, so it's not a collection.'

'There's no minimum number in the dictionary definition of collection,' the girl replied. 'Four is plenty.'

Eli's eyes widened in delight. He'd never heard another racer refer to the dictionary before, ever. Come to think of it, he didn't think he'd ever heard another child his age mention the dictionary either. He briefly wondered whether he should show the girl his dictionary cufflinks, but then thought better of it.

'That's ... very true,' he stammered. 'There's no minimum number for a collection, but there does need to be an *intent* to collect and some attempt at curation. You'd need to display, or organise, or label, or catalogue, or some such. Otherwise it's not a collection, but only an accumulation—'

'That's it!' the man exclaimed, thumping his fist on the table and making Eli jump. He pointed a finger at Eli and said, 'You're out! Back of the queue as a punishment for wasting time. *If* you have a moon tortoise – which I'm starting to doubt – then have him in your hands when you get to the desk next time. Otherwise you're disqualified.'

'You don't have the power to disqualify—' Eli began.

'Maybe not, but I have the power to send people to the back of the line for getting on my nerves,' the man snapped.

Eli sighed and turned away. The line was even longer now than when he'd joined. It would take at least an hour to queue up again, but it seemed there was nothing for it.

He glanced at the girl as he passed by. 'Thank you for trying to help me.'

'I wasn't trying to help you,' she replied. 'I was trying to hurry you up and get you out of the way.'

'Oh.' Eli tried not to feel too crestfallen. Of course a girl like that wouldn't waste time helping a boy like

him. She was so self-assured and capable, whereas Eli
was shy and awkward, as always.

'Nice cufflinks, though,' she added, flashing a brief,
warm smile that lit up her whole face and made Eli feel
a foot taller.

Then she swept past with her hare, and Eli made his
way to the back of the line.

CHAPTER NINE

'You're not going,' Nana said. 'I absolutely forbid it.'

Eli took a deep breath. It had been a long day after a sleepless night and he was tired. Tired of queuing, tired of waiting, and a little tired of being laughed at too, if he was honest. The restaurant had closed and the customers all long since gone home, leaving Eli and Nana alone at one of the tables. They each had a plate of untouched ice-cream cake in front of them, slowly melting in the heat. Fireflies blinked their bright lights in the darkness beyond the decking. And Eli's racing medallion lay on the table between them – a giant, accusing eye.

The medallions were how people back home watched the race. They were more than just discs of gold – they were actual magical eyes that broadcast everything they saw. Right now, the eye was closed, the golden lid covering the sapphire-blue eye beneath.

But once the race began, the eye would wake up. The medallions didn't broadcast non-stop – there were plenty of boring bits in a race that lasted for weeks. No one wanted to watch a racer going to the toilet, or eating a mango, or sleeping. But the medallions could sense when things got interesting or exciting, and then the giant eye would open and capture it all.

'I am going,' Eli said quietly. 'I've entered the race. It's done.'

'Then you will *unenter* and *undo* it,' Nana said, in a voice he'd never heard her use with him before. A cold voice of stone. 'You promised you would never go near the race. You promised me.'

Fleets keep their promises . . .

Eli had heard his parents say this many times. Breaking a promise now filled him with shame, but he steeled himself against it. How he felt didn't matter.

'Yes,' Eli said. 'But I was six years old and I didn't know the race would be my only chance one day. If I win, then we can get the magic ruby and we can—'

'I've already made it clear that I don't want you to find a solution,' Nana interrupted. 'You said yourself, you're not a little kid any more, so I'm extremely disappointed by this, Eli. I thought you would be mature and sensible enough to respect my wishes.'

'But you're only saying that because you don't want me in harm's way,' Eli protested.

'Of *course* I don't want you in harm's way!' Nana replied. 'If you love me, even a little, then you will throw that medallion in the bin and forget that you ever even considered entering that awful race.'

Eli gritted his teeth to prevent himself groaning out loud. He didn't know what to do and for a moment he wished there was someone else there who could tell him. But there was only him and Nana on the deck and this was a decision he had to make alone. He was trying to be brave for what felt like the first time in his life. He was trying to be selfless and put Nana first. He was trying to do the right thing. Yet here, in this moment, it suddenly seemed harder to work out what the right thing was. There were too many thoughts inside his head, all clamouring for his attention. Eli closed his eyes and took a deep breath. He didn't know what was the right thing – he could only trust his instinct.

Eli opened his eyes and forced himself to meet Nana's gaze. 'I love you,' he said, in a voice that was almost a whisper. 'And I've got this one chance to help you, like you've always helped me. I have to try.'

To his dismay, tears filled his eyes, and he thought that Nana would reach out for him like she always did.

That she would pull him into a comforting hug, and tell him to eat his cake, and that everything would be okay. But she didn't. Instead, she stood up so abruptly that her chair toppled over.

'I can't do this,' she said, her voice shaking. 'Not now. Not with you.'

A tear spilled over Eli's eyelid and ran down his cheek. He'd never argued with Nana before, not really. And he'd certainly never broken a promise before – not to her, or to anyone. It felt wrong and dishonourable and small. It made him squirm inside his own skin. But he wasn't going to back down, no matter how wretched it made him feel. He was determined to see it through, for Nana.

'Please—' Eli began.

She held up a hand to silence him. 'I've said all I'm going to,' she said. 'I'm not uttering another syllable on this subject.'

She turned and walked away, back into the house, leaving her ice-cream cake melting across her plate. Eli blinked back his tears as he gathered up the untouched desserts and took them inside. The two of them had never gone to bed cross with each other before, never. And knowing that he was the cause made guilt writhe in his stomach.

But if he didn't enter the race, then a few weeks or months from now, he'd be sitting in an unfamiliar foster home, wondering and wondering if he could have done something to help Nana if only he'd had the courage. The race started in a few days. Eli was going to join it and there was nothing Nana could do to stop him.

He spent the next few days making his arrangements – preparing packing lists, and shopping lists, and to-do lists. Eli liked a list. Lists helped break big undertakings down into little tasks and made everything feel a bit more in control. One of the first things he did was to formally notify the library and request a leave of absence. They were surprised and disappointed by the news and Eli was told that there was no guarantee that his apprenticeship would still be available when he returned. The thought of losing it made an icy sense of panic rise in his chest, but he squashed it down as best he could.

He was almost looking forward to telling Jeremiah. After all, his friend loved adventures more than anything. Surely here was one person who would applaud what Eli was trying to do, and might even respect and admire him a little for it. But it turned out that Jeremiah wasn't impressed by Eli's news at all. The two boys were sitting at the end of Paradise Pier, their feet dangling over the frothing sea below, watching Luther dive for fish. When Eli told him about the race, Jeremiah thought he was joking at first.

When he realised Eli was serious, he said, 'But you don't want to go on adventures. You've told me many times.' He straightened his back slightly and broke out in a startlingly accurate impression of Eli. *'Just because I enjoy reading about going on adventures doesn't mean I want to go on one myself. That's an entirely different thing. Entirely different.'* He raised an eyebrow at Eli. 'Those are your exact words.'

'I don't think I sounded as pompous as that when I said them,' Eli replied.

'Oh, trust me, you did.'

'Well, I don't particularly want to go on an adventure now either,' Eli replied. 'I'm doing it for Nana.'

Eli had always assumed that Jeremiah would join the race someday, but when he'd said as much a while ago, Jeremiah had shaken his head.

'It would be an adventure, sure, but I'm not likely to come first, so I wouldn't get anything out of it. Luther is amazing, but there are plenty of animals who are faster than sea phoenixes. He can't compete with an ice hare or a whirlwind jaguar. I don't sign up for anything unless I'm going to win it.'

'And never mind Humphrey,' Jeremiah said now. 'What about you? Even if by some miracle you managed to finish the Glorious Race of Magical Beasts, it wouldn't be enough. There are no prizes for coming last. And the fact is that you can't run. And neither can Humphrey. He can barely manage a brisk walk. At least you can do a sort of awkward trot, but a tortoise isn't going anywhere fast. No one enters a race with a tortoise. No one.'

'I'm going to.' Eli felt suddenly tired. 'Nana is really upset with me, and I know people will laugh, but I thought you'd believe in me, at least.'

'It's not that I don't believe in you!' Jeremiah replied. 'Of course I believe in you, it's just that . . . well, I mean, you're a librarian. You've never done a single daring or dangerous thing in your life. The race is dangerous. You know it is. And you know what you're like. You press your suits and . . .' Jeremiah waved his hand. 'You wear a tiepin. Out of choice.'

'So? Just because I wear a tiepin doesn't mean that I can't go on an adventure. It's nice of you to worry about me, though,' Eli said, desperately trying to find a positive in their exchange.

'I hate to break it to you, Eli, but I'm not just worried about you – I'm worried about *me*,' Jeremiah said. 'What happens to me if you get yourself killed? Your magic brought me here. If you die, then will I go back into the book? Would I go back to being nine years old or stay the age I am now? Or would I just stop existing altogether?'

Eli looked at him, a hollow feeling in his stomach. It hurt to know that Jeremiah was only thinking of himself, and wasn't concerned about Eli at all. 'I don't know,' he said honestly. 'I don't know what would happen to you.'

'So you're gambling with my life as well as your own?' Jeremiah's voice was suddenly cold.

Eli stood up. He hadn't expected this and he didn't feel strong enough to deal with it right now. He thought of the mistake he had made a few months ago and felt even worse. Lately, it seemed like he was getting everything wrong.

'You're right. I should have thought about it, and I didn't, so I'm sorry. But it doesn't change anything. I'm still joining the race. I have to.'

He turned and walked away before Jeremiah could see that there were tears in his eyes. He rather hoped that Jeremiah might run after him and try to make amends, but he didn't. So Eli went home and finished packing his largest briefcase. Neatly folded within were his magic keys, some tortoise jumpers, his assortment of scented candles, a few carefully selected books, some spare clothes and a travel iron. Nana still wasn't really speaking to him, and Humphrey had been asleep all evening, so once his shift at the restaurant was done, there was nothing left but to lie down and try to enjoy his final night in his own bed.

When Eli woke the next morning to find that Humphrey wasn't in his bedroom, he didn't think anything of it at first. He'd cut a little tortoise door into the lower part of his bedroom door some time ago, so that Humphrey could come and go as he pleased. He'd also built a tortoise ramp over their stairs, so Humphrey could travel to the ground floor and right out to the decking if he wanted. Eli often found him there in the morning, soaking up the early morning sun. He assumed he was out there now, and he'd collect him on his way out.

First, he dressed in his best tweed suit. He knew, of course, that a tweed suit was not a traditional choice for the race, and that it was hardly the most practical outfit for tearing around the world. But sometimes when you were about to embark on a difficult challenge, the best thing you could do was dress in a way that made you feel comfortable and the most like yourself.

'Why don't you make more of an effort to fit in?' Jeremiah had asked him, many times. 'You come to the smuggling streets in your tweed suit, calling people "good sir" and all that, and you wonder why you stick out.'

'But why should I have to change myself to fit in?' Eli asked. 'Would you? I can't imagine you ever being anyone other than who you are.'

Jeremiah had raised an eyebrow. 'But it's different. I don't . . . I mean, I don't have a hard time anywhere. It would just make things a bit easier for you, that's all.'

'I don't want things to be easier if it means not being myself.'

Eli lingered in his room long enough to write a carefully worded letter to Nana in his best penmanship, in which he tried to explain how much he loved her, how grateful he was for all she'd done and how sorry he was for hurting her. He sealed the envelope and propped it carefully on his pillow where she couldn't fail to see it. Then he took one last look at himself in the mirror, before picking up his briefcase and tortoise bag and making his way downstairs.

He found Nana in the kitchen, taking a tray of tortoise biscuits from the oven. The warm, spicy gingerbread scent made him wish with a sudden fierceness that he wasn't leaving for the race. If only he was on his way to a quiet day at the library instead. If only things were normal. But nothing was as it should be right now. Why was Nana making tortoise biscuits when the breakfast service was due to start soon? She ought to be elbow-deep in pancake mix. Perhaps she was still upset about the race and not thinking straight.

Eli cleared his throat awkwardly in the doorway and said, 'I've come to say goodbye.'

'Goodbye?' Nana spoke in an oddly bright voice but didn't turn around from the counter. 'Are you going somewhere, dear?'

Eli gripped his briefcase a little harder. 'I'm going to join the race. Like I said.'

'Oh, I don't think so, Eli. They won't let you enter without a magical beast.'

Eli glanced through the open doorway at the decking. He couldn't see Humphrey in his usual spot, but that didn't mean that he hadn't stumped off somewhere else. With a very bad feeling growing in the pit of his stomach, Eli went outside to check. But Humphrey wasn't there. Nor was he anywhere in the house.

CHAPTER TEN

Eli walked around calling Humphrey's name. But there was no sign of him and finally, Eli returned to the kitchen in defeat. 'Where's Humphrey?'

'Gone,' Nana replied. She had put the tortoise biscuits to one side and started on the pancake mix.

Eli swallowed hard. 'What do you mean, gone?'

'You can't enter the Glorious Race of Magical Beasts without a magical beast,' Nana replied, stirring a big bowl vigorously. 'So Humphrey is gone.'

'But ... but you can't take Humphrey. He's mine.'

'Not right now.' Nana finally turned to look at him, a regretful look in her eyes. 'I didn't want to take him from you, Eli, of course I didn't. I know how much you love him and he loves you. But it seems we're both doing things we never thought we'd do. I promise you he's quite safe. You can have him back once the race has started.'

She wouldn't say anything further on the subject, so Eli found himself searching the house again, as if Nana might have tucked Humphrey away in a cupboard, or under a cushion. Eli tried to swallow down his rising panic. Too late, he realised he should never have let Humphrey out of his sight. It had simply never occurred to him that Nana would take matters into her own hands.

He looked at his watch. He had less than an hour before the race started. Once the whistle blew, it would be too late. If Eli wasn't there to start with everyone else, then he'd be disqualified.

He could ask Jeremiah for help, but after their conversation at the pier he wasn't sure that his friend would be on his side. Besides, it would take time to track him down, and this was time that Eli didn't have. So he forced himself to stop, take a breath, and think. There were only so many places that Nana could have hidden Humphrey in the time available. Eli spent the next half hour scouring the Floating Quarter with no luck. He was just about to give up hope when he suddenly remembered those tortoise biscuits. The ones Nana shouldn't have been making because it was pancake hour . . .

He ran back home as fast as he could. His feet were

already rubbing themselves sore inside his smart shoes and he was sweating into his shirt. He'd never expected there to be this much running before the race had even started.

Finally he ran across the decking, where the breakfast service was now in full swing, and burst into the kitchen. Nana was bustling around with the other two chefs. Eli barely spared them a glance. Instead he went straight to the plate of biscuits. Nana had iced them with white and green frosting, but there was no disguising the soft silver glow around one of them, not if you knew what you were looking for. She'd tried to hide him at the bottom of the plate, buried beneath a pile of other biscuits, but Eli soon uncovered him. He spoke his name though Humphrey clearly wasn't able to communicate in this form because he remained silent.

Cradling the glowing biscuit in his hand, he spun around and fixed Nana with an accusing look. 'You turned him into a biscuit!'

Nana at least had the grace to look guilty. 'Eli—' she began.

'You should never turn a pet into a biscuit!' Eli exclaimed. 'That's infringing on his tortoise rights. You taught me that! What if someone had come along and eaten him?'

'You're lucky I didn't turn *you* into a biscuit!' Nana replied crossly. 'You might as well have a biscuit for a brain right now, for all the good it's doing you! And I was keeping a close eye on Humphrey. I would never have let him be eaten.'

'I only hope he's not permanently traumatised by this!' Eli said.

His gaze fell on the clock on the wall and he saw that there was no time left for arguing. He had to leave, right now, if he was to have any chance of reaching the starting line in time. He'd run out of things to say to Nana anyway, run out of ideas as to how to make things right between them. Every word he spoke only seemed to make matters worse, so he shook his head and turned towards the door.

He knew that biscuit magic didn't last long, and could only hope that Humphrey was back to his usual self by the time he reached the pier – and that no one squashed up against him too closely on the hot-air balloon, causing one of Humphrey's biscuit legs to crumble . . .

Nana didn't say anything as he picked up his briefcase, but he heard the snap of her fingers behind him, and the next moment there was no longer a biscuit in his hands but a living tortoise. Perhaps Nana had had the same concern about Humphrey being squashed on their journey through the city.

'Are you okay?' Eli asked him. 'I'm so sorry that happened to you!'

'It's all right,' Humphrey replied. 'It was quite cosy being a biscuit.'

Eli was grateful to Nana for changing Humphrey back, but also upset that their parting moments had gone this way. No warm goodbyes, no hugs. They hadn't even said that they loved each other. But at least there was the letter. He'd set down the most important things there.

He left without looking back and made his way through the city to the starting line at the end of Paradise Pier. The whole area was heaving with people. There were at least fifty contestants who'd entered the race this year, and twice as many spectators. Some were already waving flags printed with pictures of their favoured racer. There were hot food stands, and bunting, and even a brass band. There were magical beasts everywhere, growling, and chirping, and singing, and barking. A colourful spectacle of feathers, and scales, and fur, and claws. It was enough to make Eli's head spin. There were even two large blue dragons sprawled on the boardwalk, the wooden planks groaning under their weight. Eli paused at the sight of them. They were so majestic and noble – it was hard not to feel a little awed by their presence.

Eli didn't like being in big crowds, as a rule. Too many people made him feel anxious and hemmed in. Besides which, as soon as he slipped his racer's medallion around his neck, people began to look at him and point him out to one another. There had been a flurry of excitement in the city when the news spread that the famous Fleets' son was going to race and that he claimed to be a mage, but now that people saw him, Eli could practically feel the ripples of disappointment.

'But surely that *can't* be him, can it?'

Eli wondered if he'd actually heard the words, or only imagined them. He tried to tell himself it didn't matter. He was here in time. Humphrey was no longer a biscuit. Things were looking up. Then another voice filtered through to him.

'It's true! He's racing with a *moon tortoise*!'

A series of sniggers spread through the people. Eli winced, and tightened his grip on Humphrey. The tortoise didn't like all the crowd and noise either, and had retreated into his shell. Eli had been laughed at, in some shape or form, most of his life, so he'd developed quite a thick skin, and normally could ignore it, or try to pretend he hadn't heard it, but that didn't mean that it didn't hurt sometimes, or make him feel less worthwhile, less dignified, less everything. He made an effort to straighten his shoulders and was about to head towards the official starting line when, all of a sudden, Jeremiah appeared in front of him, Luther perched on his shoulder.

'Ah, there you are,' Jeremiah said. 'I was starting to think you must have changed your mind . . .' He trailed off, taking in Eli's outfit. 'You're not actually going to race dressed in a tweed suit, are you? Please tell me you at least packed some running shoes?'

Eli scowled. Why did everyone always have to make such a big deal about his suit? As usual, Jeremiah wore his captain's coat. It was a dramatic garment that reached all the way to his ankles. The outside bore the scuffs and stains of many an adventure, whilst the interior boasted a silk scarlet lining. Eli knew he'd never be able to pull off a coat like that. As for the sea boots – they were worn and comfortable, practically moulded to Jeremiah's feet and designed for someone who was going to spend hours running about the deck of a ship, often in bad weather conditions.

'Don't worry about my outfit,' Eli replied, a little more tersely than he'd meant to. 'It doesn't affect you, does it? And I've had enough to worry about this morning.'

'All right, no need to bite my head off,' Jeremiah replied.

'I'm sorry – it's nice of you to come and wave me off. It's just . . . Nana turned Humphrey into a biscuit this morning, so I've had a lot to deal with.'

Jeremiah sniggered. 'Well, you can't blame your nana for trying. And I'm sure Humphrey didn't mind. I doubt he even noticed.'

'Of *course* he noticed!' Eli realised he was shouting. 'Wouldn't *you* notice if you were turned into a biscuit? Just because Humphrey's a tortoise, and he's slow, and quiet, and keeps to himself, doesn't mean that he doesn't have feelings or that he can't be hurt!'

Jeremiah looked taken aback. Eli had never raised his voice to him before. 'Are we still talking about Humphrey?' he asked. 'Or are you just in a huff about the race?'

'Did she *really* turn me into a biscuit?' Humphrey asked from within his shell. 'I don't remember that.'

Eli ignored Humphrey's comment and looked at Jeremiah. 'I'm not in a huff! It's only that I didn't want to start . . . like this.'

He'd hoped to be calm and collected, to begin as

he meant to go on, to hold his head high with dignity. Instead he was flushed and sweating and flustered. He was aware of people pointing him out to each other and smiling as if he was a great joke. He *felt* like a joke in that moment. Even his tie was crooked, in spite of his tiepin. What if Nana was right and this was a foolish idea and he simply wasn't capable of pulling it off? Maybe he really was just putting them both through a lot of stress and upset for nothing…

Jeremiah's gaze flicked to the crowd for a moment too. Then he stepped up close to Eli, took him by the elbow and said quietly in his ear, 'Ignore them. They're not here. They don't matter. All that counts is whether you still want to enter the race, or whether you want to go home back to your normal life. So, which is it?'

'I want to go home,' Eli said at once. 'I want to go to work at the library and forget this ever happened. So much. But I'm not going to. I'm going to enter the race and I'm going to win it, for Nana.'

Jeremiah nodded. 'Then I'm right there with you.' He reached beneath his shirt and pulled out a medallion to match Eli's. 'I haven't come to wave you off – I've come to join you. I signed up yesterday. After all, why should you have all the fun? And someone has to make sure you don't get yourself killed.'

Eli felt a mixture of gratitude and annoyance. It would, perhaps, be nice to see a friendly face in the race. But on the other hand, he was tired of being patronised.

'I'm a mage, in case you'd forgotten,' Eli said. 'I didn't ask for your help and I don't need it or want it.'

'Eli,' Jeremiah replied quietly. 'Don't be a twit. I love you, but you need all the help you can get.'

There was no time to talk about it, because a warning whistle blew sharply, interrupting their conversation. All around them, racing medallions were opening their eyes. The race was about to begin, and suddenly everyone was scrambling for the starting line. As usual, the line had been placed in the sea itself, marked by an array of brightly coloured flags. Those racers with ships or aquatic animals were already gathered in the water around it. Eli saw all manner of sea vessels, from elegant ships with dozens of large white sails right down to humble rafts that bobbed precariously with every wave.

The magical sea creatures were less easy to see, but Eli spotted the silver fins of tornado dolphins, and knew that there were bound to be blizzard sharks beneath the surface too. There might even be a ninja starfish or volcano octopus. Eli recognised one of the ships – a sleek vessel called the *Spectre*. It belonged to a notoriously ruthless racer named Captain Quell, who used his ghost stingray to travel through the spirit realm. Eli's heart sank at the thought of competing with such accomplished champions, but he straightened his shoulders and stepped forward anyway.

The spectators parted to let Eli and Jeremiah through and they both hurried to the end of the boardwalk, where some organisers were handing out maps. The racers never knew the exact route the race would take. Of course, there were usually rumours, and plenty of speculation, but no one knew for sure until they received the official race map. It was rolled up like a treasure map, tied with a red ribbon and sealed with the racing seal. Eli gently broke this and eagerly unrolled the map. It had writing on the back too – a leader board of the top ten competitors, a little animal stamp next to their name to portray their magical beast. Underneath, there was also a running total of how many people were in the race, which changed magically as the race progressed. Eli saw that there were sixty-three people competing this year, although there were no names in the top ten yet as the event hadn't officially begun.

He was more interested in unrolling the scroll and

seeing the map on the other side, desperately hoping that the first round would take place near a library. Then, whilst all the other racers were running, or sailing, or flying, Eli could simply use one of his magic keys to transport himself straight there. But when he opened the map, he let out a groan.

'Ah, the Golden Sea,' Jeremiah said, peering over Eli's shoulder. 'Looks like the first checkpoint is right in the middle of it. I bet there's no library there.'

Eli gritted his teeth, annoyed by Jeremiah's self-satisfied tone.

'Actually, there are several sea libraries around the world,' he said. 'Some are underwater. Some are on little islands. There's one I know of that's right at the top of a lighthouse. Another is housed inside a library boat that travels between different ports. There's even a sunken pirate library in one of the shipwrecks near the Ice Cream Ocean—'

'That's all very well,' Jeremiah interrupted. 'But is there a library anywhere in the Golden Sea? I can't help thinking you would have led with that one first if there were.'

'No,' Eli forced himself to admit. 'There's no library anywhere in the Golden Sea.'

It was rotten luck. There were libraries everywhere.

Why did the first checkpoint have to be in one of the few places where there were literally no books at all?

'So how about it?' Jeremiah asked. 'Are you still going to say you don't want my help?'

As he spoke, he lifted the flap of his coat slightly to show Eli the inside. Within a couple of the many pockets, he caught a glimpse of two glass bottles. Eli wasn't surprised to see that one of them contained his sea chest, since Jeremiah never went anywhere without it. But inside the other was a miniature ship – complete with fleets of sails, and an octopus figurehead and an anchor.

'Let me help,' Jeremiah said. 'I'm sorry about what I said before. I shouldn't have brought up the egg-and-spoon race.'

'Beanbag race,' Eli said automatically.

'This isn't school and it's not sports day,' Jeremiah replied. 'If you want to win the Race of Glorious Beasts, then why the heck shouldn't you?'

Eli's anger with his friend suddenly ebbed away. Perhaps he hadn't been supportive immediately, but he was here now, and that was what counted.

'Thank you,' he said. 'I would very much like your help. For the record, though, I was prepared to travel over the sea.' Eli rummaged in his bag and showed

Jeremiah one of the books he'd packed: an adventure tale about a girl called Tilly who explored the world in a hot-air balloon. 'I've been in this book a few times and Tilly let me fly the balloon, so I know how to do it. I could take the balloon out of the book and fly across the ocean in it,' Eli said. 'So I'm not *totally* helpless without you. But the *Nepo* will be much faster. And . . . I'm glad you're here.'

Jeremiah grinned and clapped him on the shoulder. 'We'll show them,' he said. 'We'll show them what a librarian can do. Besides, a hot-air balloon wouldn't last long at sea. It'd get popped in the first storm. It's a good thing I'm here.'

They were just in time. Right at that moment, there was a loud blast on the starting whistle. The race had begun.

CHAPTER ELEVEN

All around them, racers were scrambling into action. Those already in the water were unfurling their sails, their magical beasts swimming and splashing through the choppy waves. Eli saw a torpedo dolphin leap right out of the water in a graceful arc, and then the large green tentacle of a volcano octopus smashed up through the surface before disappearing in a flurry of seaweed-scented bubbles.

The flying animals and their racers rose into the sky. Spectators stumbled back, hastily getting out of the way as the two dragons spread their huge wings and lumbered into the air. As always, there were several Pegasi, trotting briskly to the end of the boardwalk before spreading their white wings and lifting straight off over the water, their pearly hooves just skimming the surface before they flew up towards the clouds.

The land-bound racers were long since gone, having rushed back down the pier the moment they unrolled their maps, desperately trying to charter a boat. The cheetahs, and ostriches, and gazelles were all hot on their heels. Jeremiah reached into his coat and drew out the bottle with the ship inside.

'We'll have to swim for it,' he said. 'The water is too shallow next to the pier.'

Jeremiah drew back his arm and then threw the bottle out into the water as far as he could. It landed with a small splash, and at the same time, Jeremiah muttered under his breath, 'Hello, *Nepo*.' This caused the bottle to open and release the ship, which immediately sprang into full size. Eli knew that the bottle itself would be securely tucked away in the top drawer of the captain's desk, ready to be used again. All around them, people cried out in surprise, both at the suddenness of its arrival and at its startling and unusual appearance. The massive ship created a huge wave that surged all the way to the pier and crashed over the rails, soaking the people gathered at the end.

The *Nepo* was completely unlike the other galleons in the water. For a start, it was bright blue, with glittering golden spirals – not just the hull but the masts, and the rigging, and the sails, and even the anchor. Everything was a vibrant turquoise colour, as dazzling as a jewel, with spirals of gold fanning out across the surface. These bore a striking resemblance to the spirals of a wishing octopus – widely regarded as one of the most beautiful species in the world. And not only beautiful, but valuable too.

The *Nepo* not only resembled a wishing octopus with its colours, but it also had one for its figurehead. Instead of the typical mermaid, a blue octopus adorned the prow of Jeremiah's ship, its long tentacles sprawling down the side towards the water. Luther recognised the *Nepo* at once and spread his blue wings to soar across the water to it.

Jeremiah glanced over at Eli. 'Ready to jump?'

'Jump?' Eli looked startled. 'You mean ... you mean we're just going to leap into the water with all our clothes on?'

'Well, I don't know about you, but I didn't pack my bathing suit,' Jeremiah replied, rolling his eyes. 'It's a hot day. Our clothes will dry out quickly enough.'

'I guess so,' Eli said uncertainly. He hated to think what the salt would do to his suit. 'What about Humphrey, though? He can't swim.'

'I don't suppose you packed a tortoise raft? Or some sort of tortoise life jacket?'

Eli shook his head, immediately feeling guilty for not making Humphrey a tortoise life jacket.

Jeremiah raised an eyebrow. 'Have you prepared for this trip at all?'

Eli bristled. 'Of course. I've got a travel iron. And some spare socks. And a few notable candles, obviously, for—'

Jeremiah winced. 'Please don't tell me anything more. I can't bear it. Just put Humphrey on my back once I'm in the water.'

'That's not going to work,' Eli replied quickly. 'He'll slip off. Tortoises can't swim.'

'I know they can't swim! I might not be a tortoise expert, but I'm not an idiot either.'

Humphrey stuck his head out of his shell and said, 'I *can* swim. Tortoises are excellent swimmers.'

Eli sighed. 'Tortoises are terrible swimmers, Humphrey. I'm not falling for that again, not after you almost drowned in the fountain that time. We'll have to find something for you to float on.'

Eli knew by now that Humphrey had rather a misplaced sense of faith in his own abilities. Once he'd sworn blind that he could sword fight to an expert standard. Eli suspected that he sometimes muddled up the dreams and fantasies he had with reality. Tortoises were great dreamers.

'This is a boardwalk,' Jeremiah said. 'There must be a spare plank of wood around somewhere.'

They made their way back down the pier and soon enough found a piece of board that had once been used to advertise a funfair of some sort. It had snapped in half, meaning there was only just room for Humphrey, but Eli conceded it would have to do. Unfortunately, all of this kerfuffle had attracted quite a collection of spectators, who found it hilarious that a tortoise raft was needed in the first place.

'This is a *race*!' one of them yelled. 'You know that, right? And you're entering it with the slowest animal in the world!'

'Actually, a tortoise isn't the slowest animal in the world,' Eli replied. 'That would be the pillow snail. It can only travel an inch a minute. And the next slowest after that is the thimble starfish. It has fifteen thousand mini tube feet, but it can only travel a yard a minute.'

The heckler stared at him, his lip curling in contempt. 'Fascinating,' he sneered.

'Oh, it is!' Eli replied quickly. 'It really is! People are usually only interested in the fastest animals, but there are many fascinating creatures that make up the slowest species in the world. If you go to the animal section in the Royal Library and look under record breakers, there's an encyclopaedia that will tell you all about the other slow animals, like the banana slug, and the ocean manatee, and—'

'He doesn't really think it's fascinating, Eli, he was being sarcastic,' Jeremiah cut him off.

'Oh.' Eli felt deflated. He couldn't always tell when people were being sarcastic. He was never sarcastic himself. It seemed rude to be anything other than earnest, and it always confused him when others weren't as interested in things and keen to read about them in books as he was.

'I thought it was interesting,' a kid in the crowd piped up.

'Doesn't matter,' Jeremiah said, before Eli could start talking again. 'This isn't the moment to be a librarian. We've wasted enough time as it is. Everyone else has left except for us. Let's go.'

The two boys returned to the end of the pier. A few of the spectators trailed behind them, hoping for more laughs. Jeremiah dived into the water first. Then Eli tossed the plank of wood into the sea before lying flat on the pier and reaching down with Humphrey as far as he could. He had to let him drop the last couple of feet, but Jeremiah caught him and set him deftly on the board.

'*Promise* you won't try to swim!' Eli called down.

'All right,' Humphrey grumbled. 'I promise.'

Eli reluctantly dropped his briefcase and tortoise bag into the water, hoping his books would survive the trip. He was about to jump in himself when he spotted Vincent Tweak in the crowd. The racer wasn't rushing off to charter a ship, as Eli would have expected. Instead he was looking straight at Eli, a ferocious expression on his face. Eli stared back for a moment, confused. Surely Vincent wasn't still angry about what had happened the other night? He ought to have bigger things on his mind now that the race had started – but there was certainly something bothering him because he was pushing his way through the crowd, heading straight for Eli.

Whatever Vincent wanted, it couldn't be anything good, so Eli threw himself off the edge of the pier, trying to copy Jeremiah's dive. The problem was that Eli had never dived before, and the sight of the sea rushing up made him panic and he ended up belly flopping into the water instead. It was like landing on a slab of concrete, but worst of all was the cold. He gasped, which made him suck in seawater and start spluttering. All of which the crowd thought was hilarious.

'And to think that boy tried to claim he was a *mage*!' someone exclaimed.

'He'll never last past the knockout.'

Many people referred to the first round of the race as the 'knockout' because that's exactly what it was designed to do – knock out a good chunk of the contestants.

'Pull yourself together,' Jeremiah called over the waves. 'It's not that cold. Come on, let's get to the boat.'

Eli cast a quick glance towards the pier, but he couldn't see Vincent any more and he didn't waste time looking. He needed to put all his energy into swimming. Eli had never been in the sea fully clothed before, and he didn't know how Jeremiah managed to swim encumbered by his long coat and heavy sea boots. It was all Eli could do to stay afloat, especially as he had to push his bags along ahead of him. The two boys had a brief panic – amidst more laughs from the railings – when Humphrey, forgetting his promise, walked right off the edge of the board to plummet into the sea.

'Don't tortoises have any survival instinct at all?' Jeremiah groaned, after diving to retrieve him.

They set him back on the plank, a little embarrassed but otherwise no worse for wear. Jeremiah kept one hand on his shell to prevent him from walking off again, just in case. At last, they reached Jeremiah's ship. There was a rope ladder slung over the side for them to climb aboard, but even this was more difficult than Eli had anticipated. The ship seemed enormous in the water, towering over Eli like some sort of sea monster that might crush him. He swam forwards, but the waves battered him against the side of the ship, and he cried out as his skin scraped over rough wood and sharp barnacles.

'Grab the ladder!' Jeremiah called.

'I'm trying!' Eli gasped.

Salt water stung his eyes and burned his throat as another wave threw him against the ship hard enough to rattle his teeth. He felt a surge of panic at the thought that he'd hit his head and be knocked out, and then there'd be nothing to prevent him from being dragged beneath the hull. His flailing hands managed to make contact with the rope ladder and he grabbed on for dear life.

Eli had never climbed a rope ladder before. There were plenty of ordinary ladders at the library, of course, but library ladders had nice wide steps and railings to hold on to.

The rope ladder on Jeremiah's ship swung about with the movement of the waves, and Eli found it hard to get his shoe properly on to the rung. The rope dug into his hands, and the salt stung the cuts he'd received when he'd been thrown against the ship. It took all his strength just to cling on, his face burning at the thought of how foolish he must look to the people watching and laughing on the pier. To make matters even worse, his medallion's eye was open, meaning that all this was quite possibly being broadcast to one of the giant screens in the square.

Jeremiah had clearly had enough of being tossed about by the waves, because at that moment he slammed his fist into the side of the ship and yelled, '*Nepo!* A little help!'

There was a creaking, groaning noise which sounded a bit like the wood settling at first, as if the *Nepo* were just an ordinary ship. But in fact, it was nothing of the sort. The laughing and sniggering on the pier suddenly changed to shouts of alarm as a giant tentacle looped up out of the water. The tentacle was the same turquoise colour as the ship, adorned with golden spirals that glittered in the sun, along with pearly white suckers. The tentacle wrapped itself gently around Eli's waist and plucked him from the ladder.

'It's going to eat him alive!' someone screamed from the pier.

Eli knew that from the boardwalk it must look as if a giant sea monster had appeared beneath the ship.

It wouldn't occur to anyone that the ship itself had tentacles, or that it was alive, but both of these things were true. The *Nepo* deposited Eli gently on the deck, where he sprawled in a sad starfish shape, trying to catch his breath. Jeremiah deftly climbed aboard one-handed, with Humphrey tucked under his other arm, while the *Nepo* hooked their bags out of the water.

Jeremiah had come across Nepo in the first chapter of his book. Back then, she was an injured octopus, trying to protect her young from a group of poachers. They'd captured Nepo in a magic net that prevented her from using her wish magic. That was when Jeremiah arrived. He managed to chase off the poachers and rescue the octopuses, and when he removed the net around Nepo, she rewarded his good deed by using her wish to turn herself into a ship for him. Her babies travelled with them for a while, hitching a ride on the anchor until they were old enough to go their own way. Then it was just Jeremiah and Nepo, sailing the seas and having adventures. And it turned out that a ship that had once been a wishing octopus was no ordinary vessel. There was no other ship in the world that had tentacles and, inevitably, someone on the boardwalk recognised it.

'That's the ship from *The Seafaring Adventures and*

Exploits of Jeremiah Jones!' someone cried. 'Look, look! It's the *Nepo*!'

This was quickly followed by other shouts audible over the water.

'What's a Nepo?'

'I knew I recognised it!'

'Who's Jeremiah Jones?'

'How did the ship come out of the book?'

'What book?'

'Will someone please explain what's going on?'

Eli met Jeremiah's eyes. They'd never gone to any great lengths to hide Jeremiah's past. He hadn't changed his name in the end. But it had always been an unspoken agreement that it was something best kept secret, if possible. You couldn't know how people might react to magic. A character coming to life from a book might make them nervous. Then they could start saying that Jeremiah should be put back, or suggest that he wasn't a real person and so didn't have the same rights as everyone else. Either way, they'd thought it best not to find out. Until now.

'Don't worry,' Jeremiah said quietly, seeing Eli's crestfallen face. 'It would have come out at some point.'

Perhaps Jeremiah was right, but Eli couldn't help thinking that this was about the worst way they could have started. Their medallions still had their eyes open, so Jeremiah leaned closer to Eli's and spoke directly into it. 'My name is Jeremiah Jones and, yes, I came out of a book, and my ship is a magical octopus and I can fight sharks with my bare hands. Deal with it.'

Eli felt a prickle of guilt. It was his fault Jeremiah was here, his fault that everyone now knew who he was. Just because a medallion had its eye open didn't mean that the footage was necessarily being shown on the screens back home. After all, there were sixty-three racers, and their medallions might all be recording. Only one person's feed could be shown at any one time. But the eyes had a knack for knowing what people would find most gripping, and Eli would bet money that Jeremiah's words had just echoed out across the square.

'Chop, chop,' Jeremiah said. 'We're trying to win a race, in case you'd forgotten.'

He offered Eli his hand to help him to his feet. Luther was perched on the ship's railings, watching proceedings with a superior expression, and Humphrey was stumping contentedly about the deck. Eli knew from previous visits to the ship that there were many trapdoors Humphrey could fall into, or coils of rope to get tangled in, and that they would need to tortoise-proof everything later. But right now, it was time to get under way. A ship this size would normally require a crew of at least twenty men, but fortunately, the *Nepo* was no ordinary ship, and all she required was the word from her captain.

'Set a course,' Jeremiah told her. 'For the Golden Sea. And, *Nepo*? Sail as fast as you can.'

CHAPTER TWELVE

Eli was glad when the *Nepo* set sail, away from Harmonia's port. The city was his home, and he loved it there, but for now it was a relief to leave the jeers and disbelieving looks behind. And Vincent Tweak as well. When Eli mentioned to Jeremiah that he'd seen him on the pier, his friend said that he had probably been considering trying to hitch a ride on their ship but thought better of it when he noticed the tentacles. Eli hoped that was all it was, but something about Tweak bothered him. Before long, though, they were overtaking many of the seafaring racers. In Jeremiah's book, the *Nepo* was described as famously, unnaturally fast because she didn't only rely on the wind in her sails. As a part-octopus ship, the *Nepo* could also use her large, strong tentacles to propel herself through the water.

They passed the racers on rafts first, before rapidly overtaking some of the other sailing vessels too. The racers stared up at the *Nepo* with astounded, angry faces. No ship should be able to move that quickly, especially as there wasn't much wind today. One of the racers threw his ninja starfish on board, and the creature managed to spin around, cutting a few ropes, until Jeremiah snatched it straight from the air and threw it out to sea like a Frisbee.

It was a common thing for contestants to lash out at one another, so Eli wasn't surprised when a blizzard shark and tornado dolphin tried to send them off course with their whirlwinds, but the *Nepo* passed through both so quickly that she was mostly unscathed.

Eventually, they'd left many of the other boats behind and it was just the *Nepo*, alone on the open waters. Eli took the map from his pocket to check the leader board. All race maps were waterproof, so it hadn't suffered from its dip in the sea. He saw that the number of racers had already dropped by two down to sixty-one. Those two racers must have either broken a rule or perhaps been separated from their beasts. Eli hoped one of them was the one who'd sent the starfish to attack them. Either way, he felt like he could finally breathe a little easier. Even the medallions had closed their eyes – presumably they weren't that interested in the two boys tortoise-proofing the deck. Once they'd made it as safe as possible for Humphrey, Eli set his books and other belongings out to dry in the sun.

'So you really did bring a travel iron,' Jeremiah said, peering over his shoulder and shaking his head. 'I was hoping you were joking about that. Your old cabin is set up as you left it, if you want to get changed out of your wet stuff.' His lip twitched slightly. 'Nothing is ironed, though.'

'Thanks. And . . . not just for the cabin, but thanks for coming and helping me too. It means a lot.'

In fact, it meant everything. Eli knew he'd probably still be on the shore doubting himself if it weren't for Jeremiah. With his friend by his side, at least he stood a chance. Not only that, but it would be good to spend more time together, like they used to – before Eli got his job at the library and Jeremiah had started drifting away from him.

'Of course,' Jeremiah replied, already turning and walking towards the ship's wheel. 'No way I'd let you do this by yourself.'

Eli's shoes and socks were soaked, and he squelched his way across the deck to the nearest trapdoor. He climbed down the ladder to the corridor beneath, closing the door behind him so that Humphrey wouldn't topple in. As soon as Eli's feet touched the floor, the lamps on the walls lit up around him.

The interior of the *Nepo* was just as striking and unusual as the outside. It was the most beautiful jewel of a ship, with blue and gold tiles upon the floor and shining polished wooden panels on the walls. There were brass lamps with blue glass lampshades fastened at intervals along the walls in the corridor, along with hung paintings of wishing octopus and other sea life.

'Hello again, *Nepo*,' he said, running his fingers gently along the wall as he walked down the corridor. 'It's good to see you.'

He weaved his way through the maze of the ship until he came to the cabin Jeremiah had given him when he first stepped aboard years ago. In the books, Jeremiah was always very possessive and protective of the ship, and only ever allowed daytime visitors. No one was permitted to stay overnight – until Eli.

His cabin was just down the hall from Jeremiah's captain's quarters. When Eli opened the door and stepped inside, it was like coming back to his second home. It was the same kind of feeling he got whenever he was in the Royal Library. The cabin was neat and compact – everything had to have its own space in a ship, most things were nailed down, and the orderliness of it appealed to Eli. There was a single bed, a desk and chair, and a fitted wardrobe. A porthole let in plenty of sunlight, and Eli didn't even change out of his wet clothes before sitting himself at the desk and rolling out the map. On the back he could see the ten racers in the lead and wasn't surprised to note that they all had ocean creatures.

He turned the scroll over and traced his finger across the Golden Sea. The race covered such vast distances and Eli knew he could be away for weeks. He could only hope he returned home in time to make a difference to Nana. As he studied the map, he saw there were a couple of symbols printed on the Golden Sea, warning of pufferfish and sharks. There were also symbols for lighthouses, and a few small islands. All this was to be expected but, curiously, there were also three tree symbols in a little row, right in the middle of the sea, where the race checkpoint was marked with a red arrow. Eli peered at this, and realised they must be headed for a sea forest. Neat letters on the map said it was called the Forest of Bottles.

There weren't many forests in Harmonia, but Eli had visited various ones around the world during his trips to forest libraries. His favourites included the treehouse library in the Forest of Bear and the Pixie Tree Library in the fairy woods of Pook. Eli liked trees very much. Not only did they provide the paper for books, but they were quiet, and wise, and serene. There was something lovely and soothing about a tree. He'd never been to a sea forest, though, and didn't know much about them. And that simply wouldn't do.

He got up, stripped off his wet clothes and hung them to dry. A quick rummage in the wardrobe and he had a clean pair of trousers, sea boots and a plain white shirt to wear. Then he dug his keys out of his other trousers and left his cabin, making his way to the *Nepo*'s library. It contained a vast collection of books all relating in some way to the sea. It was sure to have some information about sea forests.

The library was Eli's favourite room on board the *Nepo*, and he felt a little shiver of excitement as he opened the door and stepped inside. Being surrounded by books made him relax and breathe easier at once. The library was a huge room at the heart of the ship, with double-height rows of bookshelves lining the walls. In between these were giant portholes providing views of the sparkling blue sea beyond.

A spiral staircase made of shells led to the second

storey above, where mother-of-pearl railings glimmered softly in the sunlight. Tall-backed captain's chairs dotted around made the perfect place to curl up with a stack of books. Giant shells served as tables, and there was always a tea tray somewhere, set with an elegant silver teapot containing hot, sweet tea, a teacup decorated with octopus tentacles and a matching plate holding three fish-shaped biscuits – chocolate and sea salt flavour. The *Nepo* certainly knew how to make people comfortable in a library.

As well as the portholes, there was also a chandelier in the shape of an octopus hung from the ceiling. The bookshelves themselves weren't made from wood, but from pale pink coral. The room smelled of old scrolls and leather-bound books, mixed with the faint hint of salty seaweed.

Eli climbed the shell staircase. He quickly located the section on sea geography and soon enough he was tucked into one of the captain's chairs with a large book open across his lap. There was a double-page entry about the sea forest in the Golden Sea. The trees were unlike anything Eli had ever heard about, quite different from those on land. He spent some time reading every word, soaking up the knowledge for later. Then there was nothing to do but wait.

The *Nepo* sailed swiftly, though Eli knew that the magical water beasts would help their racers travel fast too. He saw several rainbows arcing over the water, which were bound to mark the trail of a rainbow panther, and he felt another twinge of worry about Vincent. The panthers could only create a limited number of rainbows a day, normally between five and ten, but those could take them a long way. All the flying creatures would probably need to stop to rest at some point, on an island or cloud city, or else their racers would charter a boat for some of it. As they spent the next few days sailing, they spotted more than the usual number of extreme weather phenomena on the horizon, thanks to the racing blizzard sharks and tornado dolphins.

The *Nepo* could see these things coming, and would alter course of her own accord, but it slowed them down each time they had to do this. Still, they were making good progress and flew past several more ships. The *Nepo* gave them a wide berth in order to avoid any attack, and before long – to Eli's delight – they'd managed to inch their way onto the leader board at number ten.

It was quite an advantage having a sentient ship, especially since Humphrey had a real knack for finding danger and managed to stump his way right off the edge of the ship the first night. The *Nepo* deftly scooped him up with one of her tentacles and deposited him through the porthole into Eli's cabin. Eli fashioned him a little tortoise life jacket after that, by cutting up one of the human ones. He fastened it around Humphrey, deciding he should wear it for the duration of their voyage.

After organising the tortoise life jacket, Eli spent the rest of his time in the library, poring over maps, trying to predict what route the race was likely to take. Jeremiah, by contrast, preferred to lounge about on the deck, playing his harmonica. They had enough dried food and supplies in the galley to make up their meals, although Jeremiah warned that they would need to resupply at some point. The *Nepo* could create hot tea and chocolate biscuits out of seemingly nothing, but that was about the extent of it.

On the fourth day, they passed several more racing ships – narrowly avoiding the clutches of a volcano octopus – before reaching the edge of the Golden Sea. Through the ship's telescopes, Eli saw that there were at least three ships sailing ahead of them. He recognised Captain Quell's ship, the *Spectre*. He wasn't sure about the others, but knew from the weather that there must be a blizzard shark up ahead somewhere. He could see from the leader board that he and Jeremiah were currently in joint fourth place! If racers were travelling or working in a team then their names showed up together. Eli saw Captain Quell's name in first place, followed by three racers working together in second place and then another single name in third place. Eli knew that he would never have been fourth if it wasn't for the *Nepo* and felt a great swell of hope and pride. Despite all that business at the pier, they were doing fantastically well. He hardly dared to think it, but with Jeremiah helping him, he might have a chance of reaching that prize ...

Finally, after another day of sailing, the Forest of Bottles came into sight around midday. Just as the book had described, the trees were made of bone-white coral, reaching high into the sky, with elegant, leafless branches that twisted and arched above the water. Colourful starfish clung to the trunks almost all the way to the top. There were no leaves, but each tree had glass bottles hanging from its branches on loops of seaweed. Some were large, and some tiny; some looked relatively pristine, whereas others must have been in the sea for a long time and were covered in algae and barnacles. The colour of glass varied from clear to pale blue and bottle green. Most of the bottles contained messages written on rolled-up scrolls, but a few contained golden musical notes that floated about inside.

'Those ones with the notes are messages sent by mermaids,' Eli said, consulting the book he'd brought up on deck. 'These are all the messages in bottles that were thrown into the ocean but never reached the person they were meant for. The sea forest collects them from the water. It says here that most of the messages are thought to be distress calls from people who've been shipwrecked or lost at sea. Some are love notes or messages to people who've died. There are also rumoured to be some pirate treasure maps.'

'Well, it all seems peaceful enough,' Jeremiah said, looking at the bottles sparkling in the sun. 'So what's the catch?'

'According to the book, the forest belongs to Aqua, the mermaid queen,' Eli replied. 'And no one's allowed to open the bottles. She's afraid that some of them might contain mermaid secrets. There might be pirate curses in some of them too.'

'What's a pirate curse?' Jeremiah asked at once.

'I'm not sure,' Eli replied. 'But I don't think we should find out. The book says Queen Aqua has created an official position for her court known as the Uncorker of Ocean Bottles. Anyone else who opens one will face her wrath.'

'Hmm.' Jeremiah gazed thoughtfully at the sea forest. 'How big is her wrath likely to be, do you think?'

'The book didn't say,' Eli replied. 'No human has ever even seen Queen Aqua. She might never have existed, for all we know, or her reign could have ended years ago. Still ... perhaps we should try to warn the other racers? If one of them opens a bottle, then they might get hurt.'

'So much the better,' Jeremiah replied, with a hard glint in his eye. 'We're competing with them, remember? Anything that hurts them is good for us.'

'Even if we're being purely selfish, we could still get caught in the crossfire of a mermaid attack or an unleashed pirate curse,' Eli protested, shuddering at the thought. Dark butterflies swooped in the pit of his stomach at the thought of all the unknown dangers of the knockout round.

'Did you just call me "purely selfish"?' Jeremiah asked, raising his eyebrows.

'I didn't mean—'

Jeremiah waved a hand. 'Never mind. Look, I don't think we can warn anyone even if we wanted to.

There are already ships entering the forest ahead of us. Besides, you said yourself that Queen Aqua might not even exist. And I bet the racers will be focusing on finding the next checkpoint anyway, so they won't pay much attention to the bottles. Either way, we've got to follow the others.' Jeremiah patted the side of the *Nepo* and said, 'Steady as she goes.'

CHAPTER THIRTEEN

The ship glided forward through the waves and soon entered the forest. The eyes of Jeremiah and Eli's medallions both opened, sensing that they had reached their first destination and hoping for interesting and perilous events to occur. The water in this part of the ocean was crystal clear, and when Eli peered over the edge of the ship he saw that the pale coral trunks plunged down into the water as far as the eye could see. The trees were covered with sea life beneath the surface – not just starfish, but seaweed, and molluscs, and colourful corals.

Eli couldn't help thinking that the forest was oddly quiet, with no sign of any animal or bird life. He'd thought there would at least be seagulls roosting here. The gulls in Harmonia were a noisy, raucous bunch, always shrieking over scraps of fish guts down at the pier. But there wasn't so much as a single feather in the

Forest of Bottles. The only sound was the faint chink of glass knocking against coral. Eli shivered as a sense of foreboding washed over him. This was a sad, haunted place and he knew there were dangers lurking beneath the surface.

Now that they were closer, he saw that some of the bottles had sand and shells in them. Others must have been sent by sea witches because they contained small bones and dried, shrivelled-up seahorses, and lumpy black-wax skulls. The pirate messages were easy to spot because they bore the grinning Jolly Roger on the cork or bottle. A few of the bottles were so tiny that Eli thought they must have been cast into the water by sea fairies. It made him shiver a little to think that most of these messages were probably SOSs that had never reached their destination.

'Where is the checkpoint likely to be, do you think?' Jeremiah asked, peering through the pale trunks.

'The middle of the forest, probably,' Eli said. 'That's what they usually do for forests.'

They had to go slowly because the trees were bunched quite close together at points and there was only just room for the ship to squeeze through. They soon caught up with the three other ships that had been ahead of them. Aside from Captain Quell's vessel, there was a galleon rather like the *Nepo*. The racer on the deck was a woman with long blonde hair tucked beneath a peaked cap. She wore a blue fisherman's coat that reached to her ankles. Eli spotted the gliding flash of a fin in the water behind her ship, but couldn't tell if the magical beast was a torpedo dolphin or a blizzard shark. He realised she must be the one who'd formed the team he'd seen on the leader board because there were two other racers on the deck of her ship – one with a flying monkey and another with a lava cheetah. It wasn't unusual for racers to form partnerships to begin with, or else a single round could weed out all the swimming, or flying, or running animals. It was everyone for themselves towards the end, though.

The third vessel was a little sailing ship, and Eli saw that the racer on board was the girl he had met briefly back at Harmonia. He could see the sparkle of her ice hare at her feet and the bright red flash of her glasses. He was surprised to see a land racer here who wasn't part of a team, but her boat didn't look large enough to contain anyone below decks. Her long hair was tied up in a high ponytail, but otherwise she looked much as before, in her white breeches, black top and riding boots. She noticed him looking and lifted her hand in a greeting. Eli waved back, feeling oddly pleased that she recognised him.

They sailed on in a convoy, but didn't see any maps. Eli began to feel a bit nervous. The race organisers always put out enough maps for all the contestants. Most people wanted to win honourably, though it wasn't unheard of for an unscrupulous racer to take multiple maps, or destroy some of them, but he knew from the leader board that their group was the first to arrive. So where were all the maps?

'Aha!' Jeremiah suddenly exclaimed. 'I see what they've done. The maps are in the bottles, look.'

He pointed ahead to where Captain Quell was leaning from the side of his ship to pluck a bottle from a nearby tree. He deftly uncorked it and tipped out a scroll tied with ribbons and sealed with the racing crest. Eli knew the map would show the location of the next checkpoint in the race and he very much hoped that it might be somewhere with a library.

Seeing Captain Quell's discovery, the other racers turned their attention towards the trees, looking for maps inside the bottles.

'Take care!' Eli called across the water. 'The forest belongs to Aqua, the mermaid queen. No one's allowed to open the bottles that belong to her.'

Eli didn't know whether the others might already be aware of this, but it seemed sensible to warn them, just in case. The fisherwoman and the girl with the ice hare both raised their hands in acknowledgement. Jeremiah steered the *Nepo* to a nearby tree and carefully reached up to a low branch. Eli held his breath, watching him nervously. Some of the bottles were tied on with rope that had rotted in the sun and salt, to the point that it would probably snap if anyone brushed up against it. Fortunately, Jeremiah plucked two maps free without touching anything belonging to the mermaid queen.

The other racers all managed to find maps too, and the four ships began to sail quietly out of the forest in a convoy. Eli breathed a little sigh of relief. He guessed this location would be much more difficult for the racers that followed. They would find the low-hanging maps all gone and have to venture into the trees themselves, meaning they were far more likely to dislodge one of the other bottles and therefore disturb Aqua. Eli was glad he wouldn't be around when that happened and was about to reach for the new map to see where they were headed next when a burst of colours exploded over their heads.

Eli looked up to see a rainbow arcing towards them, as if an invisible brush was painting it across the sky. The rainbow came down to land right on the deck of the dark-haired girl's ship. She gave a cry that was part annoyance and part indignation as a rainbow panther appeared, galloping along the colours to land in a snarling heap on her boat. A racer clung to the panther's back and Eli saw that it was none other than Vincent Tweak. He was surprised to see him, as his name hadn't been in the top ten of the leader board the last time Eli had looked, but his latest rainbow had obviously allowed him to jump ahead. His long blond hair was swept back from his face and he was panting with the effort of their race across the sky.

'Hey!' The girl rounded on him. 'No stowaways! Find your own vessel.'

Vincent ignored her. He was gazing around, and Eli guessed he was looking for the maps. But then his gaze fell on the *Nepo*. His eyes narrowed and he reached up to grab on to a nearby tree, swinging himself up into the branches, followed by his panther.

'Careful!' Eli yelled. 'Most of those bottles belong to Queen Aqua. She'll punish you if you take one.'

Vincent's lip curled. 'I don't care about mermaid bottles.'

He dropped into a crouch. His eyes were still fixed on the *Nepo*, which was about to sail past, and Eli suddenly had the strongest feeling that Vincent was going to leap on to their ship. But then his rainbow panther took a step along the branch, dislodging one of the bottles in the process. It fell from the tree to land on the surface of the water, and they could all see it wasn't a map, but an SOS.

For a moment, there was a horrified silence. The racers on the other ships all froze. But nothing happened. Eli let out his breath in relief. Maybe the information about Queen Aqua was incorrect, after all.

'No mermaid queen,' Vincent scoffed. He pointed at Eli and said, 'You're a liar as well as a thief.'

Eli glared at him. It was especially irritating to be accused of stealing when all he'd done was snatch back his own tortoise. And even then, it had been Jeremiah who'd actually retrieved him. He was about to say something when the trees around them suddenly began to shake.

The coral branches trembled, and the bottles clanked together with a ringing sound. The water had been calm before, but now it churned itself up into foaming white crests. The other racers lost no time sailing their ships onward, eager to leave the forest behind. Vincent grabbed on to the shaking tree to avoid being thrown into the water. The next moment, the *Nepo* had sailed right past him.

'Is it an underwater earthquake?' Jeremiah asked, gripping the ship's railings for support.

Eli was more concerned about his tortoise. 'Where's Humphrey?' he cried, panicked. 'And is he wearing his life jacket?'

'He's right here by my foot,' Jeremiah replied. 'Tuck him somewhere safe, would you? I have a feeling things are about to get messy.'

He sounded quite pleased by the idea, but Eli was dismayed. They couldn't afford for anything to slow them down. Nevertheless, he took Humphrey and put him in one of the life-jacket boxes with a hastily whispered apology. He was just closing the lid when Captain Quell shouted from his boat in an alarmed voice. 'There's something in the water! Something big!'

Eli and Jeremiah both peered over the edge, but the sea was so rough that it was difficult to see. Then, all of a sudden, the water calmed once again, the final bubbles popping away into nothing. And Eli saw it – the gigantic shape at the edge of the forest. It was so large that it was difficult to take it all in in one glance, and Eli couldn't make sense of what he was looking at to begin with. For a moment he thought perhaps there was a whale gliding around beneath them, but then the creature twisted over and he saw the flash of a gleaming crown and realised he was staring into a huge blue eye.

He stumbled away from the railings so quickly that he tripped over a coil of rope on the deck and sat down with a thump.

'It's Queen Aqua!' he gasped. 'She's real! And she's a colossal mermaid.'

The books hadn't mentioned that fact. An ordinary mermaid queen would be bad enough, but a gigantic one was ten times worse. Eli felt his insides turn to ice.

Jeremiah frowned. '*Colossal* mermaid? I thought those were just a myth?'

But at that moment, the mermaid rose straight up out of the water. The pointed tips of her golden crown came first, closely followed by her hair. She didn't have lustrous, flowing locks, like the mermaids Eli had seen in paintings. Her hair was a wild tangle of seaweed and brown fronds of kelp, with bits of rope and fishing net tangled up in it. Her white skin was streaked with algae, and studded with shells and barnacles, sea snails and molluscs. The small ocean creatures also spread across her shoulders and arms and even dotted her face.

As Queen Aqua rose higher and higher out of the water, Eli cowered beneath her furious expression and storm-filled eyes. He could practically hear the shouts of excitement from the spectators watching back home. Water ran off Queen Aqua in great streams that soaked the deck of their ship. The shells and molluscs were so dense around her torso that they were like armour. Eli doubted there was any harpoon in the world that could pierce through. At her waist, her skin gave way to flashing green scales, each one as tall as Eli himself.

Vincent lost no time in scrambling on to his panther's back and the next moment, a rainbow burst through the air, dislodging dozens more bottles. The panther climbed the rainbow as nimbly as if it were a staircase. It quickly gathered speed and the next second the beast was racing along the rainbow stripes, going higher and higher, until it was clear over the other side. When it reached the water, Eli knew it would create a second rainbow to run along, and a third, and it would soon be miles from the forest.

Queen Aqua gazed down at the four remaining racing boats and then opened her mouth. No words came out – or not any that they could understand, anyway. Instead, she let out a piercing, blood-curdling cry that made all the bottles clink against each other once again. It was a dreadful sound, ferocious and terrible and wild. And it wasn't only noise that came out of her mouth, but a flock of birds too. They had bright orange beaks and wings like tattered sails.

'Oh no!' Eli cried. 'Those are doom puffins!'

CHAPTER FOURTEEN

'Doom puffins?' Jeremiah sounded aghast. 'That's not an actual thing! Is it?'

'Yes, yes, they're real! And look!' Eli pointed into the sky. 'There are stormgulls and peril parrots up there too! They're disaster birds. They sink ships!' He racked his brain for any useful facts from the book of birds back in the Royal Library. 'They punch holes in the sails and the hull,' he said. 'They're very strong and bloodthirsty.'

'Can you put Aqua in a book?' Jeremiah yelled.

As well as taking characters out of books, Eli could also put people in them. Animals too, potentially, but he needed to have a book in his hand and he also needed to know their name. He'd first discovered this ability back at school, during a particularly unpleasant lunchtime when he was being tormented by a bully named Tom Penman. One moment he was there, ripping up Eli's homework, and the next he had vanished inside the book Eli was trying to read.

Eli had been as surprised as anyone, and it had taken him a little while to work out how to bring Tom back. Unfortunately, he'd gone into rather a spooky book, with a cursed castle, and a lot of skeletons, and a very hairy spider. When Nana helped him get Tom out, they'd sat him down with a mug of hot chocolate until he stopped shaking, and then suggested that it might be better if he didn't talk too much about what had happened. Eli's secret remained secure, but he found that he was never too bothered by bullies at school again after that.

In this case, however, he had no idea what the disaster birds were called – if they even had names – and Queen Aqua was sinking down beneath the sea, apparently content to let the birds carry out her punishment. She probably would have been too big for him to put into a book anyway – he couldn't think of any he'd brought with him that would be suitable – and in a matter of moments, the mermaid queen was gone.

The air was thick with disaster birds, all diving towards the ship. The *Nepo* unfurled its tentacles and, fast as a whip, they knocked the birds from the air before they could get too close. The birds retreated, squawking indignantly, and quickly seemed to decide that the *Nepo* wasn't worth the effort. They turned their attention to the other ships instead.

Captain Quell's boat immediately descended beneath the water and Eli supposed it was following the ghost stingray into the spirit realm. The fisherwoman's boat suffered a few slashes to its sails, but her magical beast quickly came to her aid. The blizzard shark erupted from the sea in a blast of ice and snow, thrashing and snapping at any bird that came too close. Once again, the disaster birds shrank back, and before long they were all turning their attention on the dark-haired girl's boat. Unfortunately, there wasn't much that the ice hare could do to stop them. The girl swung the bow from her back and managed to take down some of the birds with her arrows, but she wasn't able to keep them all at bay on her own.

'This isn't fair!' Eli exclaimed. 'They're ganging up on her.'

'Not our problem,' Jeremiah replied at once. 'We should copy the fisherwoman and be on our way.'

The fisherwoman was, indeed, making use of the birds being distracted, and was already some distance across the water.

'But they're going to sink her ship!' Eli said. 'And none of this is her fault.'

Eli had always had a very strong sense of fairness and he especially disliked seeing anyone being ganged up on. It reminded him of his own days of being bullied at school.

'She shouldn't have joined the race if she's not able to handle herself,' Jeremiah replied.

He practically had to shout over the noise of the birds. They shrieked loudly as they dived at the girl's ship over and over again, shredding her sails and punching holes in the hull. In another few moments, the ship was taking on water. It all happened very quickly after that. One moment the girl and her hare were on the deck of the boat, the next they were in the water as the masts sank beneath the surface in a flurry of bubbles.

Eli hoped the birds would withdraw now that they'd sunk the ship, but instead they started to dive at the girl, pecking with their beaks and slashing with their claws. She shouted at them angrily, but couldn't use her bow and arrow now that she needed both arms for swimming. The birds were diving at the hare too, and they heard it squeal as a doom puffin pulled out a chunk of its fur.

Eli was appalled. They would both surely drown. For a terrible, dark flash of a moment, he saw his parents' deaths played out on the big screens in the square, the crowd falling into a stunned silence, everyone glued to the footage in fascinated horror as an avalanche swept them both from the summit of Bleak Mountain. A needless death was going to happen again unless someone did something. Eli wouldn't stand by and watch it happen, he wouldn't. He started towards the railings with some vague idea of leaping in, but Jeremiah swiftly grabbed the back of his collar and dragged him away.

'Oh, no, you don't. You'll sink like a stone. We might just as well send Humphrey to rescue them.'

Eli shoved his friend away. 'The birds will drown them!'

They heard another cry from the hare in the water below. The girl had an arrow in her hand and managed to stab the bird attacking her beast, but there were still dozens more swooping and diving at them. Fortunately, the sight seemed to be too much for Jeremiah too, because he thumped the railing and shouted, '*Nepo!* Get them out!'

At once, the *Nepo*'s tentacles unfurled and reached across the water to scoop up the girl and her hare. The ship lifted them right out of the water and used its other tentacles to bat away any disaster birds who came too close. A moment later, they were deposited on the deck in a soaking-wet heap, and Jeremiah was barking more orders at the *Nepo*.

'Get us out of here! As fast as you can.'

The *Nepo* didn't need telling twice. The sails unfurled and it set a course out of the Forest of Bottles at top speed. A few of the disaster birds trailed after them, but soon lost interest when the *Nepo*'s huge tentacles swatted them from the sky as if they were flies. Eli hurried over to the girl and tried to help her to her feet, but she pushed his hand away and scrambled towards her hare instead.

'Is she all right?' Eli asked, crouching beside them anxiously.

'She's got a few scratches from those horrible things,' the girl replied. Her hair had come loose from its ponytail, and she pushed it out of her face impatiently. 'They don't look too bad, but I'll need to clean them.'

'You've got cuts on your arms too,' Eli pointed out. 'I'll get the first-aid bag.'

He darted off and quickly returned with bandages and antiseptic wipes. By the time the hare and the girl were patched up, they had left the Forest of Bottles far behind.

'Well,' Jeremiah said, appearing beside them. 'That was exciting, wasn't it? Is everyone okay?'

'We're all right,' the girl said. She stood up with the hare in her arms. 'Thank you for helping. That was decent of you. I'm Raven, by the way.'

Eli gave her a shy smile. 'I'm Elijah Cassius Dewey Fleet. But my friends call me Eli.'

'Oh, I know who you are,' she replied. 'You're the boy with the moon tortoise. And the dictionary cufflinks.'

'I'm wearing encyclopaedia cufflinks today.' Eli started to hold his wrists up to show her, but then her mention of Humphrey made him remember that the tortoise was still in the life-jacket box. He hurried over to retrieve him and returned to set him down next to the ice hare. Humphrey stretched his neck out of the shell to peer at the hare for a moment, then went stumping past him, on his way to important tortoise business elsewhere.

'Incredible,' Raven said, staring. 'Everyone was talking about you two back at Harmonia. What's next? Someone trying to reach the finish line with a sticky-toed newt?'

'I'm rather fond of sticky-toed newts actually,' Jeremiah said. 'Besides, you're one to talk. I didn't see your magical beast being much use against the doom puffins.'

'We're doing very well so far,' Eli pointed out quietly, feeling a flash of hurt.

'I suppose you are,' Raven replied. 'Sorry, I didn't mean to be rude. It's just . . . a moon tortoise? Seriously?'

'Well, what about your ice hare?' Jeremiah replied. 'Don't you realise it's a faery animal?'

The girl raised an eyebrow. 'Well, that's convenient, seeing as I'm half faery.'

Jeremiah scoffed. 'Sure! Although, funnily enough, I don't see any wings. And even if you've got some faery blood in you, you're obviously too big to ride an ice hare.'

Eli tried to shush him, but Jeremiah was on a roll.

'What?' he asked. 'Pardon me if it's impolite to point out that this hare will be squashed flat if she tries to sit on it. In fact, if you try to sit on him then I'm taking him off you.'

'She's a she,' Raven said. 'And I *am* half faery.' She scraped her hair back and Eli realised that the tips of her ears were pointed. She nodded down at her hare. 'This is Perrie. And I can ride her because I can switch between human and faery size.'

She screwed her eyes up tight and the next moment she disappeared with a faint *pop*. But then Eli realised she hadn't disappeared, after all – she had only shrunk.

She was still standing on the deck, but she was now the height of a faery – the perfect size for riding an ice hare. She hopped on Perrie's back, and Eli saw that the saddle was a perfect fit for her.

'That's amazing,' he said. 'I've never met a person who's half human and half faery before.'

'And I've never met a mage,' Raven replied. 'Or a fictional character.'

Eli turned towards Jeremiah to introduce him properly, but he'd taken himself off to the other side of the deck, where he was dragging one of the lifeboats out from under its tarpaulin.

'What are you doing?' Eli called.

Jeremiah paused and looked up. 'Isn't it obvious? I'm getting a boat for our uninvited guest.'

Eli's mouth fell open. 'You can't just set her adrift in the middle of the Golden Sea!'

'I can and I'm going to,' Jeremiah replied firmly. 'The danger is past. Queen Aqua and her birds have gone. The Forest of Bottles will soon be lost on the horizon. We can't go picking up every waif and stray who comes along. We'll never win that way. Sorry, Eli, but if you're racing with a tortoise then you need all the help you can get. Besides, the *Nepo*'s lifeboats are much nicer than normal ones. Look, they come with a picnic basket, and there's a blanket, and a portable barbecue, and—'

'No,' Eli said firmly. 'I'm not setting anyone adrift.'

It was a very dangerous thing to be all alone and lost at sea. Racers had died that way in the past and Eli didn't want that on his conscience. He liked Raven because she was tough and knew how to use a dictionary, but he would have done the same for any racer, even Vincent Tweak. His parents had raced this way too. They didn't work in partnership with anyone, but they never sabotaged other racers, they never put anyone in danger and if anyone was hurt or in desperate need of assistance then they would stop to help if they could.

We win honourably, Eli's mum had said. *Or not at all.*

'I can pay for our voyage,' Raven said, transforming back into human size. 'Just drop me off at the nearest port en route to the Island of Joo-Joo Bubs.'

'What makes you think that's where we're heading next?' Jeremiah asked, fixing her with a suspicious look. 'You haven't opened your racing map yet. I saw it fall out of your pocket on the ship.'

'Oh, I … I saw the fisherwoman's map,' Raven quickly said.

'I don't see how,' Jeremiah replied. 'Since she was on

a different boat from you altogether. You must think we're pretty stupid.'

Raven shrugged. 'Well, you are trying to race with a tortoise,' she pointed out. 'But, all right, yes, I already knew the next location. In fact, I know all the racing checkpoints.'

'Impossible,' Jeremiah scoffed. 'They don't tell the racers in advance.'

'That doesn't mean someone can't find out if they're really determined and a little bit sneaky,' Raven replied.

Eli took his map from his pocket, broke the seal and unrolled it. 'She's right,' he said. 'Our next stop is the Island of Joo-Joo Bubs.'

He flipped the map over to look at the leader board on the other side and saw that he, Eli and Raven were now all taking the third place together.

He frowned. 'That's odd. Where's Vincent Tweak? He was the first to leave the sea forest, so he ought to be in first place, but it's still showing as Captain Quell.'

'Is that the blond boy who barged on to my boat?' Raven said, wrinkling her nose.

'Yes, that's him. He was in the lead, but he's not showing in the top ten at all.'

'Who cares?' Jeremiah put in. 'He probably just sent his rainbow in the wrong direction or something. Let's concentrate on ourselves. I've never heard of the Island of Joo-Joo Bubs, but it looks remote. Too remote for a library.'

Eli felt a big smile spread across his face. 'Actually,' he said, 'the Island of Joo-Joo Bubs is home to the lighthouse library I mentioned before. We can travel directly there.'

'Good,' Jeremiah said. 'Some luck at last.'

'Um, I hate to break it to you, but the Island of Joo-Joo Bubs is several days' sail away,' Raven replied. 'Not only that, but the most direct route will take you through seas containing whirlpools and salt sharks.'

'Not for us,' Jeremiah grinned.

'I'm a book mage,' Eli said. 'And I've got keys that can take us to any library in the world.'

Raven looked as if she couldn't quite decide whether he was joking or not.

'Well,' she said. 'This I'd like to see.'

CHAPTER FIFTEEN

Eli was itching to summon the keys and travel to the lighthouse library at once, but it wasn't quite that straightforward. First, they needed somewhere to dock so that Jeremiah could shrink the *Nepo* back into its glass bottle. If they travelled directly from the boat, then they would be forced to leave it behind. And it wouldn't work to head straight for the nearest bit of rock or uninhabited island because there would need to be a door somewhere to use the key on.

They consulted the sea maps and eventually decided to set sail for the Milkshake Islands. These were quiet, and peaceful – mostly taken up with dairy farms and the cows who provided milk for popular milkshake bars in cities like Harmonia.

'There's bound to be a door there somewhere we can use,' Eli said.

'And nothing too dangerous,' Jeremiah agreed. 'I'll set a course. We'll probably reach it by the morning if we sail on through the night.' He glanced at Raven. 'So we're definitely not getting a lifeboat out?'

Eli shook his head. He looked at Raven. 'You're welcome to travel with us to the Island of Joo-Joo Bubs. We can go our separate ways after that.'

'Thanks,' Raven replied. 'That works for me.'

'What is a joo-joo bub anyway?' Jeremiah asked.

'I'm not sure,' Eli replied. 'But that's what libraries are for. I don't actually know where to start with the joo-joo bubs, though. I've got no idea whether they're a type of animal, or plant, or seaweed, or something else altogether.'

'For all we know,' Raven said, 'a joo-joo bub could be some sort of slobbering monster.'

'It sounds jollier than that to me,' Jeremiah replied. 'Like it ought to be something bouncy.'

'Well, as we've got no idea where to start, it might take a little while to narrow down the right book,' Eli said. 'If I had some help, then it could really speed up—'

'Don't look at me.' Jeremiah cut him off. 'Being around that many books makes me feel twitchy and itchy. Besides, someone needs to steer the ship.'

Eli frowned. 'The *Nepo* can sail herself—'

'Sure, but she likes to have me around for moral support,' Jeremiah said.

'You'd still be with her in the library,' Eli protested. 'It's all part of the same ship.'

'A captain's place is on the deck,' Jeremiah insisted. 'Especially if there are whirlpools and salt sharks on the horizon.'

The *Nepo* backed up Jeremiah's point just then by unfurling one of her long blue tentacles and plonking a captain's hat on his head.

'Thanks,' he said, grinning as he straightened the hat.

'We're heading for the Milkshake Islands,' Raven pointed out. 'There's nothing on the horizon except sleepy cows and cold strawberry drinks.'

'Ooh, I could really go for a cold strawberry drink right about now,' Jeremiah said. 'Anyway, I'll leave you to it. I've got important captain's stuff to do.'

He turned and walked away. Eli sighed and looked at Raven. 'He's gone off to snooze in a hammock somewhere.'

'Why did he enter the race if he doesn't care about winning?' Raven asked, perplexed.

'He just came to keep an eye on me,' Eli replied. He felt a sudden surge of embarrassment. He'd made it sound as if Jeremiah was his babysitter.

'Well, I'll help you in the library,' Raven said. 'I like books. And we need to know what we're up against.'

'Thank you,' Eli replied. 'Would you like to get cleaned up first? You must feel sticky after being in the sea. There are probably some spare dry clothes around here somewhere and I can show you where the bathroom is.'

Once Raven had showered and changed into a dry set of sailing clothes, she joined Eli in the library. Jeremiah had always been weirdly unimpressed by the glorious room, so it was a delight to Eli to show it to someone who appreciated it.

'Well, this is just … it's incredible!' Raven said, staring around in awe.

Perrie had come with her and hopped off into the stacks, eager to explore. Eli sat at one of the desks, a pile of books in front of him. He gestured to them and said, 'I'm just checking the indexes for any mention of joo-joo bubs. No luck so far.'

'Right. I'll join you.'

Raven selected some books and sat down at the table opposite Eli. Together, they went through volume after volume, flicking pages and checking indexes. Eli quickly found he enjoyed Raven's company. She made a comment every now and then, or else drew his attention to something she'd read in a book, but mostly they worked together quietly. Things were very rarely quiet when Jeremiah was around, and it made a pleasant change to share some calm companionship within the haven of a library. Yet the hours dragged slowly by, and soon the afternoon melted into the evening and they still hadn't found a single mention of joo-joo bubs anywhere. Eli sighed and looked up to see that the sea outside had been painted golden by the sunset.

Raven closed a book with a thud and said, 'This is hopeless. I don't suppose this library has any sort of librarian at all?'

Eli shook his head. 'No one's allowed to stay on board the *Nepo*. Well ... no one but us. It's one of Jeremiah's rules. He likes to travel alone.'

'Is he really from a book?' Raven asked, looking curious.

Eli nodded. 'I took him out when we were little.'

'Why?'

'I was lonely.' Eli blushed. It sounded worse out loud. 'I, um, I'd always wanted a brother. And Jeremiah was ... well, he's my favourite character. Who doesn't want to be best friends with their favourite character?'

'Amazing.' Raven looked a little envious. 'I can think of several characters I'd take out of books if I could.

And he's just lived in our world ever since? Even though he's not a real person?'

Eli was shocked to hear her say such a thing. This was exactly the sort of thinking he'd worried about, and the reason he'd wanted to keep Jeremiah's origins a secret. 'Oh, but he *is* a real person! He's as real as you and me!'

'I like to think so,' Jeremiah said.

Eli flinched and turned to see his friend standing in the doorway. It was rotten luck that he couldn't have arrived when they were discussing indexes or librarians. It had to be when Raven had just said something like that, something that would definitely sting. Jeremiah's tone had been light enough, but he didn't look happy at all. And to make matters worse, Eli heard the soft, distinctive *click* of another padlock clicking open on the sea chest. As always, Jeremiah shuddered at the sound and went pale.

'I'm sorry. I didn't mean to insult you,' Raven said, looking uncomfortable. 'I've just ... never met a fictional character before, so I'm trying to understand, that's all.'

Jeremiah shrugged. 'I don't care what you think of me. I only came to say that dinner is served in the dining room. I thought you might be hungry as the two of you have been down here for hours.'

Eli's feeling of guilt intensified. It was nice of Jeremiah to have prepared food for them, which made it even worse that he'd walked in to find himself being discussed. Although he hadn't *walked* in, as such – he was lingering in the doorway. Eli didn't think he'd ever seen Jeremiah cross the threshold into this room.

'But if you want dinner then you'd best head to the dining room before I eat it all.' His eyes flicked to Raven. 'I might not be quite as real as *you* are, but I'm real enough to get a bit peckish from time to time.'

He turned on his heel and walked away before they could reply. Raven grimaced. 'I've offended him, haven't I?'

'You said he wasn't a real person,' Eli said. 'Of course you offended him. But Jeremiah doesn't like many people anyway. He *does* have a huge appetite, though, so we'd best get to the dining room. I'll put away the books later.'

They got up from the table, stretching out muscles that were stiff from sitting still for so long. Then they each collected up their magical beast and Eli led the way down the corridor.

'This is an extraordinary ship,' Raven said, gazing at the octopus paintings on the wall as they passed by. 'I've never seen anything like it.'

'It's Jeremiah's pride and joy,' Eli replied. 'He loves the *Nepo*.'

They reached the dining room, and Eli opened the door to reveal a large room dominated by a long wooden table. The polished wood glowed in the golden light spilling in through the windows, and the table was set with the *Nepo*'s china. The plates and bowls were blue and white, painted with elegant octopus tentacles, and the goblets were made from cut glass. The dining room walls were covered in soft green wallpaper depicting twisting strands of seaweed. If you looked closely, you could see little octopus babies playing within the fronds.

Jeremiah had made his famous seafood stew, which was just about one of the most delicious things Eli had ever tasted. They'd run out of bread, but Jeremiah had set out some crackers, spread with the last of their butter to go with it. The table was easily large enough to seat twenty people, and Jeremiah had taken his usual place at the head of the table. He barely glanced at Eli and Raven as they joined him. Even the chairs were fancy, with tall backs painted with different octopuses. Jeremiah's was a wishing octopus, whereas Eli's chair had a munchkin octopus and Raven's was a ghost octopus.

'I didn't expect a room like this,' Raven said. 'It's very beautiful.'

Eli got the sense she was trying to make up for her earlier misstep, but Jeremiah clearly wasn't in the mood for reconciliation.

'I suppose you thought someone like me would have a dirty galley crawling with sea roaches,' he remarked.

'Of course not!' Raven replied. She reached for her spoon and dipped it hastily into her stew. 'It's just ... you don't normally find such beautiful things on board a ship, that's all.'

'The *Nepo* is no ordinary ship,' Jeremiah said. There was a spiky edge to his tone, and an awkward silence fell around the table.

In an attempt to clear the air, Eli said, 'We haven't had any luck at all with the joo-joo bubs.'

'Then it will just have to be a happy surprise when we get there,' Jeremiah replied. 'I'm sure we can deal with them, whatever they are.'

Eli wasn't so sure. Getting himself out of sticky situations was what Jeremiah excelled at, but most people didn't wrestle with sharks and live to tell the tale. Still, if there were no answers to be found in the library, then he wasn't sure what else they could do.

And it wasn't as if any of the other racers were likely to have much idea about the joo-joo bubs either.

'If there's a lighthouse with a library in it, then the island can't be all bad,' Raven said. 'This soup is delicious, by the way.'

'It's not a soup, it's a stew,' Jeremiah snapped. 'But how wonderful that it meets your high standards. I'm so relieved.'

Eli winced at the coldness of Jeremiah's tone. Raven slowly laid down her spoon.

'Okay.' She stood up calmly. 'You clearly don't want me here, and I'd hate to be an unwelcome guest at the table, so Perrie and I will take ourselves up on deck where we won't be a bother to anyone.'

She walked off, her ice hare hopping along at her heels. For a moment, there was silence. And then Eli burst out, 'Why do you have to be like that?'

Jeremiah pushed his bowl away and folded his arms over his chest. 'Like what?'

'You know what. You like to make out you're hard and heartless, for some reason, but you're the one who told the *Nepo* to fish Raven out of the sea in the first place.'

'I didn't want the hare to drown, that's all,' Jeremiah replied with a shrug. 'I like hares. They have nice ears.'

'You go to the effort of preparing a meal for her, but then you're rude.'

'*Was* I rude?' Jeremiah asked. 'Really? I don't see how. I only said I was glad that she liked the stew. Besides, I still don't understand why she's here in the first place. I might have asked the *Nepo* to fish her out of the sea, but I wasn't expecting her to stay on board forever – you're the one who insisted on that. So, this is . . . what is this, exactly? Some sort of crush?'

Eli blushed. 'No! She needed our help. And it was the right thing to do.'

Jeremiah rolled his eyes. 'Whatever. If you'll excuse me, I think I've lost my appetite too.'

He stood up and walked out of the room. Eli sighed and ate his dinner in a glum mood. This seemed a poor way to have their first meal together. He'd enjoyed working with Raven in the library and had almost made the mistake of thinking of her as a teammate but, of course, she wasn't. She was a competitor, who would soon leave the *Nepo*. Chances were that they wouldn't see her again, except in passing, for the duration of the race. Eli felt a pang of regret at the thought. He would have liked to get to know Raven better and to see if they might become friends. He was glad of Humphrey, tucked beneath his chair, quietly humming himself to sleep. Jeremiah could be such hard work sometimes that his tortoise's gentle, peaceful company came as something of a relief.

After eating, Eli checked the leader board again. They were still travelling in third place and there was still no sign of Vincent in the top ten. That should have been reassuring, but Eli just felt unnerved. There was something that wasn't right about Vincent. Eli wondered whether he might be from a racing family that bore a grudge against his parents. Theo and Lara hadn't made many enemies because of the honourable way they raced, but perhaps they'd managed a last-minute win and a Tweak had come second and resented the loss?

There had been sixty-one racers before the first round, but Eli saw that there were only twenty contestants listed now. He guessed that some of the bottles that had fallen into the water at the sea forest had contained racing maps. They must have sunk or else bobbed off out to sea. And he knew from previous races that many of the contestants would have turned back when they realised the danger. Squaring up against colossal mermaids and doom puffins wasn't for everyone. Eli felt a flicker of pride that they'd successfully faced the first round and were now on to the second.

He left Humphrey asleep under the table and made his way up on deck for some air. It was dark and a silvery moon bathed the ship and sea in a pale light. There was a rhythmic *whoosh, whoosh* as the ship cut through the waves, along with the sighing of the wind whistling around the sails. Eli thought he was alone at first, but then he noticed that Jeremiah was at the helm, his hands draped loosely over the large wheel.

Jeremiah probably didn't notice Eli from this far away, but the moonlight painted him in a stark silhouette. His captain's coat flapped around his legs, and there was something about the angle of his chin and the way he held himself that suddenly made Eli feel he could believe the theory about Jeremiah being an outcast prince. He had a prince's pride, that was for sure. Luther perched on a railing nearby, quietly loyal as ever.

'It got lonely sometimes,' Jeremiah had said to Eli once, on one of the rare occasions when he'd opened up a little bit about his past. 'With only Luther and Nepo for company, I mean. You've always said that when I came out of the book I helped save you, but it worked the other way around too.'

Eli felt a sudden surge of an emotion that was both sad and sweet. He loved Jeremiah, but he worried about him too. And recently, more and more, it had felt as if they were coming to the end of something. That things were about to change and that he and Jeremiah were growing apart somehow. It made Eli feel melancholy for something he hadn't even lost yet. So he gave himself a little shake and, as always when he was feeling unsettled, he headed for the library.

CHAPTER SIXTEEN

If there was anything Eli loved more than the Royal Library first thing in the morning, it was a library on board a ship at midnight. There might not have been bats swooping in through the windows, but there was moonlight winking on inky waves beyond the portholes, and the soothing rocking motion of the *Nepo* as it glided over the vast ocean. The lamps glowed softly on the walls and it seemed to Eli that the books rustled their many pages, just a little, when he walked in, as if they were welcoming him.

He wasn't planning on doing any more joo-joo bub research. They'd be at the Milkshake Islands in the morning and Eli needed to be ready with the library key. He took a seat at a table and had just spread all his keys across the surface when Raven walked in. She'd changed into her racing outfit, and Eli wondered whether there was some sort of faery charm on the clothing to keep it so pristine and white.

'Oh,' Raven said. 'I wasn't expecting to find anyone here. Thanks for the cheese and biscuits, by the way.'

Eli looked blank. 'What cheese and biscuits?'

'A plate was left outside my door.'

'It wasn't me. It must have been Jeremiah.'

Raven shook her head. 'I can't work him out.'

Eli knew his friend could be waspish sometimes, but he was a good soul underneath.

'I guess he didn't want you to go hungry,' Eli said. 'I'm sorry about Jeremiah. He's—'

Raven waved his words away. 'It's his ship; he can be however he likes. And I *did* insult him first, even if it was by accident. I couldn't sleep. Do you mind if I join you?'

'Oh, no, please do. I thought I'd start looking for the key,' Eli said. 'The one for the lighthouse library.'

'Is that them?' Raven asked, drawing up a chair on the opposite side of him. 'Your magic keys?'

'Yes, except for this one.' Eli indicated a large key with a metal tentacle wrapped around it. 'That's the *Nepo*'s library key. The others are mine, though.'

'But there are only, what, twenty keys on that ring?' Raven said. 'And there must be thousands and thousands of libraries in the world.'

'That's right,' Eli said. 'I only have a few keys on the ring at any one time. If I want a key that isn't there, I have to summon it.'

'And how does that work?' Raven asked, sounding curious.

'I have to look for the key in my mind,' Eli said. 'And concentrate on it really hard. I'm, um, not that good at summoning yet, though. I've mostly just visited whatever library happens to have its key on my ring, so I've not had much practice. I might not manage to find the right one straight away.'

Raven gazed at the keys on the table between them. 'Well, I'm still kind of thinking that you're playing a joke on me, so I'll be amazed if any keys appear at all, frankly.'

Eli wasn't surprised – he knew he didn't look or act the way people expected from a mage. But he found he was rather looking forward to proving that he was more than what he seemed.

He gave a small smile. 'There's no time to lose.'

He picked up the bunch of keys, immediately reassured by the cold, clanking weight of them. Then he closed his eyes and focused as hard as he could on the Island of Joo-Joo Bubs. It was made more difficult by the fact that he had never been there, never even seen any pictures of it. He had no idea what the landscape looked like, or what types of birds and animals there were, or what the air smelled like. The only thing he knew for sure was that it had a lighthouse library. He focused on this fact as hard as he could and, before long, he felt the faint tingle of approaching keys.

When they appeared in the air around him, they let off a single, singing note, like a bell ringing in its tower. Raven gasped and when Eli opened his eyes, he saw several dozen keys suspended in the air around them – almost but not quite there, fading in and out like ghost keys. They jingled softly as they became more and more solid until, finally, they tumbled to the floor one by one and were silent.

'Well,' Raven said, staring down at them. 'That was quite something.'

'Hopefully the right key is in there somewhere,' Eli said, chewing at his lip. 'I don't know what it looks like, though. If I can't sense which key it is then we might have to try a few.'

They got up from their chairs and collected the keys together. There were twenty of them, and Eli's heart sank at the thought of the time it would take to try them all. He gazed down at the selection on the table for a moment before reaching out and picking a small green key.

'It might be this one,' he said. The uncertainty in his voice was obvious, even to him. He sighed. 'But I'm really not sure.'

'One way to find out,' Raven replied.

They walked to the library door and Eli inserted the key into the lock. He sensed that Raven still half expected nothing but the *Nepo*'s corridor to appear on the other side, but the moment the door opened, they were both knocked off their feet by a great torrent of water. Eli got a glimpse of the underwater cave beyond, shelves cut directly into the rock and framed seaweed bookmark collections on the walls. He didn't have time to take in much more because water was still rushing through, so he put his shoulder to the door and slammed it closed. Raven was on her feet, dripping wet, staring at him with an impressed expression.

'Wow,' she said. 'It was the wrong one, but that's still a neat trick.'

Eli looked around at the pools of water on the library floor and shook his head. 'It must have been some sort of mermaid or water sprite library. That happened back home once. My nana was ever so cross. I live with her, you see.'

'I know,' Raven replied. 'At least, I guessed because I know what happened to your parents. Anyone who knows anything about the race knows about the Fleets. I'm sorry that happened to you.'

Eli nodded. He appreciated people didn't always know what to say about his parents, and he wasn't always sure what he wanted them to say either. If they avoided mentioning them, then it was like they'd never existed at all, and Eli hated that. But if they brought them up then Eli had to speak about it without getting emotional, and that was hard too. He was grateful to Raven for acknowledging their existence without bombarding him with questions.

'I had my nana,' he said. He tried to dry his hands on his trousers, but since they were wet too it didn't really help. 'She was there for me. That's why I have to be there for her now. She's ill – really ill. But if I win the race then I can sell the magic and buy a special ruby to make her better. What about you?' he asked, keen to change the subject before he could get too upset. 'Why did you enter the race?'

'Oh, I … I want to save a tree,' Raven replied, using her hands to wring out her hair.

'A tree?'

'It probably doesn't seem like much to you. Not if you're worried about your grandmother. But this is a special tree. How much do you know about faery forests?'

'Not a lot,' Eli admitted.

'Every faery forest has a unique tree at the heart of it. It's the source of all the forest's magic, and you can tell which one it is because it glitters. But lately, our tree has glittered less and less. The magic is fading.'

Eli frowned. 'So what will happen if it runs out?'

Raven shrugged. 'I'm not exactly sure. But faery forests need magic to survive.'

There were some contestants who entered the Glorious Race of Magical Beasts simply for the thrill of it. And others who used the magic prize for some puffed-up, silly sort of purpose. Like last year's winner, Benedict Bruce, who'd used it to create a fantastical sky carousel, featuring various magical beasts. He'd since earned a small fortune charging people to ride it. Eli had hoped that Raven wouldn't have an important reason for being in the race because the fact was that only one of them could win. It looked like Raven might be having a similar thought, because the atmosphere between them suddenly felt a bit subdued.

'Well,' Raven said. 'We should tidy up.'

Fortunately, most of the water was contained to the floor, and none of the books or furniture had been damaged. Eli and Raven found mops in a cupboard down the corridor and used these to soak up the worst of it.

'I'm going to need another shower,' Raven said. 'But perhaps I'll wait until you've finished going through the keys.'

'I guess it's more likely to happen because any library near the lighthouse one has a good chance of being underwater,' Eli replied, feeling a little bereft.

He returned to the keys and settled his gaze on each one in turn, trying to coax one of them into calling out to him. Finally, he selected one made from shining blue glass, studded with dainty glass starfish.

'I've got a good feeling about this one,' he said, staring down at it. 'Yes. This could be it.'

He and Raven returned to the doorway and inserted the key in the lock. When Eli opened the door, no water rushed out to greet them this time. Instead, the door swung inwards into a pretty grotto of a room. There were chips of pale blue shell studded all over the floor, the walls and the ceiling. The dappled light filtering in through the windows told Eli that this was an underwater library, even before they saw the outline of a dolphin gliding past one of the windows.

'Well, it's obviously not this one,' Raven said.

Eli was about to agree and close the door when he

paused. 'Actually, perhaps we should check? For all we know, the lighthouse is underwater.'

'Good point,' Raven replied. 'It would be a useless sort of lighthouse, but I guess it's possible.'

'Let me just grab the *Nepo*'s key so we can get back.'

He hurried over to the table and plucked up the tentacle key. He quickly threaded it on to the chain around his neck next to the one for his little library back home, and then he and Raven stepped over the threshold. It was jarring to suddenly be on a floor that didn't move. The *Nepo* was always rolling and shifting, rocking with the water. The sudden switch to a perfectly stable floor made both Eli and Raven stumble. They had a look around and quickly confirmed this wasn't the lighthouse library. Every single book on the shelves was about terrapins and there was a painting on the wall of Kallie, the terrapin princess.

'We must be in her underwater palace,' Eli whispered to Raven. 'I don't think she's supposed to like visitors very much. I once read that she has guard terrapins with jewelled shells and a nasty bite.'

They hastily used the tentacle key to return to the *Nepo*'s library. After that, there was nothing for it but to spend the next hour trying the other keys one by one. They found themselves in a little beach shack library, and then one on a sailing boat, and after that there was an island library, and even a selection of books on a raft that Eli guessed had once been a castaway's library. Strangely, they found themselves in a couple more princess libraries too – the cloud library of a sky princess and the camel library of a desert princess. Next there was one that plainly belonged to a faery princess, filled with flowers and the scent of rain.

'It doesn't make sense!' Eli exclaimed, closing yet another door and putting the key aside. 'The libraries on rafts and beaches might be somewhere near the Island of Joo-Joo Bubs, and at least they're something to do with the sea, but I have no idea why princess libraries are appearing too.' He glanced at Raven, feeling embarrassed about his lack of success. 'Did you hear the rumour that a princess has joined the race this year?'

She nodded. 'Everyone was talking about that.' She gestured towards the table and said, 'There's one key left. Shall we?'

Eli picked it up and inserted it into the lock. He wasn't feeling too hopeful by this point but, finally, they opened the door to a room that was perfectly circular.

'That's it!' Eli exclaimed. 'It's got to be.'

It was obviously night at the lighthouse too because

the windows were completely dark, meaning they couldn't see anything of the island beyond. But from the doorway they could make out a plaque on the wall reading: *The Island of Joo-Joo Bubs Lighthouse*. Eli closed the door in relief and strung the key on to the chain around his neck, along with the other two.

'There's still time to get a couple of hours' sleep in before sunrise.' Eli gave Raven an apologetic look. 'Sorry that took so long.'

'Are you kidding? That was amazing! Now we'll be able to jump straight into the lead.' She gave Eli an appraising look. 'Maybe you're not such a lost cause with your tortoise, after all.'

Eli gave a small smile. He was used to people underestimating him. Perhaps this race would be a chance, for the first time in his life, to show people that a bookish boy with a briefcase could achieve remarkable things too.

CHAPTER SEVENTEEN

Eli opened his eyes to sunlight streaming in through his porthole window. When he'd gone to bed, they'd still been out at sea, with only the vast ocean surrounding them on all sides, but now he saw that they'd arrived at the Milkshake Islands. It was a tropical, picturesque sight, with palm trees waving gently in the breeze and golden sand warming in the sunlight.

He got out of bed and looked at the leader board. Their detour to the Milkshake Islands meant that they'd dropped to eighth place, but Eli wasn't too worried about that as the library key would mean that they would soon leap straight into the lead. He was concerned about what they would find on the Island of Joo-Joo Bubs, however. If the first round of the race was known for being a knockout, the second round was generally thought of as the trick one. It could seem deceptively simple at first, but there was always some secret lurking beneath the surface.

Eli especially disliked the fact that they hadn't been able to discover anything about the island or what a joo-joo bub even was. He wanted something to focus on, so he took out a new suit and then used his travel iron to smooth any creases. Having a freshly ironed suit with nice crisp edges made him feel just a tiny bit more capable and a little less out of his depth. He dug Humphrey out of the corner he'd wedged himself into and then made his way up on deck. He was relieved to see that they'd docked at a pier this time, meaning that he'd be able to simply walk off the ship rather than plunge into the sea again.

Raven must have been up even earlier because Eli spotted her walking down the pier, a cardboard tray of milkshakes in her hands. When she joined him on deck a moment later, he thought the milkshakes looked amazing close up, with lots of squirty cream on top and cold beads of condensation running down the side of the cups.

'Here, this one's for you,' Raven said, handing him one. 'I didn't know what flavours you like, so I just guessed and picked coffee.'

'That's my favourite!' Eli exclaimed. 'Thank you.'

'It's the least I can do.' Raven spotted Jeremiah coming up on deck and said, 'And don't think I forgot you, Captain. Strawberry milkshake, as requested.'

She handed him a bright pink cup with a bunch of unicorn sprinkles scattered over the cream.

'I asked them to put extra sprinkles on yours to cheer you up,' she said.

Jeremiah raised an eyebrow. 'I didn't realise I need cheering up,' he said. 'But a strawberry milkshake is a great way to start the day.'

'Now we're even,' Raven said, looking pleased.

Jeremiah raised his eyebrows. 'Even? Is this a magic milkshake? Is there, perhaps, a little wizard or enchantress at the bottom of the cup? Because otherwise I'm not sure that a milkshake is quite the same thing as saving someone from attacking doom birds and giving them a lift all the way to the Island of Joo-Joo Bubs.'

'Don't forget the cheese and biscuits you left outside my door,' Raven said.

'Guests don't go hungry on the *Nepo*,' Jeremiah replied, but not in a particularly friendly way.

'You could just say thank you for the milkshake,' Eli said, rolling his eyes.

'Haven't I already?'

'No,' Eli and Raven both said at the same time.

They didn't find out whether or not Jeremiah was actually going to thank Raven, because right at that moment, a harbour master began shouting at them from the pier, saying that they'd not paid the correct berthing fees, and Jeremiah had to hurry to sort it all out. After that, they set about gathering up their belongings. Eli packed everything as neatly as he could, stored Humphrey securely in his tortoise bag and then joined the others to walk down to the pier. Luther swooped ahead of them and Perrie hopped close to Raven's booted heels. As soon as they stepped on to the island, Jeremiah fished his magic bottle out of his coat and whispered the ship's name. At once, the *Nepo* was swept up in a magical wind that sucked it right back into the glass bottle.

'Amazing,' Raven said, peering in at it. 'That's quite a trick.'

'Eli's turn next,' Jeremiah said, tucking the bottle into his bag as Luther settled on his shoulder. 'Did you find the right key last night?'

'I've got it here.' Eli drew the key out from beneath his shirt and slipped it from the chain. 'We just need a door.'

They walked down the pier and stopped at the harbour master's hut.

'Hey!' a voice shouted. 'You can't go in there! That's my office!'

The sudden shout made Eli jump, causing him to drop the key. It clanged on to the wooden planks and then slipped straight through the gap, into the water with a soft splash.

'Oh, for heaven's sake.' Jeremiah sighed. 'I'll get it.'

Luther flew up to perch on the roof of the building as Jeremiah dropped straight off the edge of the pier and into the water. Several things happened at once then – the harbour master hurried towards them, Raven whipped her bow from her back and notched an arrow to ward him off – and a rainbow exploded on to the scene. A snarling panther raced from the colours, with Vincent Tweak clinging to his back.

Eli stared, his head in a whirl as the people on the dock began to shout. What was Vincent doing here? The Milkshake Islands were in the wrong direction. None of the other racers had any reason to be out this way ... And then Eli noticed something for the first time. Vincent wasn't wearing a racer's medallion. He wasn't part of the race. That was why he hadn't appeared in the leader board.

'You're racing the wrong way, idiot!' Raven called.

Vincent's lip curled in a smirk as he hopped from

his panther's back. 'I'm not a racer,' he said. 'I'm a bounty hunter.'

Eli had heard of such people, of course. They specialised in tracking down wanted criminals, but Eli had never committed a crime in his life, so why was Vincent pursuing him? Could he have found out before everyone else that he was a mage? Might some faraway king have sent him because he wanted Eli to do magical and important things in his court? But then he felt Humphrey shuffling about in his tortoise bag and he remembered that some bounty hunters didn't go after criminals – they went after magical beasts, either to sell or to add to some wealthy person's private collection.

'You've been following me because you're after Humphrey!' Eli exclaimed.

'I don't care about your moon tortoise! I mean, I'd get a decent sum for him, but that's not why I'm here.'

'Well, then, why *are* you here?' Eli asked, frustration bubbling up inside him. 'What do you want?'

Jeremiah gripped the side of the boardwalk just then and hauled himself up on to the pier, dripping wet, just as Vincent smiled and said in an icy tone, 'Lionel Gaskins sends his regards.' His gaze flicked between Jeremiah and Eli. 'To both of you.'

Eli drew in his breath sharply and Jeremiah went very still. This was it, Eli realised – this was the moment Jeremiah found out what he'd done.

Raven looked blank. 'Who's Lionel Gaskins?'

'Hey!' The harbour master had arrived, and brought several large friends with him. 'We don't want any racing mania here. It'll upset our cows. And if the cows are upset they don't produce milk, and then no one gets any milkshakes.'

'I don't care about the race or your cows,' Vincent snapped. He pointed at Eli. 'This boy has stolen something and I've come to get it back.'

Jeremiah laughed, although it seemed to Eli that there was something forced about it. 'Do you honestly think you're just going to put me in your pocket and take me home to Gaskins? Tell him I'm not interested and that he should just go and annoy some other poor character.'

Eli found he could hardly dare breathe. This was his fault. He'd written to Gaskins after reading that interview. He felt he owed the author an explanation for his writer's block, so he'd confessed about Jeremiah.

He'd put a spell on the words so that they'd disappear once they were read, and he didn't own up to being a mage himself, but he explained that Jeremiah had been taken out of the book and that Eli was a librarian and so could be trusted to look out for him and keep him safe. He'd reasoned that this way Lionel Gaskins would at least know what had happened and could give up his attempts at a sequel, putting his efforts instead into developing a new character for a new story.

But instead, he had received a string of very angry letters from Gaskins, demanding the name of the mage and that Jeremiah be put back where he belonged at once. Eli hadn't replied to any of them because he didn't know what to say. He wished he'd never written in the first place. There had been no letters in weeks, though, so he'd hoped that Gaskins had finally given up. It had never occurred to him for a moment that he'd take matters into his own hands by sending a bounty hunter.

'I thought you'd still be nine years old,' Vincent admitted, glaring at Jeremiah. 'And that would have made things a bit easier. But Gaskins wants to write a sequel and he needs you to do it, so whether you like it or not, you're coming with me.'

'You are ALL ordered to leave this pier at once!' the harbour master said. 'Get out your magic ships and rainbows and *go*!'

'With pleasure,' Vincent replied. He leapt on to his panther's back in one fluid movement, a rainbow shot into the sky and then they were racing up it.

Eli couldn't work out what was happening at first. Had Vincent given up? But then, to his horror, he took one of the pistols from its holster and pointed it straight at Luther, who'd flown away from the roof when the rainbow erupted.

'No!' Jeremiah yelled, as Vincent pulled the trigger.

It wasn't a bullet that came out, but a net, attached to a long coil of rope. It plucked Luther straight from the air, folding up his wings so he couldn't fly. Eli guessed Gaskins had told Vincent that anywhere Luther went, Jeremiah would go too. He'd have no choice but to return to the author if he captured his bird. Even Jeremiah Jones couldn't climb a rainbow with his bare hands, and perhaps Vincent would have got away if Raven hadn't fired her arrow. It grazed Vincent's arm and he fell from his panther with a yell.

Unfortunately, he crashed right through the roof of a cowshed, which definitely counted as upsetting the cows. Everyone raced to the scene and there was much mooing and shouting as Jeremiah extracted Luther from the wreckage. Thankfully, he seemed to be unharmed, and the children were all far more concerned about the phoenix than they were about Vincent, who was loudly exclaiming over his bleeding arm.

Jeremiah gave Raven a grateful slap on the back. '*Now* we're even,' he said.

'You're under arrest!' the harbour master thundered. 'ALL of you!'

It turned out it wasn't very easy to arrest someone when their panther was snarling at you, so Vincent managed to make his rainbow getaway, but the others weren't so lucky. The Milkshake Islands didn't generally suffer from too much crime and so the children were all herded into one cell in the local police station, along with their magical beasts.

They tried various pleas and arguments to be released, but with no luck, and the hours ticked away maddeningly. Eli saw their names slip off the top ten of the leader board and the number of contestants went down from twenty to fifteen. Jeremiah kept saying he couldn't understand how Gaskins had managed to track him down after all this time, and Eli simply couldn't bear to own up to the letter. Jeremiah would be furious and definitely see it as a betrayal. It would have to come out eventually, of course, but the thought of the conversation made Eli's stomach feel tangled up in knots. Right now, though, they needed to focus on getting out of here. There was no keyhole inside the cell to use the library key that Jeremiah had plucked from the water.

'I guess it's up to me to get us out of here,' Jeremiah sighed.

'That seems fair,' Raven grumbled. 'Since it's your fault we're here in the first place.'

Jeremiah had nothing to say to that and Eli kept quiet too.

Fortunately, it wasn't the first time Jeremiah had ever been locked in a cell and his book mentioned that – using only his shoelaces, a phoenix feather, a teaspoon and a bit of pluck – Jeremiah could break out from behind any bars that tried to hold him. On this occasion, he had the laces, feather and pluck, but no teaspoon, so it was taking rather a long time.

'I could probably do it faster,' Humphrey grumbled to Eli. 'Tortoises are excellent at prison breaks.'

'We'll be out soon,' Eli soothed him.

In fact, it was almost lunchtime when Jeremiah finally managed to click open the lock of their cell. The children tumbled out and raced to the nearest door.

The noise alerted the constable, who came charging after them, but Eli put the key into the lock and pushed the door. It swung open into the lighthouse library they had seen before. The children and their animals lost no time in shooting through the door and closing it swiftly behind them.

CHAPTER EIGHTEEN

The Milkshake Islands were lost from view, and the children found themselves hundreds of miles away on the Island of Joo-Joo Bubs. Eli hoped that they'd left Vincent far behind too, but it worried him that the bounty hunter could be hot on their heels even now . . . The lighthouse library was awash with sunlight – it gleamed off the wooden floor and the spines of the books in the small, circular room. There was space for one armchair and a table, but it was otherwise clear of furniture. Eli noticed that the shelves were filled with books about magic. There were volumes on card tricks and illusions, coin tricks and sleight of hand, magicians' tips and stage magic guides.

Jeremiah walked to the nearest window and peered out at the island. 'Ah,' he said. 'I think I know what a joo-joo bub is.'

Eli and Raven hurried over to join him. All of their racing medallions had opened their eyes, watchful for any exciting moments. Eli saw that the library was located on one of the lighthouse's upper floors and so they had a good view of the island. It was small enough that they could see right to the other side of it – really, the island was nothing more than a small rock in the middle of the ocean. And it was completely covered in a carpet of strange flowers. They had long stems, turquoise-blue petals and a bubblegum scent that reached the children all the way at the top of the lighthouse. But the really odd thing about them was that they seemed to be made – entirely – from balloons.

'Well, balloon flowers aren't too bad,' Raven said. 'They don't look like they're about to attack us anyway.'

'I can't see a checkpoint,' Eli said, frowning. 'Surely we should be able to spot it from here? It looks like we have a view of the whole island.'

'Maybe something happened with the racers who got here before us and the maps were destroyed?' Jeremiah suggested. 'We're behind now, aren't we?'

They'd lost valuable time at the Milkshake Islands. Eli saw that the number of racers had decreased even further since he last checked and there were now only thirteen of them left. He, Jeremiah and Raven were in joint ninth place. The only racer behind them was named Kali Krag and the tiny blue dragon stamped beside her name said she was a dragonrider. There was no mention of Vincent, of course. Eli hated the fact that they had no idea how close to them the bounty hunter was. Raven's arrow had gone into his arm, and hopefully that would slow him down, but Eli didn't think he'd give up easily. What if the bounty hunter *did* manage to capture Jeremiah? Would Gaskins find some way to get him back in the book? Would Eli ever be able to get him back? For a moment he wondered once again whether he should tell Jeremiah the truth about the letter he'd sent to Gaskins. He hated keeping secrets from his friend, but the middle of the race was just the worst moment to have that argument. He told himself it made sense to wait until things were calm and quiet. It wasn't lying – not really. It was just ... managing the timing.

'The second round is always trickier than it appears,' Raven said, sounding worried. 'Maybe there are some maps hidden amongst those balloon flowers.'

They hurried to the door.

'I hope there's a safe route down those cliffs,' Eli said as they went.

The island rose straight up out of the water and it would be a long, long jump to the ocean below.

Knowing his luck, he was bound to break his arm, or at least a finger.

'Maybe there's a nice little staircase cut into the rock you can use once we've found the map,' Jeremiah suggested. His tone was a bit sarcastic and Eli could tell he was still shaken because of the run-in with Vincent. 'Otherwise, we might just have to lower you down on a rope.'

'We didn't bring any rope,' Eli pointed out.

Jeremiah rolled his eyes. 'I was joking. You don't really want to be lowered down on a rope, do you? Like some sort of cow?'

Eli blushed, wishing the subject of rope had never come up in the first place.

They ran down the spiral staircase towards the exit, and Eli immediately spotted about a dozen bolts drawn across the door, as if there was something on the other side that the occupant really, really didn't want to come in. That couldn't be a good sign, and Eli felt a flash of worry. The children had almost reached it when a voice rang out behind them.

'Stop! I don't know how you got inside the lighthouse, but you absolutely *cannot* step outside!'

They turned to see a man standing in a doorway. Eli caught a glimpse of a living room behind him, with soft rugs and plush armchairs. He could hear a cat purring somewhere within. The man was very tall – so tall that he had to stoop a little to prevent his head from banging on the doorframe. He wore a smart navy-blue suit and a bow tie, which immediately made Eli feel a certain kinship with him. It looked like he had attempted to comb his white hair neatly back, but several wisps of it had escaped and stuck out at funny angles that gave him a bit of a frazzled appearance. He wore a pair of shabby but comfy-looking slippers on his feet and he had a kindly face, although he was staring at them with an appalled expression.

'Are you the lighthouse keeper?' Eli asked. 'I'm very sorry for the intrusion, but we're taking part in the Glorious Race of Magical Beasts, you see, and—'

The man groaned. 'Yes, yes, I know all about that. Several racers have already perished.'

Jeremiah raised an eyebrow. He reached up to stroke Luther, who'd settled on his shoulder. 'No offence, but how dangerous can bubblegum-scented balloon flowers possibly be? I don't want to brag, but I've been known to fight sharks with my bare hands and—'

'There are no flowers out there!' the man cut him off.
Eli glanced at the other two. They'd all seen the

flowers – hundreds of them. But then, Eli had known they had to be more than they seemed.

'There are no flowers,' the man insisted. 'Only joo-joo bubs. And I'm not a lighthouse keeper. I'm Thin Sir.'

Raven and Jeremiah both looked blank, but Eli recognised the name. 'You're a magician,' he said, realisation dawning. Magicians didn't have quite as much power as mages, but they could still do some amazing things. Eli recalled reading about this man in a book about the world's most renowned magicians and racked his brain for the details. 'You used to specialise in balloon magic,' he said. 'But then one day you vanished. No one has seen or heard from you in years and everyone thought you were ...'

He trailed off. It seemed rude and unnecessary to point out that people all thought he was dead. Just at that moment, the purring sound got louder and the cat trotted out to join its master. Only, it was no ordinary cat. It was made entirely from balloons. Thin Sir scooped him up and the balloon creature purred contentedly in his arms.

'I retired,' he said. 'I had to because of the joo-joo bubs. They're ...' He swallowed so hard his Adam's apple bobbed in his throat. 'It's difficult to explain to non-magic people, but the joo-joo bubs started out as balloons. For balloon-animal magic, you know. And then one day they refused to stay in the shapes I'd designed for them and started to create forms of their own. They're chameleon-like. They take whatever form suits them in the moment. That's why you saw flowers. They're sneaky, you see – they take a harmless-looking shape to try to lure people out.'

'All right, but even if they can turn into other things, I still don't see what the big deal is,' Jeremiah said. 'Surely any shape they take is harmless enough if they're made of balloons. Even if they turned themselves into balloon tigers, they wouldn't be able to attack us with balloon teeth, would they?'

'They don't want to attack you,' Thin Sir said. 'They want to turn you into a balloon.' He gestured with the cat in his arms. 'What do you think happened to Tigger here? He used to be a real furry cat until I left a window open one day, and then he went outside and a joo-joo bub got him. All it takes is one touch, and you'll be transformed into a balloon forever.'

CHAPTER NINETEEN

The children exchanged wary glances. Nobody much fancied being turned into a balloon person.

'It would certainly be difficult to fight sharks as a balloon boy,' Jeremiah mused. 'And I'm sure it would complicate life in a lot of other ways too. But we only have his word that's what the joo-joo bubs want. For all we know, it's a lot of twaddle to put us off reaching the checkpoint.'

It had been known to happen. The race organisers occasionally paid actors to mislead and complicate things. But Eli suspected they didn't need to do that in this case. He'd seen the number of racers on the leader board go down. *Something* had knocked people out of the race here.

'There's no checkpoint out there,' Thin Sir quickly said. 'The organisers would never have been able to set foot on the island. This isn't a ploy, I swear it. Every word I've told you is the truth.'

'And I *have* heard of Thin Sir,' Eli pointed out. 'He's definitely a real magician.'

'But we don't even know that this *is* Thin Sir,' Jeremiah pointed out. 'The race organisers might just be using the legend of him.'

'Look, what does it matter whether he's a real person or not, telling the truth or not?' Raven cut in. 'We know there's a checkpoint on the island here somewhere, and we need to find it to get to the next part of the race. We can't stay hiding in this lighthouse.'

Eli knew she was right. Whatever was out there, they would just have to face it.

'Thank you for the warning,' he said to Thin Sir. 'But we've got to go.'

The magician shook his head sadly. 'I've done what I can,' he said. 'If you step out of that door, then be warned, I will lock it behind you immediately and I won't open it again, no matter how much you scream or beg. I can't risk a joo-joo bub getting in here. If you're determined to be turned into balloon people, then so be it.'

'Eli probably wouldn't even notice, to be fair,' Jeremiah said. 'Not so long as he was still allowed to be a librarian. And to tend to his candle collection, of course. Come to think of it, I'm not sure your life would change in any way at all if you were turned into a balloon.'

'Ha ha,' Eli replied 'You're very funny. But if you're done making jokes at my expense, shall we get a move on?'

'May the gods have mercy on your souls,' Thin Sir said sombrely.

'What a cheerful pep talk,' Jeremiah said. He glanced at the other two. There was a gleam in his eye and Eli could tell he was looking forward to throwing himself into whatever danger waited on the other side of the door. 'Are we ready?'

'Let me just get my bow,' Raven said, slinging it from her back and plucking an arrow from the quiver. 'It might come in handy if we're under balloon attack.'

Eli rummaged in his bag too and retrieved a candle. Jeremiah checked to make sure the *Nepo*'s bottle was within easy grabbing distance. Then they began sliding open the bolts. The door swung outwards and they stepped over the threshold. The blue balloon flowers filled the island before them, looking innocent and rather jolly as they bobbed about in the sea breeze. True to his word, Thin Sir slammed the door closed and they all heard the scrape of the many bolts being drawn across again.

The moment the final one clicked into place, something changed. The flowers began to morph and stretch before their eyes. Eli wouldn't have believed that something as innocent as a balloon could take on a sinister form, but the creatures that appeared before them were strangely unnerving. They had taken on the shapes of children, a mix of boys and girls. Their balloon heads lolled to the side slightly, giving them the appearance of dolls, or puppets whose strings had been cut. The boy balloons had black hair and wore blue shorts, whilst the girls had yellow plaits and pink dresses.

But the most horrible thing of all about them was their arms. They were extra long, fashioned from multiple balloons so that they stretched on and on, until they were three or four times as long as they should have been. Their heads all swivelled towards Eli and his friends on the lighthouse steps and their red balloon lips stretched into ghastly smiles. Then one of them spoke in a squeaky balloon voice.

'Hello, friends. Shall we play the tickle game?'

The other balloon children reached out their long arms eagerly.

'Urgh!' Jeremiah shuddered. 'Yuck, no, I don't think we will!'

The balloon children's smiles abruptly turned upside down into big frowny faces. Eli swallowed hard and resisted the urge to take a step back.

'Everyone who comes to the Island of Joo-Joo Bubs *must* play the tickle game!' the balloon boy snarled. 'It's the law.'

'Your law has no power over us,' Jeremiah replied.

'If you don't play,' the balloon boy replied, 'then you don't get these.'

The joo-joo bubs stood back a little to reveal a crate filled with rolled-up maps. Eli saw that the crate had a parachute attached to it and guessed that it had been airdropped on to the island, presumably so that the messenger wasn't turned into a balloon. But the worst sight of all was the balloon woman. They hadn't seen her before because she was slumped against the crate, but now Eli got a clear view and realised there was something horribly familiar about her. She wore a long blue balloon coat and had blonde balloon hair trailing from beneath a balloon cap. She held a balloon shark in her lap and balloon tears ran down her cheek. It was hard to tell for sure, but Eli had the terrible feeling this was the fisherwoman racer they'd seen in the first round. He shivered at the thought of sharing such a fate and wondered whether there might be other balloon racers on the island too. The joo-joo bubs only allowed them a brief glimpse before they crowded back around the crate once again. Then they were surging forwards, long arms outstretched, fingers reaching eagerly.

Raven was already notching an arrow to her bow, but she looked worried. 'There are too many of them,' she said. 'I can shoot arrows quickly, but I can't pop them all at once. You two will have to help.' She glanced over her shoulder at Jeremiah. 'Do you have any kind of weapon on you?'

He shook his head. 'I usually fight with my hands.'

'Huh,' Raven grunted. 'Not much use when touching one of those things will turn you into a balloon. Did you see the fisherwoman? There's no way I'm ending up like her. Looks like it's going to be up to me to save our skins.'

'Perhaps I can find a rock or something,' Jeremiah said, staring around.

Neither of them paid much heed to Eli, since they both knew he wouldn't have any weapons and would be no good at fighting. They therefore failed to notice that he was hastily unscrewing the lid from the jar of his scented candle with trembling hands. The label on the side stated that this one was 'Old Bookshop Scent' – a mix of paper and ink, leather sofas, and wood-fire smoke. Eli wasn't sure how much it would help, but it was the only thing he could think to offer in this sort of situation. He couldn't get the image of the balloon fisherwoman out of his mind, and all of a sudden the chances of them escaping this island in one piece seemed slim. But at least the candle would give them the chance to catch their breaths and think about what to do next. Desperately trying to still the shaking in his hands, Eli carefully set the candle on the lighthouse steps. He grabbed a box of matches from his pocket just as the nearest joo-joo bub lunged at them. Raven fired her arrow and it went straight into the balloon boy with a satisfying pop. He collapsed at their feet in little ribbons of shredded balloon.

'Nice shot,' Jeremiah said.

But the balloon's demise seemed to enrage the other joo-joo bubs, who all rushed forwards at once, reaching with their grasping balloon fingers. Raven launched another arrow at the nearest one, just as Eli set his lit match to the wick of the candle. It caught alight and, at once, a building sprang up around them. It was small and crooked, with sloping floors and exposed wooden beams. It was, in fact, an old bookshop, filled with bookcases and shelves full of leather-bound volumes. A comfy-looking leather sofa sat beside a crackling fire. The shop had formed around the lighthouse, so the steps and front door were still there, and an entire wall was made up of the white bricks of the lighthouse.

It was all very lovely and peaceful, except for the fact that when it had sprung up around the children it had also trapped several joo-joo bubs in with them. Still, seven or eight of the creatures was preferable to the dozens that were already squashing their balloon faces up against the windows outside. Raven lost no time in firing arrows at the remainder, whilst Jeremiah polished off two more by snatching up a pyramid-shaped paperweight from the counter and using the pointy end to pop them. Soon there were no joo-joo bubs left in the shop, only the ribbons of their popped balloons.

The danger wasn't over yet, though, because the creatures were reaching their fingers in under the door, the pink sausage-like balloons stretching longer and longer towards them. The children popped the fingers with Raven's arrows and then quickly blocked up the gap under the door using the heaviest hardbacks they could find. One determined joo-joo bub attempted to climb down the chimney, but immediately popped upon landing in the fire, and the remaining creatures stayed away from the roof after that.

'Well, this is a neat trick,' Raven said, staring around at the shop whilst leaning over to catch her breath.

'Thanks,' Eli replied, setting the candle carefully on the counter. 'I like candle making and I realised a while ago that I can make magic candles if they're something to do with books or reading. I thought it would give us time to come up with a plan.'

'Let's come up with one quickly, then,' Jeremiah said.

Eli glanced at his friend and was surprised to see that he'd started sweating.

'You're the only one who hasn't really contributed so far,' Raven pointed out. 'We'd have been sitting ducks out there if it wasn't for my arrows and Eli's candle.'

Eli felt a surprised flicker of pride at her words. He *had* contributed, and suddenly felt a tiny bit proud of himself. Maybe there might be some good parts about being a mage, after all.

'I would have thought of something to save us all at the last minute,' Jeremiah replied in a dismissive tone.

'It's true, he probably would have,' Eli said. 'He's kind of known for getting out of fantastically dangerous situations without even a scratch.'

He tried to be cheered by the thought. Surely Jeremiah

would come up with a masterful plan to get them past the joo-joo bubs? Still, escape seemed a long way off.

'Perhaps you might volunteer a solution now,' Raven suggested to Jeremiah. She glanced at the windows. Each one was filled with joo-joo bubs pressing their faces against the glass in a disturbing manner. 'Shall we draw the curtains?' Raven said. 'It's putting me off, seeing their creepy faces staring in like that.'

The children hurried to cover the windows, and Eli took the opportunity to say quietly to Jeremiah, 'What's wrong?'

'Nothing,' he said at once. 'Why would you think something's wrong?'

'Perhaps because you look like you're about to be sick,' Raven said. 'I guess the joo-joo bubs were a bit harrowing, to be fair.'

'Don't be ridiculous,' Jeremiah snapped. 'I'm Jeremiah Jones – I'm not scared of balloon children.'

'Well, *something* is making you sweat.'

Eli knew Raven was right. Jeremiah's hands were shaking slightly too. It didn't make sense. Usually, after something dangerous like shark fighting, Jeremiah was on top of the world. Eli gazed around the shop for an explanation, but there was nothing in there with them except ... books. He recalled how Jeremiah had never set foot in the Royal Library back in Harmonia, and Eli had never seen him inside the *Nepo*'s library either. He'd come as far as the doorway, but had never crossed the threshold.

'Are you . . . afraid of the books?' he asked.

Eli assumed his friend would deny it. After all, Jeremiah Jones wasn't afraid of anything. But instead he met Eli's eyes and said, 'Wouldn't you be? If you'd spent years locked up inside one. Someone else choosing what you'll do and who'll you be. Every decision mapped out for you. Every moment of your life decided in advance.'

Eli felt another shiver of guilt. He'd taken Jeremiah from his book, given him a taste of freedom and then endangered it all with his letter to Gaskins. Vincent could be on his way here right now. And even if he wasn't, there was nothing to stop Gaskins from employing one bounty hunter after the other until he got what he wanted – Jeremiah trapped inside the pages of a story once again.

'But . . . but you're here now,' Eli pointed out, desperately looking for a positive. 'Lionel Gaskins isn't deciding for you any more.'

'I'm afraid of being dragged back into a book.' Jeremiah looked at the shelves suspiciously. 'I can feel them hungering for me. They know I'm here.

It's like … like two magnets getting drawn towards each other.'

Eli glanced at the bookshelves. He could sense things from books sometimes – normally a warm, friendly sort of welcome whenever he entered a library. But now that Jeremiah mentioned it, there did seem to be a bit of a charged atmosphere in the room, a watchful sort of hunger …

'So there you have it – I'm afraid of books,' Jeremiah said with a scowl. 'Go ahead and have a laugh at my expense.'

Raven shook her head. 'Everyone is afraid of something,' she said quietly. 'And none of us wants to spend any longer in this shop than we have to. So I think I've got a plan – or half of one. If I shrink down to faery form and ride Perrie then I should be able to outrun the joo-joo bubs to the checkpoint and collect maps for everyone. There's an island about five miles west from here called Grasshopper Island. Perrie can sprint across the ocean to it and then you two can follow on in the *Nepo* and pick me up there. In exchange I'd like you to take me to the last checkpoint.'

Eli nodded. 'Agreed.'

'Seems fair,' Jeremiah said.

Raven gave him a suspicious look. 'And don't think

about trying to double-cross me and leave me behind because I'll be the one with the maps. You'll be disqualified if you don't come and get them.'

'I don't go back on my agreements,' Jeremiah said. 'But nice to know you have such a high opinion of me.'

'How are you going to get past the joo-joo bubs, though?' Eli asked. 'Even if you can outrun them, one might manage to touch you as you go past.'

'Well, that's where you two will have to help,' Raven said. 'I'll need you to create a diversion, just long enough for me to open the door and get a head start.'

'No problem,' Jeremiah replied. 'Diversions are one of my specialities.'

'Tortoises are excellent at creating diversions!' Humphrey piped up from inside his bag. 'I can help.'

'Is there a way up on to the roof?' Jeremiah asked.

'Um, not really,' Eli replied. 'I mean, the shop has drainpipes that you'd probably be able to shimmy up, but you can't get to those without going outside.'

Jeremiah went over to the nearest window and twitched the curtain back. 'They're still there,' he said, letting the curtain fall. 'Determined little things. All right, well, what about the upper floor?'

'There's a staircase in the office at the back,' Eli said, pointing at the door behind the till.

'Good. I can climb out on the windowsill and get to the roof from there.'

'But how are you going to create a diversion on the roof without anything to help you?' Eli asked.

In the book, whenever Jeremiah needed to create a diversion, he was usually on a desert island, or the deck of a pirate ship, and there were parrots, and coconuts, and extravagant hats, and pirate dogs, and various other things that made for excellent diversion plans. But here and now, there were only books. And much as Eli loved books, he didn't think the joo-joo bubs were likely to sit down nicely for a story . . .

But then he remembered the books he'd packed, and it occurred to him that perhaps the joo-joo bubs would sit down for a story, after all.

'What about this?' He pulled a book from his bag and showed it to Jeremiah. It was about a magician who could perform spectacular living firework displays. 'I've been in that one a few times and am quite friendly with Jax, the magician. I'm sure if I bring her out, along with one of her fireworks, then she'll be happy to create a small diversion for us.'

'All right. Worth a try,' Jeremiah said.

Eli felt a small burst of pleasure that a book was coming in useful in a situation like this. For once, he wasn't a spectator or a sidekick – he was the person wielding the magic and saving the day ... Then he thought of the next steps and his worries crowded back in all at once.

'How are we going to get off the island?' he asked Jeremiah. 'We haven't got ice hares we can ride past the joo-joo bubs.'

'If we don't need to collect maps then we can just leap into the sea straight from the nearest cliff and swim to the *Nepo*,' Jeremiah said, like it was nothing.

Eli was aghast. 'But ... but I *can't*,' he practically wailed. 'The cliffs are hundreds of feet high. I can't jump from a height like that – I could barely manage it from the docks back at Harmonia. Besides, what if there are rocks at the bottom?'

Jeremiah folded his arms over his chest. 'Well, I'm not sure what you want me to say, Eli. What did you expect from the Glorious Race of Magical Beasts? You must have known there would be leaping from great heights, and dodging rocks, and swimming for your life, and running faster than you'd ever run before in your life. You were the one who insisted you could do it. But if you've changed your mind then we can just bow out of the race right now and go home.'

Eli frowned. Jeremiah was right. If he wanted to save

Nana's life, then he had to do all these things he was afraid of. He didn't think he would ever have been able to do it for himself, but he *had* to do it for her.

'You can do it, Eli,' Humphrey said quietly. 'You can do anything.'

Eli wished he could be comforted by Humphrey's faith in him, but if it was anything like the faith the tortoise had in his own abilities then it was probably wildly unfounded. Still, he forced himself to grit his teeth and nod. The sooner this was all over, the sooner he could be back amongst his books and bats. How he longed for the hush of the stacks, where the only activity was the gentle rustle of turning pages, and the only danger of injury was the occasional paper cut.

'Just run straight to the cliff edge and jump into the sea,' Jeremiah said. 'Try to avoid any rocks, if you can. I'll be right beside you and we can swim to the *Nepo* together.'

Eli felt sick at the thought, but there didn't seem to be any other choice. Raven gave him an encouraging pat on the arm.

'You can do it,' she said.

'Librarians aren't made for jumping off cliff edges,' Eli groaned. He lowered his voice so that Humphrey wouldn't hear and added, 'Nor are tortoises.'

'Well, this is why everyone thought you were a joke contestant to begin with,' Raven said. 'Perhaps some still do. It's up to you to prove them wrong.'

Eli nodded and looked down at the book in his hands, concentrating his thoughts as hard as he could on the magician inside.

'Jax,' he muttered. 'Jax Flazzle.'

There was a faint whistling noise, which quickly turned into a gust of wind, and all of a sudden the pages of the book fluttered wildly and then a girl stepped right out of them. She was about their age, with lilac-coloured hair that stuck up from her head in spikes. She wore a long, bright pink coat over a striped dress, and lightning-coloured boots. She grinned when she saw Eli and said, 'Hello! I wondered when I might see you again.'

Jax always seemed perfectly happy in her fictional world. In fact, all the characters Eli had met seemed the same. Except Jeremiah.

'Hi, Jax,' Eli said. 'I've got a favour to ask.'

He quickly explained what was happening outside with the joo-joo bubs and asked if they could have one of her fireworks to create a diversion.

'Of course! I have just the thing.' Jax pulled a firework from her coat pocket and pointed at the fireplace. 'Just set it off in there. Make sure it's pointed straight up the chimney, though, if you don't want to lose your eyebrows.'

'Thank you so much.'

Jax handed over the firework. 'Catch you later, Eli. Come visit again soon.'

Eli told her he would and then he gathered his thoughts and spoke her name to put her back in the book. She disappeared in a blast of magical air, leaving the three racers to look at the firework. It was a chunky thing, covered in electric-yellow foil and patterns of sparkly dragonflies.

'Do you want to take up position by the door?' Eli said to Raven.

She shrank herself to faery size and climbed on to the saddle on Perrie's back. The hare seemed to sense that racing was imminent. Her long ears twitched with excitement and she was practically trembling with anticipation. Jeremiah went over and grabbed the bolt, ready to draw it across.

Eli put his tortoise bag back on, then went to the fire and carefully reached in to place the firework upright on top of the burning logs. The flames lapped up at it and the wick caught light with a pop and sizzle. Eli hurried to the window and twitched the curtain aside to peer out at the joo-joo bubs.

'Get ready,' he said. 'There should be something any minute now . . .'

He'd barely finished speaking before the wick burned down, the firework caught and jets of sparkling yellow light were shooting from the firework and going straight up the chimney. The next moment there was the sound of excitable shouting outside and the joo-joo bub faces disappeared from the windows as they drew back to stare up at the roof.

'Go!' Jeremiah cried, throwing open the door.

In the blink of an eye, Raven shot through it. Eli snatched up his briefcase and he and Jeremiah hurried out after her. It was time to leave the Island of Joo-Joo Bubs.

CHAPTER TWENTY

Raven and Perrie sprinted across the island so fast that they were just a pale blur. In a matter of moments, they were racing past the maps – hopefully snatching three up along the way – and then carried on going right off the edge of the island. The fisherwoman had gone, and Eli wondered whether she'd wandered off or been blown away out to sea. It was a horrible thought either way, and he shuddered. But at least they had a plan now. Eli had never seen an ice hare run in real life before, and they really were lightning fast.

Eli set off with Jeremiah. He knew the joo-joo bubs wouldn't be distracted by the fireworks forever and that they had to run as fast as they could, but he couldn't resist a glance back, curious to see what kind of diversion Jax had provided. He saw that the air above the shop was full of firework dragonflies, their long tails sizzling and sparkling as they swooped and hovered. The joo-joo bubs were oohing and aahing, pointing into the sky, and even clapping their hands in delight.

Eli glanced back around at Jeremiah, but his grin faltered. For an odd flicker of a moment Jeremiah had seemed ... insubstantial somehow. Almost as if he were a bit blurred around the edges. But now he looked completely ordinary and Eli told himself it must have been the dazzle of the fireworks affecting his eyes. The next moment a spark fell from one of the dragonflies, landed on a balloon child below and immediately popped its balloon head. Then the joo-joo bubs were all shrieking in panic and scrabbling to get away from the fireworks, which, unfortunately, meant they all started to run straight towards the boys.

'Run!' Jeremiah gasped.

'I'm already running!' Eli panted.

Jeremiah was moving ahead and glanced back in frustration. 'That's not running!'

Eli managed to get one foot to pound clumsily in front of the other, but his briefcase bashed and bounced against the side of his leg, and he was breathless within seconds. The soft spots at the back of his heel and the edge of his little toe smarted and stung where they rubbed against the leather. He slipped and slid across the grass, desperately trying to go as fast as he could, but feeling like he was just running on the spot and pinwheeling his arms.

'Is that a joke?' Jeremiah yelled, sprinting back to grab him by the arm. 'Stop messing about and *run*!'

Eli threw himself forwards, with Jeremiah half dragging him along. Luckily, the balloon children weren't exactly designed for running either, and they bounced and bobbed behind them. The dragonfly fireworks had followed them too, and a few more sparks rained down to pop some unlucky joo-joo bubs, but that only made the ones that remained run even faster, and Eli could practically feel their fingers reaching and stretching towards him. The island wasn't big, and the cliff edge was coming up fast. Eli could hardly believe he was going to leap – it was like something from a nightmare. He could hear the squeak of balloon shoes behind him and redoubled his efforts.

Every bone in his body screamed at him to stop when he reached the edge, but Jeremiah's words from the bookshop came back to him and he knew that jumping was all part of the race, part of what he'd signed up for, and part of proving to himself and the world that he could do this. The eye of his medallion was wide open, ready to capture the terrifying descent in all its glory. He was about to leap when Humphrey suddenly piped up, 'Eli!'

He spoke so sharply that Eli came to an abrupt halt, thinking that Humphrey must have spotted danger.

'I'd like *The Dance of Jemimah* read out at my party,' the old tortoise said. 'I should have thought of it earlier.'

Before Eli could groan out a response, Jeremiah grabbed his arm.

'When I said you had to jump, I didn't mean throw yourself off blindly! We can't do it here – look at all those rocks. Do you want to be pulverised? Come on.'

He tugged him a little way further along the cliff and then said, 'Yes, here is good.'

The joo-joo bubs squeaked along the cliffs in pursuit as Jeremiah plucked the magic bottle from his pocket. He drew back his arm and hurled it out to sea, muttering the words beneath his breath. 'Hello, *Nepo*.'

Once again, the ship appeared seemingly out of thin air, causing waves to ripple out around it. Eli was relieved to see the beautiful blue-and-gold ship – but they still had to get to it. The approaching joo-joo bubs had clearly spotted it too because they raised their squeaky voices in dismay at the prospect of their prey escaping.

'Can you jump, or do you want me to chuck you in?' Jeremiah asked.

'I can jump!' Eli exclaimed indignantly.

'Do it now, then,' Jeremiah replied.

And with that, he leapt from the top of the cliff, his long coat flapping around him. Luther was right behind, swooping towards the *Nepo*. The joo-joo bubs were almost within touching distance of Eli now, so there was no time to hesitate. Gripping his briefcase hard enough to make his knuckles turn white, he jumped over the edge of the cliff, hearing Humphrey let out an excited yelp. There was a stomach-churning moment when he seemed to hang suspended in mid-air, and then the ocean was rushing up to meet him with startling speed.

Eli couldn't help it – he screamed all the way down. He didn't even attempt a dive this time, but remained ramrod straight, his hands clenched into fists at his sides. He hit the surface shoes first and plummeted beneath the waves shockingly fast and surprisingly far. Eli half expected his feet to touch the seabed. Bubbles exploded all around him and his yells were abruptly cut off.

The sea felt cold as ice, and his whole body trembled with the shock of it. The salt stung his throat and eyes, and the sound of the waves echoed around inside his ears as if he were trapped in a giant shell. To his dismay, he couldn't work out which way was up and which was down. His lungs screamed for air as he kicked and thrashed, but he just seemed to turn over and over and never reach the surface.

At last, a hand clamped on his elbow and Jeremiah was beside him in the water, helping him kick his way up. His head broke the surface and he gratefully sucked in big lungfuls of air.

'Are you all right, Humphrey?' he gasped.

'All right?' the tortoise replied. 'I'm fantastic. That was *amazing*! Let's do it again!'

Fortunately, the joo-joo bubs didn't look like they were going to follow over the edge of the cliff. Eli guessed that being made from balloons meant they were wary of the rocks too. But that didn't stop them from growing and stretching their arms to reach down the cliff towards them.

'Come on,' Jeremiah gasped. 'Let's get out of here.'

The two boys swam towards the *Nepo*. Eli wondered how long the joo-joo bubs' arms would stretch and had the horrible image of the *Nepo* itself being turned into a giant balloon ship. A balloon vessel wouldn't get far before a shark, or a rock, or even a particularly sharp barnacle popped it. Fortunately, it turned out the joo-joo bubs could only extend their arms so far before the sea breeze became too much for them. With chilling howls of defeat, they drew their arms back in and stood wailing on the cliff edge.

The *Nepo* didn't need Jeremiah to tell her this time, and unfurled a tentacle of her own accord to pluck Eli from the sea and deposit him on deck, where he landed in a gasping heap. Jeremiah shimmied up the ladder and joined him a moment later. They turned back in time to see that Kali Krag, the final racer, had arrived at the island with her massive blue dragon. Its fire-breathing roar easily scattered the joo-joo bubs, and Kali scooped up a map without ever setting foot on land. To Eli's relief, she made no attempt to sabotage the *Nepo* – perhaps she didn't see the point, as they were now officially in last place. Instead, the dragon spread its wings and disappeared into the sky, leaving the *Nepo* to unfurl its sails and set off at full steam ahead.

Chapter Twenty-One

Eli dug Humphrey out of his bag. All the excitement had made the moon tortoise sleepy, and he gave a big yawn that showed off his bright pink tongue.

'I think I might take a little nap,' he said, and stumped off to find a sunny spot. Jeremiah remained on deck to steer a course towards Raven, whilst Eli returned to his cabin. As a way of self-soothing, he turned his attention to his sodden tweed suit. His jacket was structured tweed and so it wouldn't like being wet. Eli knew from the last time this had happened that the lapels, wadding, pocket flaps and vents would likely shrink or pucker or a combination of the two. Either way, his jacket would end up being a bit misshapen. And he'd lost his tiepin altogether when he'd jumped into the sea. In short, Eli was feeling rather messy, and bedraggled, and entirely unlike himself. This jacket might be beyond repair, but at least he could turn his attention to the others he'd packed.

He spent some time carefully steaming them with his travel iron and then spritzing with the travel-sized bottle of cedar-scented cashmere spray. After that he polished his shoes, and by the time he'd showered and washed and combed his hair, he was feeling a little more like himself again. But they were still in last place. Only just in the running. There was a long way to go to catch up. He could feel his chances of reaching the prize rapidly slipping through his fingers.

They'd almost reached Grasshopper Island, at least. They didn't have to sail all the way up to it in the end because Raven spotted them first, and sprinted across the water on Perrie's back. Once they'd welcomed her on board she transformed into her human size and said, 'You managed to escape the clutches of the joo-joo bubs then? I half thought you might both be balloon boys by now.' She smiled at Eli. 'It's good to see you in one piece.'

'You too,' he replied.

'Have you looked at the map?' Jeremiah asked.

'Yes. The last round is in the tiger temple.'

Eli unrolled the map Raven handed him and saw she was correct. The next, and last, checkpoint was at the tiger temple, in a country called Roopa. None of them had ever been to Roopa before, but they'd heard of it. It was a small country, taken up mostly with jungle. It was ruled over by a benevolent tiger princess, who was known for her love of beautiful gardens.

'It's said to be bursting with flowers,' Raven said.

'And tigers,' Eli said, feeling worried. How on earth were they going to get past them?

'A jungle country full of tigers doesn't sound like the kind of place that has many libraries,' Jeremiah remarked.

'Actually, there's at least one library there,' Raven replied. 'The Library of Miniature Books.'

'Hmm.' Jeremiah narrowed his eyes. 'And you know about this how?'

Raven rolled her eyes. 'Some of us do know things about places other than our homes,' she said. 'But, actually, I know about it because the library was a gift from the faeries to Topaz, the tiger princess. The tiger temple belongs to her too.'

'Well, it's good news about the library,' Eli said. 'It means we can use the keys to travel straight there.'

'I suppose so,' Jeremiah replied. 'Libraries aren't normally dangerous, at least. A bit like museums. Dusty and boring, maybe, but not dangerous.'

'Museums aren't dusty and boring!' Eli protested, quite horrified to hear anyone say such a thing. 'And libraries aren't either. Some libraries can be a bit dangerous, actually. Like the library of Kalkatraz Prison, where some of the most dangerous criminals in the world live. And the Night Library, which is the domain of vampires, bad faeries and night sprites. But museums are almost always safe.' He loved museums almost as much as he loved libraries. 'They're fascinating and informative.'

'That depends what type of museum it is,' Jeremiah said. 'If it was a shark museum or something, then, yeah, maybe it might not be completely boring. But people don't make museums about interesting things like sharks. It's always something painfully dull.' He flicked a glance at Eli. 'Like stamps.'

Eli felt a little hurt. 'Now you're deliberately picking something you know I'm interested in, just to be mean. I suppose you thought I'd be embarrassed if Raven found out about the stamps.'

The guilty flicker in Jeremiah's eyes told him he was correct.

Eli stood up a little straighter. 'Maybe you don't know me as well as you think. When have I ever changed myself to try to fit in? People have always laughed at me for being a bit different, but I *like* who I am, and I'm not changing for anyone.'

'Hear, hear,' Humphrey said, stumping up to affectionately headbutt Eli's foot.

'Good for you,' Raven said approvingly.

Eli turned to her and said, 'Thanks. And I'm not at all embarrassed to say that I collect stamps. Did you know that the first one in the world was created in Harmonia? It was called the Penny Royal and had an image of the *Queen Marjory* galleon.'

He wasn't sure what Raven's reaction to this would be. She liked the dictionary and knew some cool words, so he hoped she wouldn't laugh at him about the stamp collection, like some of the kids at school. He didn't expect she would actually be interested in the stamps, because no one ever was, but she might be kind enough to make a polite comment.

Instead, she said, 'So you're a philatelist then, not just a collector?'

Eli felt a little jolt of delight. 'I ... why, yes, I am!' He beamed at Raven. 'I've never met anyone who knew what a philatelist was before. Except for Mr Robinson – one of the librarians at the library – he's a stamp enthusiast too, you see.'

'So what *is* a philatelist?' Jeremiah asked, folding

his arms over his chest. 'Just a fancy word for stamp collector?'

'Well, no, not quite. I mean, there's often some overlap between a stamp collector and a philatelist, of course, but philately is the *study* of stamp production, so, technically, you could be a philatelist without actually owning a single stamp, which is quite fascinating, and—'

'It's not fascinating,' Jeremiah interrupted bluntly. 'And it's a ridiculous thing for there to be an actual word for.'

'There are philatelic clubs all over the world,' Eli pointed out. 'At the Royal Philatelic Society there's even a gift shop with some very lovely tea towels and tote bags. And in their tea rooms you can enjoy a postal-service-themed afternoon tea and—'

'Eli, look at my face,' Jeremiah said. 'Do I appear even remotely interested? Remember we talked about how to tell if someone's interested in what you're telling them?'

'You asked him what a philatelist is,' Raven pointed out. 'Why ask the question if you don't want to hear the answer?'

'I wanted a *brief* answer, not a lecture,' Jeremiah replied. 'Not everyone is as much of a word lover as you.'

'A logophile,' Eli couldn't prevent himself from muttering.

'Sorry?'

'It's just ... that's the word for someone who loves words,' Eli said. 'Logophile.'

'Can we get back to the matter at hand?' Jeremiah jabbed a finger at the map. 'We need to get to the tiger temple, in case you'd forgotten. I'll set a course to use the magic keys.'

He stalked off then, without another word.

Eli flashed Raven an apologetic smile. 'Do you really like stamps?' he asked. 'Or were you just saying that to spite Jeremiah?'

'Oh, no, I've been a member of the Faery Philatelic Club since I was five,' Raven said. 'You can get one of their starter packs for free if you send them a stamped envelope. Last year I won the young collector of the year award for my butterfly stamp collection.'

Eli thought this was quite possibly the most wonderful thing he had ever heard. Not only was Raven interested in something he loved – something that everyone else seemed to think was a bit nerdy – but she liked it enough to enter competitions and win awards too. She wasn't trying to hide her interest in stamps or play it down. It seemed to Eli that Raven was just as happy in her own shoes as he was in his, and he admired her for that.

'I'm going to start on bugs next,' Raven went on. She looked at Eli. 'I'll show you my collection one day, if you like. They're faery stamps, though, so you'll need a magnifying glass to see them properly.'

'I would *love* that,' Eli replied, with a little more enthusiasm than he'd meant to show.

Reluctantly, though, he accepted that their stamp conversation would have to be resumed another time. There was research to be done, so he said goodbye to Raven and made his way to the library with Humphrey. It didn't take long to find out more about the tiger temple.

'It's here,' Eli said, taking a map back on deck to show Jeremiah. 'Just a few miles away from the Library of Miniature Books.' Eli couldn't prevent himself from beaming and wondered why Jeremiah didn't look more pleased. He gave his friend a nudge. 'This is good news,' he said. 'It means we have a chance of catching up. We just have to figure out some way of getting past the tigers.'

'Oh, is that all?' Jeremiah asked sarcastically. 'How do you even know that Roopa is the right destination? Think about it. Raven might have forged the map – we only have her word that this is the one she picked up on the Island of Joo-Joo Bubs. Perhaps she has her own reason for wanting to get to Roopa.'

Eli shook his head. 'Faeries can't lie.'

'She's only half faery,' Jeremiah pointed out.

'Well, I trust her anyway,' Eli replied.

He didn't like the expression on Jeremiah's face. He could feel the tenseness coming off him, that sense that something wasn't quite right. The same thing had happened once or twice in Harmonia, usually right before Jeremiah had failed to turn up for an arranged meeting. And Eli really couldn't afford for Jeremiah to draw away from him now, not in the middle of the race.

'Raven isn't your friend,' Jeremiah went on. 'She's your competitor. If she can double-cross you, she will. She wants to win the race as much as you do.'

'Not everyone is dishonourable,' Eli protested. 'I wouldn't double-cross her.'

'Yes, but you're . . .' Jeremiah waved his hand vaguely. 'You're unique. Most people aren't like you. You told me Raven wants the magic to save the forest she lives in, and that the faeries can't survive there without magic. So she's got a lot of people relying on her, hasn't she? And her loyalty has got to be to them, not you. You need to remember that.'

Eli felt a niggling sense of discomfort and doubt. He wanted things to be uncomplicated and pleasant, and for people to be straightforward and decent with one another. That was how things were in the library staffroom, but he knew full well that wasn't how the Glorious Race of Magical Beasts worked. It was everyone for themselves.

'Look,' he sighed, 'whether you want to trust Raven or not, the map she's given us is the only one we've got. We have no choice but to go to the tiger temple.'

Jeremiah shrugged. 'Whatever. You're the boss of this daft enterprise. I just wish you'd be a little less trusting. People would take advantage of you if I wasn't here.'

Eli folded his arms over his chest. 'I can look out for myself. And anyway, you *are* here. You're not ... you're not having second thoughts about helping me win the race, are you?'

Eli hoped Jeremiah would assure him that *of course* he wasn't having second thoughts, and that Jeremiah Jones always saw an adventure through to the end. But, instead, he said, 'There's land not far from here – Goat Island. I spotted it on the map. We should arrive a couple of hours after sunset and then you can use your key.'

He spoke lightly enough, but his hands were holding the ship's wheel so tightly that his knuckles were white.

'Okay. Thank you.' Eli was about to turn away when he paused and cleared his throat. His next words came out awkwardly, but he knew he had to say them anyway. 'Is everything all right?'

'You mean aside from the fact that we're trying to win an impossible race with a joke tortoise whilst running away from a bounty hunter?' Jeremiah asked. He was gazing at the horizon rather than Eli. 'Sure. Right as rain.'

'I know you're upset about Vincent,' Eli said. 'And once the race is over, we'll figure out what to do about him, I promise. But ... it seemed like maybe there was something wrong back in Harmonia too, before we even knew about Vincent. Is something else going on?'

Jeremiah glanced at him and – just for a moment – Eli thought that he was going to open up and say something, something significant, something that would change things. But then his eyes narrowed and he said, 'I'm not sure what you mean. Is there something *you're* not telling *me*?'

Eli paused, before shaking his head. He couldn't

confess to the letter he'd sent Gaskins right now, he just couldn't. Jeremiah would be so angry.

Jeremiah turned back to the horizon and said, 'That's that all sorted out, then. You worry too much, Eli. And, speaking of rain, it looks like we have some coming up.' He nodded towards the clouds gathering in the sky ahead. 'You'd best get below deck before you ruin another suit.'

CHAPTER TWENTY-TWO

Eli left with a bad feeling in the pit of his stomach. The rain came soon afterwards, pummelling against the portholes. The orange glow of the lamps made the *Nepo* cosy below deck, but Eli knew everything would be drenched and windswept above.

'Jeremiah isn't still out there, is he?' Raven asked, frowning up at the ceiling. She and Eli were having dinner in the dining room, but Jeremiah hadn't joined them. Perrie was lying with her nose between her paws next to the fire, and Humphrey was tucked inside his shell beneath Eli's chair. He was wearing his tortoise life jacket, his silvery moonlight shining out softly around it.

'Jeremiah likes rain,' Eli replied. 'He's a pluviophile.'

He was about to explain what the word meant when Raven said, 'A pluviophile is a person who finds pleasure and peace of mind during rainy days. It means someone sitting on sheltered decking with a hot drink and a book, looking out at the rain whilst being warm and dry themselves. There's got to be a different word for what Jeremiah's doing – standing on the deck of a tossing ship, alone in the dark, whilst it hammers it down. He must be cold, wet and miserable up there. That's not being a pluviophile, that's ... I don't know, someone doing some kind of penance.'

Eli wondered if she could be right. It was pitch black outside now, and the *Nepo* was rocking quite alarmingly on the waves. The deck would be drenched and slippery underfoot, and the salt spray would sting your eyes, and the wind would make your hands numb with cold. Eli wondered whether he should try taking a plate of food up, but what would be the point? It would be soaked and spoiled the moment he stepped outside. Plus, Eli didn't have Jeremiah's sea legs. When the weather was like this, Eli was nervous of losing his footing and being swept overboard.

'Sometimes he just likes to be alone,' he said, trying to reassure himself as much as anything. 'And he probably wants to make sure that the weather doesn't blow us off course and that we reach Goat Island as quickly as possible—'

'*Goat Island?*' Raven cut him off. 'But ... we're not going there, are we? That can't be right.'

'Jeremiah said it was the nearest land,' Eli said. 'He checked the map.'

'Yes, it's the nearest,' Raven replied. 'But it's literally a rock with a few goats on it. There are no buildings there, no doors. You won't be able to use the library key. It's no use to us.'

Eli frowned. 'But ... Jeremiah knows that I need a door ...'

He trailed away as a flash of lightning forked through the air outside, quickly followed by the deep rumble of thunder. At the back of his mind it occurred to him that the storm beasts would be doing well right about now.

'Perhaps he's not as much of an ally as you think,' Raven said, sounding alarmed. 'Maybe he's going to drop us off at Goat Island and leave us there, whilst he carries on to try to win the race himself.'

'He wouldn't do that,' Eli protested. His head was starting to throb. The situation with Jeremiah was making him miserable. How he longed for everything to go back to being simple.

'Everyone wants magic, Eli,' Raven pointed out. 'I bet there's something Jeremiah could use that prize for. Why else did he enter the race? Think about it. You said he joined to accompany you, but he didn't actually have to sign up to do that, did he? He could have just tagged along without a medallion of his own.'

'You're wrong,' Eli said. 'You've got to be.'

He couldn't believe Jeremiah would betray him like that, he just couldn't. And yet … something was certainly wrong. He could feel it. The racing medallions seemed to sense impending excitement and/or doom too, because both Eli's and Raven's suddenly had their eyes wide open, watching and waiting for something to happen.

'I'll go and talk to him,' Eli said, standing up from the table. 'Maybe he made a mistake about Goat Island.'

Yet at the back of Eli's mind was a little voice whispering that Jeremiah Jones didn't make mistakes. He always knew exactly what he was doing.

'I'll come with you,' Raven said. 'I want to hear for myself what's going on.'

Eli thought about trying to dissuade her. After all, Jeremiah was far less likely to open up with her around. But she had every right to know what was happening, and he couldn't think of a way to make her stay. Perrie raised her head from her position by the fire, her long ears twitching as she sensed something was happening.

'You stay right where you are, P,' Raven said, reaching down to scratch the hare behind her ears. 'I want you warm, and safe, and dry.'

'That goes for you too, Humphrey,' Eli said, quite unnecessarily, as it was clear that the tortoise was sound asleep. Even so, Eli scooped him up from beneath his chair and deposited him on the rug beside Perrie so that he would have company if he woke up while they were gone.

Then they made their way up through the ship. Eli had never been on deck in truly bad weather before. When he and Jeremiah had been younger and gone off on voyages together, they had always chosen bright, sunny, calm days. In fact, come to think of it, Eli supposed those outings hadn't really been adventures at all, although they had seemed so to him at the time. Looking back, he could see them for what they had truly been – mostly picnics in the sun, with a bit of sea swimming, and an occasional island beach to hang hammocks and collect coconuts and make rafts. Jeremiah had told Eli back at Harmonia that he didn't really know what an adventure was, and perhaps he'd been right.

When Eli pushed open the hatch to climb up on deck, he was immediately drenched with the water flowing over the boards. It was so cold that he cried out with the shock of it. Jeremiah's words from that long-ago conversation came back to him:

He didn't say the cold was sharp as knives that would peel your skin off . . .

He didn't say that the salt spray stung my eyes so badly I could hardly keep them open . . .

For the first time, Eli could properly understand what Jeremiah had been saying back then. The reality of being on the deck of a ship in the middle of a storm wasn't what Eli had imagined at all. He realised there were parts of his friend's life inside the book that had been far more painful and gruelling than Eli had appreciated. No wonder Jeremiah had such a horror of vanishing back within the pages. The shriek of the wind sounded like wounded animals, and the sails stretching into the night sky above them snapped and flapped so ferociously that Eli felt the urge to cover his head with his hands in case the masts should be ripped up and crash down on top of him. The rain was like icy needles, diving over and over again into his eyes and mouth and skin.

Raven was certainly right. Jeremiah wasn't on deck

because he was enjoying the rain as a pluviophile. No one would be here unless they absolutely had to be, unless something critical was at stake.

It was difficult to see up on deck in the storm. The clouds covered the moon and stars, and the ship tilted and lurched on the waves so violently that it was impossible to properly distinguish the sea from the sky. It was so bad that Eli wondered if Raven would turn back after all. The rain splattered against the lenses of her glasses, but she remained by his side as they staggered and slid over the deck. Each time a flash of lightning forked through the air, the deck would be lit with brilliant yellow light. But the next moment they'd be plunged into darkness once more, and it would be even harder to see where they were going.

Fortunately, Eli knew where Jeremiah was likely to be – at the wheel. On the next lightning flash, he saw his friend starkly outlined against the sky for a moment. His boots were planted firmly to steady himself on the deck and he gripped the navigational wheel with both hands. He was, of course, dripping wet, and there was something about the set of his shoulders and the angle of his chin that showed how determined and tense he was, as if battling against some great foe. If this had been a normal ship, Eli would have thought he was trying to keep the ship steady in the storm, but he knew the *Nepo* could do this on her own. So what was Jeremiah battling against?

Eli raised his voice to shout his friend's name, but it was immediately lost in the gale. He'd never felt so small and insignificant, and now even the mighty *Nepo* seemed frail in the face of the storm's great fury. A huge wave crashed over the deck, sending Eli and Raven sprawling. They had to grab on to coils of rope to stop themselves being washed right over the side. It seemed to Eli that the ocean might take the *Nepo* altogether. After all, ships did sink in storms.

Maybe this wasn't the time to confront Jeremiah; maybe explanations about Goat Island could wait until the storm had passed ... Yet somehow he knew this *couldn't* wait. Eli and Raven struggled to their feet and in another few moments they'd reached Jeremiah at the wheel. He couldn't have looked more appalled if a real-life devil had appeared before him.

'What are you *doing*?' he yelled above the roar of the waves. 'Get below!'

Eli shook his head. 'Something's wrong!' he shouted. He put his hand on Jeremiah's shoulder and was shocked to feel that he was trembling – his friend who wasn't scared of anything. 'I want to help!'

Jeremiah turned to look at him, and in that moment a flash of lightning lit up the deck and Eli saw an expression on the other boy's face that chilled him to his core. Jeremiah was afraid, but it was more than that. There was anguish burning in his eyes like two red-hot coals.

'I'm sorry!' he panted. 'I think . . . I think it's already too late!'

Eli frowned. 'Too late for *what*?' If he could only get to the bottom of whatever the problem was then perhaps he could help do something about it. 'I know you're not steadying the ship, so what are you trying to *do*?'

'I'M TRYING TO STAY HERE!' Jeremiah roared over the wind. 'I'm trying to keep the *Nepo* here!'

There was a wild look in his eye and his knuckles were white where they gripped the wheel, as if whatever he was doing was taking every ounce of his strength.

'What do you mean?' Raven yelled. 'You're not making any sense!'

'The book!' Jeremiah gasped. 'It wants us! It wants us back, it . . .'

He broke off with a groan and slumped on to his knees, his hands torn from the wheel to press flat against the soaking boards. Alarmed, Eli crouched beside him, but before he could ask if he was all right, Jeremiah gripped both his arms and said urgently, 'Keep your head above the water!'

'What? What are you—'

'Just keep your head above the water, okay? Kick as hard as you can. Do whatever you have to. I'll come for you, I promise. You just have to hang on.'

Eli shook his head. He didn't understand, and the not understanding frightened him, and so did the storm, and the cold, and the dark. But before he could say another word, Jeremiah had vanished.

One moment he was there, water streaming from the ends of his black hair and dripping from the ragged hem of his captain's coat. And the next, he was gone, as if he'd never been there to begin with. There wasn't a single trace of him left, but his words still echoed inside Eli's head.

The book ...

It wants us back ...

Eli looked up in time to see Luther vanish from the rigging. And, suddenly, he knew what was going to happen next. He stared at Raven with an expression of terror on his face.

'The ship!' he gasped. 'It's going to disappear too.'

'*What?*' Raven looked like she was about to be sick.

'But . . . but we're at sea in the middle of a storm! What about the animals?'

Eli thought of Humphrey snoozing innocently by the fire and horror prickled over his skin. Was there any chance at all that they might reach them in time? And even if they did, would it do any good? There were rowing boats on board the *Nepo* that could be used as lifeboats, but they were part of the book too and would disappear along with the rest of the ship.

They had to at least try to reach Humphrey and Perrie, so Eli scrambled to his feet, and he and Raven sprinted over the deck. But then suddenly they weren't running any more, they were falling, because there wasn't a deck, there was no longer even a ship. In the blink of an eye, the *Nepo* had vanished back into the pages it had come from, leaving Eli and Raven suspended several storeys in the air, with nothing but the stormy sea below them. It was impossible, unthinkable, yet it had happened, and they were plummeting down, down, down towards the black, hungry waves.

CHAPTER TWENTY-THREE

Eli's hands reached blindly for Humphrey, hoping that by some miracle they might make contact with the tortoise's shell on the way down. The thought of his pet being lost alone at sea was unbearable. Even with his life jacket on, the tortoise would be at the mercy of the waves, completely helpless, and would surely drown.

And in those endless moments before he plunged into the sea, Eli knew he had failed in every way that mattered. He had let Humphrey down – his sweet-natured, magical pet who trusted him utterly and relied upon him for everything. He'd let Jeremiah down because his magic was supposed to be holding him here, but suddenly wasn't working for reasons Eli couldn't understand. He'd let Raven down – having promised her safe passage on board a ship that was no longer there. And he'd let Nana down, robbing her of those last months they might have had together – the only thing she'd ever asked him for. Now there would be no one to look after her in the days to come ...

Eli tried to suck in as much air as he could in the final seconds before he plunged into the sea, but it made no difference because the force of the fall knocked all the breath from his body. And then he was plunging deep, deep below the surface, just like he had when he leapt from the Island of Joo-Joo Bubs. Only, this time, there was no Jeremiah to drag him to safety. There was no helping hand or promise of rescue. There was only the muffled roar of the waves ringing in his ears, and the echo of Jeremiah's voice.

Kick as hard as you can ...

I'll come for you, I promise ...

But Jeremiah wasn't here, and Eli didn't know what had happened, only that his friend was gone and Eli was struggling alone in the sea. He kicked and kicked as hard as he could, his lungs burning in their hunger for air. He clenched his teeth and concentrated on keeping his mouth closed, but finally he couldn't help himself – he took a big, gasping breath, even though he knew that it wouldn't help, that it would only make things worse, that it would kill him. Water rushed into his mouth, filling his throat and making him choke.

At the back of his mind, it occurred to him that there would be people watching this, in the square in Harmonia. He could imagine the grave hush that had fallen over the crowd, the fascinated solemnity that comes of watching a person die up there on the screen. He kicked, and kicked, and kicked, and kicked . . .

When his head broke the surface he felt a brief flash of triumph. He'd done it! He'd made it back on his own. But the relief was short-lived because the next second a wave crashed over his head, dragging him under once more. And no matter how many times Eli got his head above the water, there'd be another wave to drag him under, and another, and another.

He was exhausted, and the amount of seawater he'd swallowed was making him retch into the ocean. He cast about for something to grab on to, but the *Nepo* had vanished entirely, so there were no wooden planks or barrels to use as floats. He couldn't even tell where Raven was. Any thought he might have had of trying to find and save Humphrey was gone. He felt a flash of agony at the thought that he'd lost his little friend for good. All around him was noise and chaos. Crashing waves, and stinging salt, and strong currents that were like icy hands grabbing on to his legs and trying to pull him down, down, down.

I'm going to drown now, Eli thought, with sudden certainty and a strange, eerie calmness.

He couldn't tell whether he'd been in the water for a few minutes or a few hours. It didn't matter. His strength was gone. He'd given it his best shot, but sometimes a person's best just wasn't enough. He slipped beneath the surface and knew he wouldn't be able to kick his way up again. He wished he could see Nana one last time, to say sorry and goodbye. He wished he could be amongst his beloved books for a few moments too, in the soft hush of the library . . .

Then a hand clamped around his arm and pulled him up. Suddenly, Raven was there, helping him swim to the shore of the nearby island. Eli was so focused on getting there that he didn't notice when the *Nepo* suddenly appeared in the water nearby, solid and real once more. At last, he and Raven collapsed on to the wet sand, panting with the effort.

It had finally stopped raining and the soft sparkle of stars appeared in the sky above. There was a frantic splashing behind them as Jeremiah approached, dripping wet from the ocean. Eli felt a huge rush of relief at the sight of him.

'Are you okay?' he asked.

Eli was still coughing up seawater, so Raven replied instead. 'Our animals! They're still out there!'

Eli hated the thought of Humphrey alone in the dark, trying to keep his head above the water ... but then he spotted him. Humphrey's moonlight shell made him easy to see, bobbing on the surface in his life jacket, and with a tortoise's luck, he was already being carried in to shore. Eli felt tears on his cheeks as he waded into the shallows and scooped him up, grateful right down to his soul. At the same time, there was a fluttering of feathers as a large shape swooped overhead, and Luther landed on Jeremiah's shoulder.

'Help us look for Perrie,' Jeremiah said. The phoenix immediately spread his wings and took flight. Jeremiah and Raven both threw themselves into the cold water.

Eli walked up the beach, anxious to check on Humphrey, who was still tucked inside his shell.

'Are you all right?' he asked, setting the tortoise down on the sand.

'Oh, yes, I always wanted to experience a shipwrecking,' Humphrey replied. 'It's a good thing I'm such a strong swimmer— Oh, look! Seagrass!'

He stumped over and began munching happily.

But it was a less joyous return for Perrie. Luther

retrieved the hare from the ocean and flew back with her to the beach. Raven noticed the limp white shape clutched in the phoenix's claws and swam to shore. Luther set the hare down gently on the sand. Eli hurried over and they could all see at once that the little animal had died. Her white fur was sodden and she seemed very small and delicate in the moonlight. Raven buried her face in her hands and sobbed. It was like her heart was breaking into a million pieces. Eli was appalled by what had happened, but couldn't think of anything to do to help. Their magical beasts were like family. Raven couldn't possibly lose Perrie, she couldn't . . .

Then Jeremiah put his hand on her shoulder and said quietly, 'It's okay. I can fix this. I can bring Perrie back.'

Raven looked up at him, half-blinded by tears, hardly daring to believe it might be true. 'How?' she gasped.

'Luther.'

They all watched, holding their breath, as Luther hopped forwards over the sand and laid his head against Perrie's chest. A single tear trickled from the bird's blue eye and seeped into the hare's pale fur. The next moment, Luther's feathers started to dissolve into water. It seemed like the bird just melted into the sand. When the last feather vanished, there was a little explosion of salty foam that soaked away to reveal a smooth, shiny blue egg.

At the same moment, Perrie's little paws twitched and then she was standing up and shaking herself, straightening her long ears and rubbing up against Raven's legs. With a cry of delight, Raven scooped up her pet and hugged her close to her chest.

'You're okay, you're okay,' she said, over and over again. Then she looked up at Jeremiah, who'd picked up the blue egg and was holding it carefully in his hand. 'What just happened?'

'Luther is – was – a sea phoenix,' he replied. 'His tears can restore life, but he loses his own in the process.'

He looked sad and suddenly very tired. Part of Eli longed to put his hand on his friend's arm, but it felt as if the distance between them was bigger than ever. They'd both been keeping secrets from each other, and Eli worried that they would never recapture their easy friendship from before. Their chances of winning the race might be long gone by this point too.

'You mean he's . . . Luther's dead?' Raven asked.

Jeremiah nodded. 'My Luther died. He'll be reborn and it will still be Luther, but a different one. We'll have to start our friendship again from scratch and it won't be quite how it was before. He won't remember all the things we did together. He won't even know who I am.'

'I'm sorry,' Raven said. 'But why did you let this happen in the first place? You knew the *Nepo* was going to vanish. That's why you set a course for Goat Island. You let us think we were safe when we weren't.'

Jeremiah nodded. 'I know I owe you both an explanation, and I promise I'll give you one, but, for now, I don't think I can stay on my feet a second longer, and I'm just . . .' His voice caught in his throat. 'Can we get some sleep and talk in the morning?'

The last hour had been exhausting for them all, so Eli and Raven agreed the explanation could wait. It was warm on the beach, and their clothes were already drying, so they didn't bother to swim back to the *Nepo*, in the end. Instead, they found a sheltered spot of soft sand to curl up in. As Eli closed his eyes, he tried not to think about the difficult conversation with Jeremiah that was waiting for him in the morning.

CHAPTER TWENTY-FOUR

Eli woke to a goat trying to nibble his hair. He sat bolt upright on the sand, and for a moment, he couldn't remember where he was. Then the events of last night came flooding back. He ached all over, but the storm had passed, the sun was in the sky and the air smelled of surf and coconuts and . . . regrettably, goat. It was quite a strong smell, actually, and no wonder, as there must have been twenty goats on the beach, poking about in the seaweed and peering at the children curiously.

Eli saw that Raven was still asleep, curled around Perrie, who was snoozing contentedly in the crook of her arm. Humphrey was asleep inside his shell and Jeremiah was sitting further on down the beach, bending over something. When Eli walked over, he saw that it was a newly hatched Luther. There were little pieces of blue shell on the sand around the baby sea phoenix. Eli had read about how this happened, but he'd never seen it for himself. The phoenix had been an adult the whole time Eli had known him, so it was strange to look at the scrawny little baby bird scratching around excitedly in the sand and fluffing up its white baby feathers.

'You don't know me yet,' Jeremiah was saying to the chick, 'but we're old friends. You used to be very wise, but now you're a little bald thing who doesn't know much about anything, so stay close to me if you can. I'll look out for you.'

'It was nice what you did for Perrie,' Eli said.

Jeremiah didn't look around. 'It was the least I could do.' His shoulders hunched slightly. 'Come and sit down. There's something I need to tell you. Something I should have shared a while ago.'

Eli dropped down beside his friend in the sand. He had a bad feeling about whatever he was going to say. Jeremiah took a deep breath.

'I think my time here is running out. Fictional characters aren't supposed to come out of books, Eli. We're not supposed to change and get older and choose our own path. You and I both know that. And Raven was right when she said I wasn't real. I'm not. Not really. I'm just . . . I'm just an idea from someone's head.

And now the book wants me back. I can feel the pages hungering for me, trying to drag me in where I belong.'

Eli shook his head, the bad feeling growing into a sense of dread. 'You belong here with me.'

'I love being in the real world and I don't want to go back to being a nine-year-old adventurer – never growing up, or having friends, or making mistakes. But I've felt myself getting pulled back more and more lately. I can feel myself starting to fade away. And sometimes it takes all my concentration not to disappear altogether, back into the book. It happened a couple of times, in Harmonia.'

'That's why you didn't meet me when we'd arranged to,' Eli said.

Jeremiah nodded.

'But why didn't you tell me straight away?' Eli asked. 'I might be able to do something to fix this.'

He couldn't think of a single thing in that moment, but surely if he spent enough time thinking it through and poring over his books then he'd find a way? He could feel a nameless sense of panic rising inside him, and pushed it down roughly. There simply must be something he could do to fix this.

'I can't talk about it.' Jeremiah's voice dropped to a whisper. To Eli's dismay, he suddenly looked frightened. 'Talking about it makes it worse, makes it stronger.'

'Makes *what* stronger?'

Jeremiah looked at him. 'The thing. The thing inside the sea chest.'

The boys fell silent, and in the silence there came a soft *click*. Jeremiah shuddered and Eli knew that it was the sea chest coming open again inside his pocket.

'I really can't say too much because it's ... I think it's listening,' Jeremiah said. 'And the more I tell you about it, the more power it will have. But there's something in the sea chest that wants to take me back to the book. Lately it's been getting bigger, stronger, and if it ever gets out then it'll drag me back into the pages, I know it will. And even you won't be able to get me out.'

'Why not?' Eli protested. 'You don't know that. I got you out once. I could do it again.'

Jeremiah looked suddenly sad. 'When you took me out of the book you were a lonely little kid. It's different now – you have the library and a life of your own, you don't need me. Things between us have changed, we both know it's true. And after you began working at the library ... Perhaps the reason it's happening now is because you're ... well, you're outgrowing me.'

'*What?*'

Jeremiah wouldn't meet his eye. 'Sometimes I think that if I disappeared back into the book one day, you'd barely even notice.'

'But that's not true!' Eli cried. 'Of course I'd notice! I'd be devastated!'

Jeremiah's words were niggling at him.

And after you began working at the library ...

But something else had happened around that time too – Eli had sent his letter to Lionel Gaskins. All along, he'd hoped this might mean the author would give Jeremiah up gracefully, but instead he'd only redoubled his efforts to get him back.

'I'm sorry,' Eli said, his voice a whisper. 'I've just realised what's happening. And it's my fault.'

He took a deep breath and then told Jeremiah everything. There was a horrible silence once he'd finished.

Finally, Jeremiah said, 'But ... but you *know* how I feel about being trapped inside that book! You know how I hated it. Why would you risk all that by writing to Gaskins?'

'I didn't think I *was* risking anything,' Eli replied. 'I just thought I was apologizing. I mean, I stole you from him, so—'

'I am a *PERSON*!' Jeremiah shouted, making Eli jump. 'You can't steal a person, Eli! You're the wordsmith, so you know that. You steal *things* but you kidnap *people*. So, which am I to you?'

'No,' Eli said very quietly.

'No?' Jeremiah looked confused. 'No, what?'

'No, I won't let you speak to me this way. You *know* you're a person to me! You know you've *always* been a person, and that's how you came out of the book in the first place. That's what I was trying to explain to Gaskins. You belong to me because I love you. And it's got nothing to do with whether you're a fictional character or not. I belong to you too. That's what being family is. So don't you *dare* try to tell me that I don't care about you when you know it's not true.'

'Is that why you joined the race?' Raven asked.

The boys hadn't noticed her approaching, but now they looked around to see her standing on the beach nearby, with Perrie snuggled in her arms.

'What do you mean?' Jeremiah demanded.

'Well ... if you win, then you could use the magic to make yourself real,' Raven said. 'Permanently, I mean.'

Eli felt a sudden sinking feeling. Could it be true? Had Jeremiah joined for himself? And could Eli really blame him if he had? He had as much right to seek his own happiness as anyone else, after all. Eli's head suddenly felt too small for all the thoughts charging up and down inside it, all clamouring to be heard at once.

'Of course not!' Jeremiah was saying. 'I came to help Eli save his nana.'

Eli stood up. 'We've wasted enough time,' he said. 'Let's get back to the *Nepo.*'

'We can't sail anywhere on that ship!' Raven replied. 'Not now we know it could disappear out from under us at a moment's notice!'

'Even if we don't carry on with the race, we can't stay here,' Eli replied. 'There's nothing on the island but goats.'

They'd amassed quite a little crowd of interested goats by this point, all staring at them curiously whilst they munched at the various plants growing on the beach.

'What do you mean "even if we don't carry on with the race"?' Jeremiah demanded. 'Of course we're carrying on. It's the only way to help Nana.'

'I know, but I'm just ... I don't know why I ever thought I could win this.' They were still in last place, even further behind than they'd been before. Eli felt defeated, and small, and rather stupid. The feeling of arguing with his best friend in the world was horrible and made him feel angry as well as upset. Perhaps Jeremiah felt the same, because he didn't say anything further. After all, what was there left to say? Either Jeremiah trusted him or he didn't. Perhaps their years of friendship hadn't meant anything, after all.

'You know what I think?' Jeremiah began. 'I think that—'

'I don't care!' Eli snapped. 'And I don't want to hear any more of your thoughts right now. We need to move. Where's Humphrey?'

Jeremiah looked taken aback, but thankfully he clenched his jaw and didn't say another word. The three of them trudged down the beach to where Humphrey had stumped determinedly across the sand to the water and then got stuck. Fortunately, he was still wearing his life jacket, so was bobbing about in the shallows with a peaceful expression on his face. Eli waded in after him and the old tortoise said brightly, 'I've thought of another one!'

'Another what?'

'Poem. For my party. It's about glory and adventure, so I think it'll be perfect for Jeremiah to read.'

Eli remained silent. He couldn't bear to tell Humphrey that Jeremiah might not be at his party, or even in their lives at all. So he silently began an awkward doggy paddle, whilst pushing Humphrey ahead with one hand. Raven shrank herself down to faery size and climbed on to Perrie's back so the ice hare could race across the water back to the boat. And Jeremiah set baby Luther on his shoulder, where the little chick flapped his stubby wings and squawked in excitement as they swam.

They were a bedraggled group as they climbed on board the *Nepo*. Eli was glad to see the ship again but, like Raven, he didn't feel at ease on her deck any more. He rather doubted he'd ever feel safe sailing on her again. This made him feel such a wave of sorrow that suddenly he couldn't stand to be there a moment longer.

'Right,' Eli said. 'I'm going home.'

'What, for good?' Jeremiah looked shocked.

'I don't know,' Eli said honestly.

'In the meantime, perhaps you could take me to the nearest island?' Raven looked at Jeremiah.

'I'll set a course,' he said gruffly, before turning and striding across the deck.

CHAPTER TWENTY-FIVE

Eli took the key from beneath his shirt and walked over to the nearest door, Humphrey still tucked under his arm. The key clicked in the lock and the door swung open to reveal the little free library back in Harmonia. Eli stepped over the threshold, glad to leave the *Nepo* behind. He simply couldn't believe that Jeremiah had suggested that Eli didn't think of him as a real person. It was such a galaxy away from the truth, and the unfairness of it scalded. Harmonia must be a few hours behind Goat Island because it was still dark, although Eli could see the sky beginning to shine a dusky rose colour on the horizon. All was quiet and peaceful, and the restaurant's decking was deserted. To his astonishment, Eli could see a large screen erected at one end of the decking, which, even now, was replaying some of the footage from the race. Nana had never permitted this before and he was touched that she would do so now, but a bit unnerved at the same time. So many things were different and Eli didn't like change.

He paused in the tiny library, taking a moment to run his fingers over the spines of all the books he loved so dearly. At least this place was still the same. He couldn't resist glancing in his visitors book and was gladdened to see a new note in there – just a couple of lines – from someone who had borrowed and read *The China Rabbit*:

I had never heard of this book before, but it comforted me very much during a difficult week, and raised my spirits. Thank you.

Eli smiled slightly, feeling a bit of his anger fizzle away. He knew that books could do this, of course – that they had the power to lift people up, and make them feel less alone and less sad. He was always especially pleased to be responsible for introducing the right book to the right person at the right time. It was what he was meant to do – he was *good* at being a librarian, whereas it seemed to him that he was very bad at having adventures.

'Why are we back home?' Humphrey asked suddenly. 'Did we win the race already?'

'No, Humphrey,' Eli sighed. 'I don't think we're going to win the race at all.'

'But . . . but why are we back here if it isn't over?' Eli couldn't bear the confusion in the old tortoise's voice.

'I've . . . I've just come to pack a bag,' he said, thinking quickly. 'My stuff was lost in the shipwreck.'

This was true. All his candles, books and clothes were lost when the *Nepo* vanished. Apart from his keys, which had been in his pocket, his things had all been in his cabin, so Eli guessed they had been scattered across the ocean by now. He still wasn't sure whether he was actually going to pack a bag or not, but he didn't want to have that conversation with Humphrey right now.

'Why don't you go into your shell and have a snooze?' he suggested. 'You must be tired.'

'All right, I wouldn't mind a snooze, now you mention it. Don't dilly-dally too long, though; we *are* in a race, in case you'd forgotten.'

'I know, I know.'

As Eli tiptoed from his library and across the deck, he caught the familiar whiff of coffee and chocolate sauce. The breakfast service would start soon and he could almost smell the pancake batter frying in the pan. His stomach rumbled as he crept upstairs and he felt a sudden wave of homesickness so strong he actually whimpered. Perhaps it would be better for everyone to stay home for good, and not return to the *Nepo* …

As he let himself into his comfortable, cosy bedroom and set Humphrey down in the corner, he'd almost made up his mind to stay. Just drop out of the race now and admit defeat. He wasn't cut out for this, and he wasn't going to win. He'd made so many mistakes, they were in last place, Humphrey had nearly drowned, Jeremiah was furious and so was Eli. He didn't think he could face going back and continuing their conversation. It seemed easier to hold on to his anger. Perhaps this was it for him and Jeremiah. For the first time in his life, Eli felt the urge to throw something. He didn't give in to the feeling because he didn't want to frighten Humphrey, but magic crackled between his fingertips and it was a painful effort not to give in.

But then his gaze fell on his chest of drawers. There was a large, leather-bound dictionary on top. It had been a gift from his parents and was one of his most prized possessions. Inside was an inscription:

To our gentle, loving, wonderful son. May you succeed at anything you put your mind to. Much love, Mummy and Daddy. xxxx

Eli had always loved the book because it made him feel like his parents had understood him, that they'd loved him for who he was. They hadn't minded that he wasn't like them, that he preferred books and learning to voyages and exploits. But now, beside the dictionary was another book of a similar size – one that hadn't been there before. He walked over and saw that it was a thesaurus, bound in the same handsome blue leather as the dictionary. When he flipped open the cover, he saw that some words had been written in his grandmother's neat handwriting.

For my dear Eli. The bravest boy I've ever known. All my love, Nana. xxxx

Eli stared at the words, his head swimming. This book hadn't been here when he left. Nana must have bought it after he'd left for the race, and put it in his room for him to find when he returned. He realised there were tears in his eyes which he suddenly had to blink away. No one had ever called him brave before. Eli knew that he was quiet, and studious, and thoughtful, and kind, and various other commendable things. But surely not brave. Why, he had trembled most of the way through the race so far ...

And now, beside the dictionary definition of brave. He knew that it did not mean to be unafraid, but rather to face the fear willingly, to endure the danger, to show courage. Perhaps he *was* brave. Perhaps he could do this impossible thing. Perhaps he could pick himself up one last time to make things right with his best friend and see it through to the end. And if he didn't win, well, at least he would have given it his absolute best shot. Nana's voice echoed inside his head:

Sometimes you just have to give yourself a stern talking-to and get on with things, whether you feel like it or not . . .

He put the book down, then went to the cupboard, where he yanked a fresh suit from its hanger. Within five minutes, he was dressed, with a smart new tiepin and a pair of gleaming alphabet cufflinks. Then he pulled out a satchel and restocked it with some candles and carefully selected books, including a harmless one about flowers in case he wanted to put anyone within its pages, and a book about venomous bugs and how to create antivenom, which might come in handy if they were heading to the jungle. Finally, he scooped up Humphrey and then glanced towards his bedroom door. It was so very tempting to go downstairs and find Nana. He could hear noises coming from the kitchen now, and knew that she'd probably be down there, preparing the pancake batter. It would be wonderful to see her, even only briefly. But he feared that if he did that now, then he'd never have the strength to return to the race.

So he turned away and walked up to the wardrobe, where he selected the right key and inserted it into the lock. A moment later, he was back on board the *Nepo*. It was time to make their way to the final round – but there was something important he had to do first.

CHAPTER TWENTY-SIX

It didn't take Eli long to find Jeremiah. He always said a captain's place was on the deck and sure enough, he was there at the rails, looking out to sea with baby Luther perched on his shoulder. Eli approached his friend feeling both hopeful and cautious. He was halfway between wanting to hold on to his anger and wanting to let it go. He was suddenly afraid that Jeremiah wouldn't want to fix their friendship as much as he did.

Nevertheless, he took a deep breath, joined his friend and said, 'If I'd known that Gaskins was going to send a bounty hunter after you then I never would have written to him. You can believe it or not, but it's the truth. I wrestled with the decision for weeks. I was trying to do the right thing. Now I know I got it wrong. I'm not perfect, okay? I make mistakes. So do you. So does everyone.'

Jeremiah turned to look at him. 'I know that you care. I care too. That's what makes this hard. But before we go on, there's something I need to say.'

Eli braced himself for more recriminations, more anger, more bitterness. Instead, Jeremiah said quietly, 'I'm sorry I got cross before.'

Eli stared at him. It was the first time he could ever remember hearing his friend apologise. Jeremiah didn't say sorry to anyone. He was always right, always.

And yet, he went on, 'I understand why you wrote to Gaskins. I don't like it. But I do understand. You wouldn't be you if you hadn't felt the need to be honest.'

'I'm sorry too,' Eli said, feeling a wave of relief and gladness. Perhaps their friendship was going to be okay, perhaps they could mend it if this was something Jeremiah wanted too. 'I never meant to put you in danger,' Eli went on. 'We'll figure it out. Once the race is over, I promise we'll find a way to keep you here.'

Jeremiah grinned and clapped him on the shoulder. 'That's enough talking.'

An hour later, the *Nepo* docked at a populated island. This gave Eli enough time to locate the correct key, so he was ready when the three of them disembarked. Jeremiah put the ship back in the bottle and then the three children gathered in front of the nearest door. This happened to belong to the harbour master, who began to tell them off for loitering, but didn't manage to finish his lecture before Eli inserted the key and the three of them stepped through into the Library of Miniature Books. As soon as they did so, they leapt up the leader board from last place to first. Eli felt a great rush of relief. Thanks to his magic library keys, they were still in with a chance.

It was broad daylight here, and they could see that the library was open because there were a few interested people milling around, peering at the tiny books in their glass cases. No one looked up or took much notice of them, and they were able to pass through the library unimpeded.

When they reached the exit, Eli turned to Raven and said, 'I guess this is where we part ways.'

He felt a pang of loss at the thought. He'd enjoyed Raven's company and regretted that the race was forcing them back into being competitors.

Raven looked troubled too. 'I wish we could carry on working as a team, but there's no prize for second place, so . . .'

Eli nodded. This was the nature of the race. They'd known that.

'Perhaps we can compare stamp collections once this is all over,' Raven said.

'I'd love that,' Eli replied.

Raven's eyes flicked to Jeremiah. 'Thank you for saving Perrie. Look after each other. And . . . I'm sorry.'

With that, she shrank herself down to faery size, hopped on to her hare's back and disappeared out of the door.

'Sorry for what?' Jeremiah said, his suspicions immediately raised.

Eli had no idea what she might have been referring to, but there was no time to wonder about it. They followed her out of the library and found themselves in a town square, much like the Royal Library back in Harmonia. The main difference was that this square was lined with tall jungle trees, long vines hanging from the branches and colourful parrots ruffling their feathers amidst the foliage. The air was warm and sticky compared with the cool interior of the library, and it felt to Eli like trying to breathe through pudding.

Just like the square at home, there were large screens set up for the local residents to watch the progress of the race. The space was currently full of spectators. Eli hadn't realised that his medallion's eye was open until he saw it broadcasting directly on to the large screens straight ahead of them. A hush fell over the crowd as they all turned to look at Eli and Jeremiah on the steps of the library. The next moment, they were breaking into applause and many people started pushing forwards, asking for autographs and racing mementos.

'Just one feather from the sea phoenix!' one woman begged, tugging at Jeremiah's sleeve. 'I can pay you handsomely for it!'

'Get off.' Jeremiah slapped her hand away. 'He's only got two feathers and he needs them both.'

'Are you really a mage?' someone shouted from the crowd. 'Do some magic!'

'Where's your tortoise?'

'Here I am!' Humphrey piped up from within the bag.

'How does it feel to be in the top two?'

'It feels like something we shouldn't fritter away by standing here answering questions,' Jeremiah snapped. 'Now, please clear a path.'

Eli couldn't see Raven anywhere in sight, and guessed she'd been able to run through the crowd unimpeded in her smaller faery form. He and Jeremiah didn't have the same advantage and he realised they might have to push their way through. But as soon as they started trying to move in earnest, the crowd changed. The entire atmosphere changed. It was no longer friendly and curious, but grim and determined.

'You can't pass through,' a woman at the front said. 'Princess Ravinia said not to let you.'

'Who's Princess Ravinia?' Jeremiah replied.

The woman gestured at the screen. 'We can see you, remember? So we know you've been travelling with Princess Ravinia. Our princess told us who she really is.'

Eli and Jeremiah slowly turned to look at each other. Raven. Ravinia.

'Princess Ravinia is friends with our princess,' a man near the front said. 'And Princess Topaz asked us to do anything in our power to help her win.'

Eli felt a small flash of hurt that Raven hadn't told them the truth. But at the same time he supposed he couldn't blame her if she'd thought it might give her an advantage later. The race made friendships difficult – impossible, really. All that mattered was reaching the finish line before anyone else.

'What are we going to do?' Eli said beneath his breath to Jeremiah. 'They're making it impossible to pass through the square.'

Jeremiah narrowed his eyes. 'Are they blocking the square? I don't see how. I mean, they're not exactly joo-joo bubs. They're just ordinary people. We can get through them, all right.'

'But how? There'd be pushing and shoving, and someone might get hurt.'

'Stop fretting. They're the ones threatening us, remember? If they don't want to get pushed and shoved then perhaps they should consider going home and putting the kettle on.'

He cleared his throat and stepped forward on the steps. 'You say you've been watching our progress through the race?'

There was a general nodding from the crowd.

'Good. Then you must know who I am?'

Eli heard a few people say Jeremiah's name aloud, along with some mutters of 'Witchcraft!' and 'Unnatural.'

Jeremiah ignored them and went on, 'And if you know who I am then you must also know all about the *Nepo*? She's part ship and part octopus, but she's completely loyal to me and she doesn't like it when obstacles get in my way. If anyone here has read my book then perhaps you remember the chapter where the *Nepo* used her tentacles to clear out an entire gang of blizzard sharks—'

'Shiver,' Eli interrupted.

Jeremiah looked at him. 'Pardon?'

'It's the collective noun,' Eli said. 'For sharks. They're not a gang – they're a shiver.'

'Thank you for the linguistic lesson,' Jeremiah said.

Eli beamed back. 'You're welcome.'

Jeremiah rolled his eyes and turned back to the crowds. 'So, yes, the *Nepo* swatted away an entire *shiver* of sharks with hardly any effort at all. I don't think a few townsfolk are going to give her much trouble, but if you want to test your luck then hang around, by all means.'

He reached into the pocket of his coat and drew out the bottle containing the *Nepo*. The mood in the crowd shifted, and people looked quite alarmed. After all, if they'd been watching the race then they would have seen how the *Nepo* burst right out of the bottle, and even without her tentacles, a huge galleon crashing down in the middle of a village square was likely to break a few cobblestones and squash anyone unfortunate enough to get in the way.

'Hang on a minute—' someone yelled.

But Jeremiah was already raising his arm. 'On the count of three!' he yelled. 'One!'

There was an immediate scrambling and scrabbling

towards the edges of the square as people fought to get out of the way.

'Two!' Jeremiah called.

'Erm, maybe you should count to ten instead?' Eli suggested, suddenly worried. 'We don't *really* want anyone to get squashed—'

'*Three!*'

Jeremiah's arm swept forwards in a perfect arc, and the bottle sailed out to the middle of the square and landed on the cobbles with a clink and clank. The thick, magical glass didn't break on impact, and the bottle bounced and rolled to a stop. There was a moment of charged silence and then, with a wicked grin, Jeremiah said quietly, 'Hello, *Nepo.*'

CHAPTER TWENTY-SEVEN

The *Nepo* burst from the bottle. Perhaps the ship had been listening to Jeremiah because she came out with her tentacles flailing more than usual. The massive galleon took up almost the entire square, and the large screens were quickly knocked over, shattering upon the cobbles. Anyone within reach found themselves batted away by the tentacles and the townsfolk scattered. Eli was concerned in case anyone had been hurt, but Jeremiah waved his fears away.

'Don't worry, I could see there was plenty of room for the ship before I opened the bottle. And if anyone got flicked by a tentacle, well, that's their own fault for poking their noses where they don't belong.'

'Still.' Eli winced as he looked at the square and the broken pieces of the screens. 'I feel bad about the damage.'

'You can feel bad later,' Jeremiah said, grabbing his arm. 'Right now, we have to get to the tiger temple.'

He was right – there was no time to lose. Most of the people from the crowd had gone completely, and those that remained were lingering at the outskirts. The *Nepo* waved her tentacles in a threatening manner just in case anyone thought about following, and so Jeremiah and Eli left without any further challenges, racing down the road towards the tiger temple.

Tall jungle trees surrounded them almost instantly, and they caught the bright flash of colourful feathers as parrots flitted to and fro above them. There were some mischievous monkeys too, who insisted on flinging peanuts at their heads.

'Pesky things,' Jeremiah said, scowling up through the trees. 'What's the collective noun for monkeys, then? A mischief of monkeys?'

'No, it's a troop,' Eli panted, pleased to be back on the topic of collective nouns. 'Mischief would be a good fit, though.'

'I quite like a shiver of sharks,' Jeremiah replied. 'I'll remember that one.'

'I think a parliament of owls is my favourite,' Eli gasped, breathless from running. 'Or, perhaps, a cauldron of bats.'

The air was unpleasantly muggy, and Eli's shirt and trousers were already damp with sweat. He shrugged off his jacket and stuffed it into his satchel, wincing a little that it was unfolded. He glanced at Jeremiah running alongside him, still wearing his long captain's coat, but as usual, his friend seemed unaffected by the weather.

'We must be getting closer,' Jeremiah said, indicating the path ahead.

Eli saw that there were stone tigers lining it. They each held a lantern full of fireflies in their mouth, creating a shimmering, otherworldly glow. It was difficult to run with a tortoise tucked under his arm, but the two boys sprinted the rest of the way. Finally, they came out into a clearing, and there was the tiger temple sprawled before them, all white stones, and tangled vines, and golden domes. On first glance, it looked like a ruin, it was so overgrown with creepers and flowers and leaves. But Eli recognised the black-and-orange-striped petals and knew that these were tiger flowers.

An orange-and-black tiled path curled around the corner. After the business at the square, Eli had thought that there might be crowds here too, but it was quiet save for the chirping of the parrots and the squawking of the monkeys.

'Come on,' Jeremiah said. 'Let's find an entrance. I bet there's more than one in a place like this. And keep your wits about you.'

Together, they made their way down the path and soon reached a pair of elegant golden gates. To Eli's dismay, a pair of living, breathing tigers guarded the entrance. Raven would have been able to slip straight between the bars in her faery form, but the boys had no hope of squeezing in like that, even without the tigers to contend with. 'Maybe they're friendly?' Jeremiah suggested. 'I mean, they're probably the princess's pets, aren't they?'

He took a step closer, perhaps thinking to test his idea, but both tigers immediately let out threatening snarls. Eli couldn't help shivering. He'd seen pictures of tigers in books, but he'd never been this close to a living one before. He could see the muscles rippling beneath their fur, and the strings of silvery drool that stretched between their jaws.

'Can you . . . I don't know . . . do some tiger taming?' Eli asked hopefully.

Jeremiah frowned. 'Sharks are more my thing, you know that.'

'Isn't there any crossover? I mean, they're both wild beasts, so—'

'The only way of dealing with two tigers would

be to injure them badly enough that they can't chase after us.'

'Oh, no!' Eli exclaimed. 'No, we mustn't hurt them.'

It was forbidden to hurt a princess's animals, but Eli wouldn't have dreamed of doing so anyway.

Jeremiah sighed. 'Look, tigers are perfect killing machines. Perhaps if I had a whip. Or a stool – that's what they use in a circus, isn't it? I might be able to keep them at bay then.'

'Oh, well, I can get you a stool,' Eli said, pleased at the chance to contribute.

He dumped his bag on the floor and put Humphrey down alongside it. The tortoise immediately popped out of his shell and began to stump towards the tigers in a friendly sort of manner and had to be quickly snatched up by Jeremiah before he could become a tiger snack.

'There's no need for that,' Humphrey protested. 'Tortoises are excellent tiger tamers.'

'Humphrey, that's really not true!' Eli groaned.

The next moment, he had a candle in his hands. As soon as he lit it, the same bookshop from before sprang up around them, with its creaking floors and overflowing shelves. There was a rickety stool behind the counter, which Eli had thought Jeremiah could brandish at the tigers to get them away from the gates – but, in fact, the tigers were trapped inside the shop with them. They didn't like this at all and immediately began to prowl about, searching for an exit. They seemed even larger inside the poky little space, especially with their hackles raised and low growls rumbling in their throats.

'Quick!' Jeremiah thrust Humphrey back to Eli. 'Let's get out through the window.'

Eli tucked Humphrey under his arm and they turned towards the window behind the counter, but they moved too quickly, and that drew the tigers' attention. One of the beasts sprang on to the counter, knocking over the till in the process. It burst open on the floor, pennies rolling out across the floor. The tiger towered over them, swiping with its massive paw as it roared in Eli's face.

Eli had once read that a tiger's roar could paralyse its prey animal, and now he understood why. He felt as if a bucket of ice water had been thrown over him. He couldn't look away from the tiger's glowing amber eyes. Humphrey had retreated into his shell completely, tucking his stumpy legs in tight.

'Get back!' Jeremiah cried, shoving Eli towards the window as he leapt in front of him, snatching up the stool and waving the legs at the tiger whilst bellowing, 'BACK! BACK!'

Eli threw open the window and scrambled out, landing in a heap on the other side. He set Humphrey down and reached through to help Jeremiah, who climbed out, still clutching the stool. Together, they slammed the window shut, just as the tiger headbutted it, all teeth and drool and snarl. Fortunately, the beast was far too large to pass through the small window. It managed to push the window back open, but then could only reach its large leg through, swiping blindly with its claws. The action reminded Eli of the cats he sometimes saw in the library courtyard, going after mice, and he felt a sudden urge to laugh. He bit his tongue, afraid he wouldn't be able to stop if he started now.

'Let's go,' Jeremiah panted, keeping a tight grip on the stool.

It wasn't over. They both knew there were bound to be more of the big cats. Apart from being a bit squashed in Jeremiah's pocket, baby Luther looked no worse for wear from the escapade, and Humphrey had finally poked his head out of the shell.

'How does the stool even work?' Eli asked as they hurried through the gate. 'Isn't it really flimsy to a tiger?'

'It's the legs,' Jeremiah replied. 'It confuses them because they can't focus on all four at once. I'm not sure how many I can fight off with this thing, though. I wish we still had the *Nepo*.'

Eli did too. They set off down the jungle path.

'Any idea which way we should go?' Jeremiah asked.

Eli shook his head. They'd only know they were in the right place when they found the checkpoint. Unlike the other times, this one wouldn't contain multiple maps, but only a single trophy. The first contestant to pick it up from the table would be the winner. Eli knew that the last checkpoint was often located at the highest part of a mountain, or darkest part of a cave, or something along those lines. When he glanced at the leader board he saw that they were in third place behind Raven and now a racer called Lola too, who must have swooped over them whilst they were walking through the jungle. Her position was rapidly switching back and forth with Raven's, which Eli guessed meant they were probably all closing in on the finish line at about the same time.

The boys ran down the jungle path, darting frequent glances into the thick undergrowth, expecting to see the orange flash of tiger stripes or the cold gleam of a predator's eye. But there was nothing out of the ordinary, and moments later they'd reached an abandoned temple that looked as if it was being taken over by the jungle. They hurried through a series of empty rooms before coming out into a courtyard, where they both stopped and stared at the sight before them.

A huge temple rose up in the shape of a tiger's head. It had massive sparkling green jewels for eyes, and it was covered in moss and vines and striped flowers. The winner's cup was right at the top of the temple, shining and silver.

And the entire place was completely overrun with tigers.

There must have been twenty or more, snoozing on the hot stones, basking in the sunshine, or lazily paddling about in the emerald-blue waters of the lake at the foot of the temple. A couple of large sapphire-coloured butterflies fluttered happily around the flowers.

Eli's first thought was that it was tranquil, and beautiful, and very special, and he felt privileged to see this many tigers in the wild. There were the usual black-and-orange ones, along with other types he hadn't even known existed. A white tiger sprawled on the temple steps, and a black tiger basked in the dappled sunlight filtering through the palms. There was a tiny tiger too, no bigger than a bird, and a massive one that was twice the size of an ordinary beast.

A flash of white suddenly caught Eli's eye and he looked over to see Raven standing on a nearby rock, Perrie at her feet. And then the other contestants arrived.

When Eli first caught sight of Lola, soaring through the sky on the back of her Pegasus, he thought that surely this must be it. She could swoop straight down to land on the top of the temple. There was a tiger lying there, but she could probably scoop up the trophy and fly away before the tiger got to her, and then it would all be over. But he couldn't let that happen. He had come all this way, the winner's cup was in sight, there had to be some means of reaching it . . .

The Pegasus flew down towards the temple and the tiger stood up. It had black and orange stripes, and Eli had thought it was like the ones guarding the gates, but he was wrong. This tiger had wings. They unfurled slowly, almost lazily, in the golden sunlight. The orange-and-black feathers were bold and beautiful, and the wings were powerful, and the tiger soared into the sky in one fluid motion, snarling a warning to stay away.

Eli heard Lola's cry of shock as she turned the Pegasus around and retreated to the safety of the clouds, where she lingered, probably trying to work out her next move. The flying tiger had alerted the others – now every single one of the big cats was awake, and alert, and looking right at them.

CHAPTER TWENTY-EIGHT

Eli was just thinking it couldn't get much worse when a fifth contestant arrived. The turquoise water of the lake began to simmer, like a pot boiling over, and then the masts of a ship appeared, followed by its pale sails. Eli immediately recognised the *Spectre* and its notorious owner, Captain Quell. Where Quell went, his ghost stingray, Shiver, wouldn't be far behind and, sure enough, the sleek, deadly fish soon floated up out of the water beside the boat.

'I'll go on alone,' Jeremiah said. 'I've got more chance of reaching the trophy that way.'

He set off without waiting for a reply, dodging past tigers, expertly using his stool to keep them back. It had turned chaotic very quickly, with racers running and scrambling, and tigers roaring. Eli was about to set off after him when his bag suddenly became so heavy that it almost dragged him to the floor. He opened it to find the interior entirely taken up with a book. The Book of Lullabies. Eli stared at it for a moment, trying to work out how it could possibly have got there. Then he remembered that when he'd gone back home he'd picked up another bag – the one he'd tucked the library ticket Giselle had given him into all those weeks ago. It was so large that Eli had to use both hands to heft it out. Its cover was inky blue, and studded with shining, gold musical notes. He flipped open the cover and scanned the contents, but Giselle had been right. There was no lullaby for curing illnesses. For a moment he felt tempted to throw it to one side so that it didn't slow him down, but then another thought occurred to him and he turned back to the book eagerly.

It contained page after page of music. There were songs for dolphins and whales, eagles and albatrosses, unicorns and dragons. Eli's fingers trembled as he flipped back to the contents, feeling a flash of triumph when he saw the tiger lullaby. But his pleasure was quickly replaced with despair, for Eli was no musician and couldn't read music. The musical notes might as well have been nonsense scrawls upon the page.

He thrust the book back in his bag and ran across the

courtyard towards Jeremiah, panting with the effort of carrying both Humphrey and his bag, which now weighed a tonne. Captain Quell's boat was quickly becoming overrun with tigers, and he'd retreated to the crow's nest for safety, shouting in a furious, helpless sort of way. Lola's Pegasus kept making attempts to fly up to the winner's cup, but the winged tigers blocked the path each time. Raven was still perched on her rock, probably trying to figure out a clear route through the tigers. And Jeremiah was focused on getting past a white tiger, but the big cat looked more irritated than intimidated by the stool.

The next second, Eli gave a horrified gasp as the tiger lifted its massive paw and swatted the stool, splintering it into bits. Jeremiah dropped the useless broken legs and threw himself to the ground as the tiger swiped at him again. There was a ripping noise as his coat tore, but luckily Jeremiah seemed unhurt as he rolled away and leapt to his feet. He grabbed on to some hanging vines and climbed these up to the nose of the tiger statue. There was a tiger crouched in one of the nostrils, but the other nostril was free and Jeremiah tucked himself up in this, panting for breath.

Suddenly, Eli knew it was time to run – faster than he'd ever run before in his life. It didn't matter how much his feet hurt, or how tired he was. It was time to be fast.

'*You're a Fleet,*' his father's voice whispered in his ear. '*You can do this.*'

Eli didn't feel his parents' presence much, normally. They were never there in the Royal Library, or the cobbled streets of Harmonia, or even at Nana's house. But all of a sudden he could sense them both in the middle of the tiger temple, could feel the faint touch of his mother's hand on his shoulder, almost see the sparkling outline of their two gazelles on either side of him. Whatever else happened next, Eli had reached the end of the race, and he was sure his parents would have been proud of him for that. Even better, he was proud of himself.

He charged forwards, full of renewed determination. He could almost hear the cheers of people watching back home and, after all, why *shouldn't* Eli win? He'd come this far. He'd faced mermaid queens, and joo-joo bubs, and survived being shipwrecked. But his feeling of triumph didn't last long. The jungle heat was making him sweat inside his tweed jacket, and his hands were particularly clammy. Humphrey's smooth shell slipped in his grip and Eli had to do an awkward half-lunge, half-stumble to try to grab him. He managed to break the tortoise's fall, but didn't quite grab hold of his shell. He could only watch in dismay as his pet slid along the ground, coming to a stop right in front of a large black tiger.

Eli was appalled. He'd practically thrown Humphrey at the beast. Even worse, the moon tortoise didn't have the sense to stay tucked inside his shell, but was stretching his neck out and peering around indignantly.

'Eli, really!' he exclaimed. 'A little care might go a long way.'

The tiger padded closer, and Eli had dreadful visions of Humphrey getting his head bitten off. The big cat stopped in front of Humphrey and lowered his head to peer at him.

'Humphrey!' Eli hissed. 'Get back into your shell and keep very still!'

'Nonsense,' Humphrey replied. 'I already told you – tortoises are excellent tiger tamers.'

Humphrey stared straight up at the tiger, his silvery light bathing everything in a soft glow. To everyone's surprise, the tiger seemed rather fascinated by Humphrey and sniffed him all over, whiskers twitching. Eli was convinced he must be sizing him up for a snack, but after a moment the tiger flopped itself down on the ground beside the tortoise and started to purr.

Eli stared. Tigers couldn't purr. He'd read that somewhere in one of the library books. None of the big cats could purr, except for leopards and ... and night tigers. These were very rare creatures, said to be entirely black except for the starlight constellations on their fur, visible only in moonlight. Now that the tiger was close to Humphrey, Eli could see the stars twinkling in its fur. For a moment, Eli wondered whether Humphrey might be able to charm the other tigers too, but none of the others were night tigers. At least it seemed that Humphrey was in no immediate danger from the tiger, so Eli made the best of the diversion and ran the last few paces to the foot of the temple.

'What are you *doing*?' Jeremiah hissed down at him. 'You're going to get yourself eaten by a tiger!'

'Catch my bag!' Eli ordered, shrugging it from his shoulder.

'What? Why?'

'There's a book in there!'

Jeremiah groaned. 'This isn't the time!'

'It's the Book of Lullabies! There's a song in there that will send the tigers to sleep if you play it on your harmonica. Page ninety-seven. Catch!'

It was an extremely heavy book, and Eli worried he

might not have enough strength to throw it all the way up to Jeremiah. Knowing his luck, it would probably fall back down on his head and squash him flat – much to the amusement of everyone at home. He thought of Nana, and the reason he'd entered the race in the first place. He thought of all the things he'd managed to do since setting out, even though no one thought he would last past the first round.

Eli drew back his arm and used all the strength in his body to hurl the bag into the air.

For a moment it looked as if it wasn't quite going to make it, but Jeremiah threw himself flat on the ground and reached down, grabbing on to the strap with his fingertips. The weight almost dragged him right over the edge, but he scrabbled backwards, causing a flurry of loose stones to rain down. The next second, he'd yanked the book out, grimacing in distaste, and was flipping through the pages, the bag falling over the edge to land at Eli's feet.

Unfortunately, the movement and the talking had attracted a couple of nearby tigers, who were prowling towards Eli and didn't look at all as if they wanted to be friends. He felt a tugging on his shoe, and when he looked down, he saw one of the faery-sized cats there, attacking his foot. Its teeth were too small to be able to bite through the leather, but Eli was still rather alarmed and called up to Jeremiah.

'Um, could you be as quick as you can? It's just that I'm getting a bit surrounded down here.'

'I'm *trying*!' Jeremiah called back, sounding a little panicked as he fumbled through the pages.

Finally, he found the right song, swept his gaze over the musical notes and then pulled his harmonica from his pocket. Eli was afraid it might be too late. The big tiger nearest him was lowering itself into a hunting crouch, lips parted in a snarl, all its fur standing on end. Jeremiah began to play the lullaby just as it was about to spring, and the tiger froze, listening.

A tiger lullaby wasn't at all like a human one. It didn't sound gentle and lilting to Eli's ears, but low and grumbling, almost like deep purring that echoed around the ruin. The effect on the tigers was immediate. They began to yawn and stretch. One by one, they flopped themselves down wherever they happened to be, put their large heads between their paws, closed their eyes and fell asleep.

Eli stared around the temple, hardly able to believe it had worked. The faery-sized tiger had curled into a little ball, with his tail over his nose, and gone to sleep on his shoe, so Eli reached down and gently

313

picked him up to set him next to one of the big cats, where he wouldn't get squashed. Then he looked up at the winner's cup, still glinting and winking in the sunshine, waiting for someone bold enough to claim it.

Eli glanced over to where Raven was poised on Perrie's back, her eyes fixed on the trophy, preparing to run. She hunkered down, tightened her grip on Perrie's reins, and then the hare was moving so quickly across the square that she was just a blur of pale fur. At the same time, Lola swooped down on her Pegasus, her route clear of obstacles now that the winged tigers had gone to sleep. Captain Quell was running from his ship too.

Eli fumbled in his bag for the appropriate book. It was the one about gardens and flowers – a nice book where no one could possibly be hurt. He'd checked thoroughly to make sure there was nothing even remotely dangerous in there, but it took a great deal of concentration and willpower to put a person within the pages. He'd never attempted to put two people into a book at once before, and wasn't even sure if it was possible, but he had to at least try. He gathered all his thoughts and energy and said in a clear, strong voice, 'Princess Ravinia and Lola! Chapter Four!'

For a moment, he didn't know if it was going to

work. Perhaps he was too tired and in need of a rest. His fingers tingled with magic and his ribs ached inside his chest. He focused his thoughts as fiercely as he possibly could, and then there was a whooshing sound and a strong breeze blew around the jungle as Raven and Lola were whisked away into the book. Eli saw their names appear on the page. He slammed the book closed, stuffed it into his bag and started running. He could see Perrie, poised at the top of the temple, but without Raven she wasn't able to claim the trophy. The Pegasus was flying around in a panicked manner, probably wondering where her rider had gone.

Eli briefly considered trying to put Captain Quell in the book too, but he was already slightly dizzy from his previous effort and didn't think he'd be able to repeat it immediately. Eli looked about in vain for a path or ladder to reach the top of the temple, but there wasn't one. He was going to have to climb, finding footholds and handholds in the stone wherever he could. He launched himself at the rocks.

In its crumbling state, there were plenty of places to get a grip, but Eli's fingers were bleeding within moments. He was making progress, though, little by little. His arms and legs burned with the effort, and he was sweating so fiercely that his shirt stuck to his back and he knew his jacket and trousers would be quite ruined. But when he looked down, he saw that the ground was further away than he'd been expecting and, in fact, he was almost halfway up the tiger's face, at the nostrils.

The stone there was more fragile than he'd realised and he grabbed the edge, only to have it crumble away in his hands. He yelped, his arms windmilling as he flailed in panic. He would have fallen all the way back to the ground if Jeremiah hadn't thrown down the harmonica and grabbed his wrist. Eli's body slammed against the stone hard enough to knock all the breath from his body and scrape the skin from the end of his nose.

He was vaguely aware that Quell had reached the bottom of the temple, and it surely wouldn't take him very long to catch up. The thought of failing now was too painful. Eli's hopes all pinned themselves on Jeremiah. Surely his friend would be able to do something at the last moment – perhaps scramble up to the top of the temple and claim the trophy on Eli's behalf. After all, he'd told Eli himself that this was why he'd entered the race in the first place.

But the moment Jeremiah had stopped playing, the tigers began to stir and twitch. The tiger that had been asleep in the nostril even reached down and took a groggy swipe at Eli where he was still dangling from Jeremiah's hand, helpless as a fish on a hook. The tiger's claw tore a hole in the lining of his jacket sleeve, missing Eli's skin by a whisker.

'Keep playing!' he shrieked at Jeremiah.

Eli dug his fingers into the stone, leaving Jeremiah free to let him go and resume the song. The tigers settled at once, but the need to keep playing meant that Jeremiah had to remain where he was. He wasn't going to be able to help Eli this time. He wasn't going to be able to win the race for him either. Eli had to finish alone.

He reached up for another fingerhold, trying to ignore the burning of his arms and the blood trickling down his fingers, making his grip slippery. He was unwise enough to glance down, and saw that Captain Quell was catching up rapidly. Perhaps Eli might be able to put Quell into the book now? Perhaps the few minutes that had passed would be enough for him to gather another burst of magical strength. But Eli didn't think that was likely. His fingers no longer fizzed with magic and a hollow feeling told him he'd used it all up. Besides, there was no way he could get a hand free to retrieve a book from his bag, even if he wanted to.

There was nothing to do but keep climbing, and

hoping, and praying. At last, Eli reached the top of the temple, his hands scrambling over rock as he struggled to pull himself over the edge. His suit was completely ruined by now, marked with dust and jungle grime, along with several holes. Eli saw the winner's cup shining on the ground, flanked by the two winged tigers. Jeremiah was still playing his lullaby, and the beasts seemed sound asleep. Eli didn't hesitate – he ran straight towards it.

The ghost stingray swooped overhead, and to Eli's dismay it took a dive at him as he approached the cup. He ducked and rolled across the ground, just in time to avoid the stinging barb of its tail, but it was clear that the magical beast didn't intend to let him anywhere near the trophy. Eli could have wept. He'd come so far, and was so very close . . .

To make matters even worse, a rainbow suddenly arced through the air, carrying the fast blur of a panther and rider, and Eli's heart sank. Vincent Tweak. The bounty hunter had probably lost track of them whilst they'd been off course around Goat Island, and perhaps he'd been busy patching up the wound to his shoulder too – but now he was here, right at the wrong moment.

The rainbow landed on top of the temple, and Vincent leapt off his panther's back to round on Eli, grabbing him roughly by the front of his shirt and shouting into his face.

'Where is he? I'm done playing games! You will give me Jeremiah and you'll give him to me now!'

'He's a person!' Eli gasped. 'It isn't possible to give away a person, even if I wanted to. Which I don't.'

He pushed Vincent away, then stumbled, falling on to his back hard enough to knock all the breath out of him. To his horror, Vincent advanced, drawing back his boot as if he intended to kick him where he lay on the ground. Eli tried to brace himself, but he could hardly breathe. Out of the corner of his eye, he saw Captain Quell pull himself up on to the temple roof. It could surely only be moments until he reached the cup.

Eli squeezed his eyes closed. This was it, he thought, the moment he lost, the moment it turned out it had all been for nothing. Not only that, but he was about to receive a kicking. He instinctively curled into a ball. He longed to be the kind of person brave enough to somehow drag himself to his feet, to be like Jeremiah and face Vincent with a calm, cool gaze and some kind of cutting remark, but the truth was he was terrified and trembling.

And yet ...

This couldn't be how it ended. Curled in a sad little ball whilst some bully took a shot at him. He had to at least try to defend himself. Eli's hand fumbled in his bag and he grabbed hold of the first book he found. There was no time to check the title. Vincent was almost upon him, his boot inches from Eli's face when Eli gasped out his name.

'Vincent Tweak! Chapter One!'

He had no idea if it would work, was still worried that he might have used up all his magic. He dug down deep, deep inside himself, scraping at the edges for anything that remained, pulling all the threads and scraps together. The act made him nauseous and his head swam alarmingly, but he concentrated all his thoughts and energy as hard as he ever had before.

Then there was a whooshing sound and a powerful gust of air. With a cry of rage, Vincent was swept away, sucked into the pages of the book. The effort, and adrenaline, and fear made Eli shake so badly he could hardly lift the book to see the title, and when he did, he flinched. There would be no pleasant gardens for Vincent. He had vanished into a book about the venoms and antivenoms of poisonous bugs.

CHAPTER TWENTY-NINE

Eli scrambled to his feet and looked up to see Captain Quell sprinting towards the cup. It was too late. There was no way that Eli could catch him up now. He started forwards anyway, because it would be impossible to simply stand there and accept defeat, but his head was spinning and his legs were shaking, and he could barely manage a tottering stagger. He could see the triumph in Captain Quell's eyes as he stretched his hand out with eager greed towards the trophy...

But then – out of nowhere – a little blue puffball of a bird dived down at the captain, squawking happily as it aimed its tiny beak straight for the man's face. It was Luther! Captain Quell roared as the bird bit him squarely on the chin. He staggered back and his hands flailed, punching through the air at the sea phoenix, but Luther was too small and fast. The bird almost seemed to bounce and zigzag through the air, easily avoiding the stingray too as it nipped at the captain's earlobes, and nose, and head – sharp little bites that sent him reeling.

Eli looked at the winner's trophy, still untouched, still unclaimed. It was only a few paces away, and yet it seemed like the longest distance and the longest run of Eli's life. His chest heaved and ached, sweat and blood made his palms sticky; he could hardly breathe, or think.

He was almost there – close enough to see the magical beasts etched into the gold of the cup – when Captain Quell suddenly managed to duck away from Luther and lunge at Eli. He crashed into him from behind, and Eli went down with a heavy thump that knocked all the air out of him. He reached forwards blindly, stretching his arms so far that he feared he might dislocate his shoulder—

And then his fingertips made contact with the cool, smooth handle of the cup. His hand closed around it and he yanked it towards him, and all of a sudden it was over, the cup was Eli's. It certainly wasn't the sort of stylish win that his parents had always pulled off, but that didn't matter one jot. He had done it. He had won. He groaned in relief, and then Captain Quell finally stood up, making it a little easier for Eli to breathe. To his surprise, the captain reached down to help him up and shook him gruffly by the hand.

'Congratulations,' he said. 'It was a good win.'

'Thank you,' Eli replied, his voice a hoarse croak.

He couldn't believe this was happening. It felt like a dream. He and Captain Quell climbed down the temple together, followed by the stingray and Luther, who had turned quite docile now that the race was over. When they reached the bottom, Eli held the cup high in both hands so that Jeremiah could see it. He saw his friend's eyes widen and he almost dropped the harmonica. The next moment an expression of pure joy lit up his face, and then he was scrambling down the temple one-handed, whilst using the other to continue the lullaby. When he reached Eli he stopped playing and pulled him into such a tight hug that Eli winced.

'Sorry!' Jeremiah said, releasing him slightly. 'I'm just ... oh, Eli, I'm just SO proud of you! You showed 'em.' He put his hand on Eli's shoulder and squeezed it. 'You showed them all. Well done. What a triumph. For you and your nana.'

Eli hardly knew what to say. He felt completely overwhelmed – with relief, and happiness, and pride. And tiredness too. When he got home, he intended to go straight to bed and sleep for a week. The tigers' ears were starting to twitch, so Jeremiah quickly began playing again. Captain Quell raised his hand in farewell and then returned to his ship.

Something nuzzled Eli's ankle and he looked down to see Perrie hopping about frantically at his feet. The Pegasus was circling the air above and the rainbow panther was anxiously pacing up and down. With a guilty start, Eli remembered the other racers and hastily pulled the books from his bag to set them free. The next moment, Lola and Raven stood before him, picking petals from their hair. Their magical beasts rushed to greet them and Raven scooped Perrie in her arms before turning to Eli.

'So you did it,' she said, nodding towards the cup with a smile that was half regretful and half admiring. 'I thought you might.'

Lola groaned, but offered reluctant congratulations to Eli before climbing on to her Pegasus's back and rising into the sky. Captain Quell's boat had already vanished beneath the waves.

'I'm not sure what to do about Vincent,' Eli said, glancing at Jeremiah. He pulled the poisonous bug book from his bag. 'I put him in the wrong one. If he stays in there, he could be bitten by something and killed.'

Jeremiah shrugged and Eli had the horrible feeling

he didn't care either way. Eli knew he couldn't leave the bounty hunter where he was, yet at the same time he wouldn't have the strength to put him straight in another book either. The decision was made for him when he saw that the book was damaged. Perhaps it had happened when Captain Quell had landed on top of him, but either way there were several ripped pages and the book's spine was broken too. A damaged book wouldn't be able to hold a real person for long.

Sure enough, the next moment the book exploded in Eli's hands, pages fluttering in the air around them as Vincent appeared, gasping for breath and brushing exoskeletons from his jacket and looking livid. When his gaze fell on Eli, a truly frightening expression came over his face, one of pure hatred. Eli felt a prickle of alarm, but took a deep breath and forced himself to meet Vincent's stare.

Jeremiah lowered the harmonica. 'I'm not coming with you,' he said. 'Do you get that? You can spend the rest of your life chasing me if you want, but you'll never collect your fee. Tell Gaskins it's over. He lost.'

'I'm not your messenger boy!' Vincent snarled.

'I'm sorry about the bug book,' Eli said, desperately hoping to smooth things over. 'I didn't plan to put you in that one, it was just the first one I grabbed.'

'How convenient!' Vincent's face was ashen and Eli realised the bug book must have been a harrowing experience.

'You didn't give me a lot of choice,' he said quietly. 'I don't want to hurt you. But if you keep coming after Jeremiah then I promise I'll put you into another bug book. And you won't get out next time.'

Eli didn't like threatening people. He didn't like it at all. He felt no surge of pleasure at Vincent's frightened expression, or the look of respect from Jeremiah. This, right here, was part of why he had never wanted anyone to know he was a mage. Because once people knew you had power then, one way or another, it seemed you'd be forced to wield it.

'Please,' Eli said. 'Just leave us alone.'

For a moment, he thought his threat had worked. Without another word, Vincent turned and stalked away, his panther slinking after him. But then he reached the spot where Humphrey still stood beside the black tiger. The tortoise was munching happily on a few green leaves poking through a gap in the stone tiles. Vincent stopped and stared at Humphrey with a vicious expression on his face, then he lifted his boot and held it right over the tortoise. Time seemed to slow and then stop altogether. Eli could sense Vincent preparing to stamp on Humphrey, shattering his shell, and he knew he'd never get there in time to prevent what was about to happen . . .

But then Jeremiah shoved him out of the way, and reached into his coat pockets. His hand came out holding the glass bottle containing his sea chest and he hurled this straight at Vincent without hesitation.

'Open!' he yelled.

The glass shattered against the side of Vincent's face, cutting the skin of his jaw. He cried out and took a staggering step back. The sea chest became full-sized as it flew free of the bottle, and Eli watched in horror as it crashed to the ground with a jarring impact. The padlock must have clicked loose again, as it had so many times before. The chest tipped on to its side and the lid finally sprang open. Eli watched in fascinated horror as the contents burst out upon the paving stones.

The thing. The thing inside the sea chest . . .

It's been getting bigger, stronger, and if it ever gets out then it'll drag me back into the pages . . .

Eli really wasn't sure what he expected to see. His mind had come up with so many possibilities when it came to the dark, dreadful secret of the sea chest. He'd imagined things with claws and teeth, forbidden treasure maps, cursed stolen jewels. But what actually came out was paper. Pages and pages of it, all turning loose and scattering. Eli looked at Jeremiah, expecting his friend to be beside himself, but he looked strangely calm.

'It's all right,' Jeremiah said. 'Really. This was coming anyway.'

'What?' Eli frowned, struggling to keep up, to understand. 'What was coming?'

Jeremiah gave him a small, sad smile as he tucked Luther into his pocket. 'The sequel.'

There was hardly any breeze in the temple courtyard, yet the pages fluttered about faster and faster, until they were swept into a sort of whirlwind. Not only that, but Eli could see other things in the whirlwind too. The ghostly outlines of sea monsters, and storms, and shipwrecks – the world that Jeremiah had left behind. And then, suddenly, from the tempest of paper curled a great, monstrous tentacle. It had the same transparent look as everything else, but it was solid enough to curl around Jeremiah's waist, squeezing until he winced.

His eyes met Eli's just once, and in them Eli saw a sort of grim resignation and sorrow.

'Thank you,' he gasped. 'For my time in the real world.'

This was a goodbye, Eli realised. The end of it all.

'No!' He grabbed Jeremiah's arm and held on as hard as he could, but it wasn't enough. His friend's sleeve was ripped from his grip as the tentacle whipped back into the whirlwind, taking Jeremiah and Luther with it. Eli ran forwards, determined to stop it. He was a mage – there must be something he could do. But the next second, the sea monsters, and storms, and shipwrecks had all vanished, and the whirlwind abruptly died, and all that was left was a neat pile of paper on the ground. Not a book – but a manuscript. The top page read: *The Further Seafaring Adventures of Jeremiah Jones.*

Eli looked up at Vincent, who seemed just as shocked by what had happened. And suddenly Eli felt a hot, fierce, terrible rush of anger rise inside him. Vincent must have seen it in his face because he took a stumbling step backwards. Eli rummaged in his bag and drew out a book. It was a book about the most dangerous animals in the world, and the cover was full of teeth and claws. Vincent had stolen away his best friend in the world and Eli might never, ever get him back. It would be so easy to punish Vincent, to put him straight in the book. He didn't even care that he'd be torn limb from limb—

Then Humphrey stumped up and said quietly, 'You're not that type of mage, Eli.'

All his anger seemed to drain out of him, leaving him with nothing but sorrow.

'Go!' he said hoarsely, glaring at Vincent. 'Get out of my sight.'

Vincent didn't need telling twice. He turned and ran to scramble on to his panther's back. The next moment they were both racing towards the exit. Tears ran down Eli's face as he bent to pick up Jeremiah's manuscript.

'We have to go,' Raven said, appearing beside him. 'The tigers are waking up.'

She was right. Without Jeremiah to play the lullaby, the big cats were yawning and stretching. There was no time to figure out what had happened or how to undo it now. Eli stuffed the manuscript into his bag and snatched up Humphrey. He expected Raven to shrink to faery size and ride away on Perrie, but she stayed by his side, which was lucky because Eli was trembling so badly he could hardly walk.

Raven half-dragged him to the nearest doorway, and Eli fumbled for the key around his neck. He inserted it into the lock and threw the door open to reveal his little free library, just as a tiger leapt towards them. Raven gave him a shove and then tumbled in behind him. They fell into the phone box together and slammed the door closed on the tiger with seconds to spare.

And then that was it. The temple and the tigers were gone. The race was over. And Eli was finally home.

CHAPTER THIRTY

Eli had completely lost track of what time or day it might be back in Harmonia, but it turned out that he and Raven arrived at Nana's Kitchen right in the middle of the dessert service. All the customers were on their feet, applauding. Before Eli could get his bearings, the door to the little free library was thrown open and he found himself being pulled out into Nana's arms. She wrapped him in a big, warm, tight hug, the winner's cup squashed between them. He breathed in the familiar smells of milk chocolate and pancake mix and allowed himself a few moments to feel safe and warm.

'Welcome home, darling boy,' Nana whispered in his ear. 'And well done. You did it.'

Before Eli could reply, Nana had reached out and pulled Raven into the hug with them.

'Come here, young miss. I know you're a princess, but I hope you don't mind if I hug you too. I want to say a big thank-you for being a friend to Eli during the race.'

Nana was right, Eli realised. Raven *had* been a friend to him during the race, and he was grateful. But there was one person who should have been here who wasn't: his best friend and book brother. Eli's chest ached with the loss of Jeremiah. His throat felt as if there was a fist squeezing around it, and when he tried to say his friend's name, only a strangled sob came out.

'Oh, my dear.' Nana rubbed his back. 'I'm so sorry about Jeremiah. I know nothing I can say will make it any easier. For now, let's get you a plate of pudding, and then it's hot baths and bed. No arguments! You must stay the night with us too,' she said to Raven. 'I'll get a bed made up for you in the living room.'

Eli was glad when Nana ushered them inside, away from all the curious glances of the customers, and sat them down at their own private table in the kitchen. Before long they each had a hot fudge pudding and a mug of hot chocolate, and the noise outside was muffled to a low hubbub. Humphrey tucked himself under the table and went to sleep, and Eli ate his pudding, glad of the warmth and the sweetness, but it was difficult to enjoy anything without Jeremiah by his side. Raven didn't seem much in a talking mood either, and concentrated on wolfing down her dessert.

'So, you're a princess,' Eli finally said, pushing his empty plate away.

'Yep.'

'Why did you keep it a secret?'

She shrugged. 'It wasn't a secret, exactly. I just didn't go around telling everyone. People treat me differently when they know I'm a princess. Like they're different to you when they know you're a mage. Besides, the tiger princess is a friend of mine. She said she'd ask her people to block the way of the other racers. I thought it might give me an advantage.' She sighed. 'Not that it did much use in the end. I'm sorry I didn't tell you the truth, Eli. I hope we can still be friends?'

Eli nodded. 'I'd like that. What will happen to your village now? Or I guess I ought to say your kingdom?'

'I don't know. I'll have to think again.'

It suddenly seemed so unfair. They both needed the magic for something important. Eli had thought he'd be overjoyed to win, but he just felt guilty, like he'd stolen happiness from other people. A thought occurred to him and he wondered whether it might be possible . . .

'There can only be one winner of the Race of Magical Beasts,' Eli said, almost to himself. 'That's what everyone always says, anyway. But who decided that in the first place? Does it have to be that way?'

'Well, there's only one prize,' Raven said with a shrug.

Nana spoke from the doorway. 'But what if the prize could be shared?'

Eli took a deep breath. She'd echoed his exact thought.

'No one's ever shared the prize before,' Raven said, looking between Eli and Nana. 'Why would they, when they could have all of it?'

Nana walked over, pulled up a chair and joined them at the table. 'Maybe because it's the right thing to do?' she said. 'For someone who helped them along the way.'

'Half the magic won't be enough to get a ruby,' Eli said. 'I want to share, but there isn't enough magic to go around.'

'Not to solve everything,' Nana agreed. 'But I expect half the magic would buy a pearl.'

A magic pearl was rather like the magic ruby, but not as good at keeping the magic inside. It leaked out much faster with a pearl.

Eli looked at Nana. 'That would buy a little more time, but not a lot.'

'It would be plenty,' she said firmly. 'It would give

334

me the years of an ordinary person. That's enough, Eli. Truly it is.'

Eli thought for a moment, then nodded and turned towards Raven. 'Nana's right. Half of the magic won't be enough to save your kingdom altogether. It won't be enough to fix things completely. But it would be something; it would be a start.'

Raven looked between them. 'That's . . . I don't know what to say. Thank you.'

Eli smiled, but all of a sudden he felt a wave of exhaustion. He didn't think he could carry on talking about it that night. He was relieved when Nana stood up and ushered them both off to bed. When he was finally back in his bedroom with Humphrey, he longed to crawl beneath the sheets, but instead he sat down on the floor, took Jeremiah's manuscript from his bag and searched for his friend with his mind. Maybe Jeremiah had been wrong. Maybe it was simply a question of bringing him back out of the book. He'd done it once, hadn't he?

But as soon as he tried, he could tell it wasn't going to work. At first he hoped that maybe he was just too tired, and perhaps it would work in the morning . . . But when he flicked through the pages, he realised that Jeremiah's character in the new book was nine years old again. Eli couldn't bring him out as a twelve-year-old because that wasn't who he was in the book any more. For a moment, he felt tempted to try to bring him out anyway. But it wouldn't be the same. It wouldn't be *his* Jeremiah. Perhaps his friend really was gone for good.

'We'll get him back,' Humphrey said, gazing up at Eli with his bright eyes. 'We won the race, didn't we? Anything is possible.'

Eli hoped he was right, but it was difficult to feel much optimism. He didn't know where to start. Inside his head, he kept replaying the moment when Jeremiah had been pulled back into the book and it had felt like there was something final and inevitable about it. At last, he left the manuscript on his desk and climbed into bed, wishing he could stay there forever. He'd have to attend the winner's ceremony tomorrow to collect his prize, which would involve more people staring at him and talking about him, and he felt he'd had enough of that to last him a lifetime. But he was quiet and alone with Humphrey for now, and that was something.

Tomorrow, he told himself as he closed his eyes. He would think about it all tomorrow.

CHAPTER THIRTY-ONE

THREE WEEKS LATER

Eli left Nana's Kitchen and made his way to the Royal Library. He could have used his magic key to get there instantly, but he enjoyed the walk and found it helped calm his thoughts. And he especially wanted to be calm today because he had a very important meeting. The restaurant was busy, as usual, but now that Nana had the magic pearl, her health was much better, and so was her magic. There was a whole fleet of chocolate penguin waiters to help her again. Eli knew Nana wouldn't be with him forever, but he was grateful for the time they still had and meant to enjoy every moment.

To Eli's relief, he'd been allowed to go back to his apprentice librarian job. He was still perfectly happy attending to his apprentice duties, including the bat droppings, and yet ... since winning the race, Eli had been daydreaming more and more about creating a library of his own, one solely dedicated to magical books. Not right now, but maybe one day.

Eli had been thinking about magic a lot too. The remaining half of the race prize had gone to Raven's kingdom, and in her last letter she'd said that the faery tree's health was already improving, with new buds and leaves on its branches. It would take time, but she was optimistic, and insisted that Eli must come and visit to see for himself, and to look at her stamp collection. Eli had always felt that trees were special – they were where books came from, after all – but now he wondered whether perhaps his mage magic might be able to do something for the tree, to help nurture it back to life. There was no way of knowing for sure, but it didn't hurt to try.

He'd always feared that revealing himself as a mage would mean he'd be dragged off into battle, or summoned by kings, but no such things had taken place yet, and perhaps they never would. Maybe, after all, he could be a mage, but use his powers as he saw fit. Perhaps he could help Raven restore her faery tree and then, when he wasn't working at the library, turn his attention to other magical trees in need of attention around the world … Eli felt quite excited by the prospect. He'd been feeling a lot more confident in himself since the race. It was a great relief that he no longer had to keep such a big secret too. For the first time, it felt as if he could truly be himself and that perhaps the mage and librarian parts of himself could exist side by side.

But there was something else that needed to be sorted out first, before any of that. Eli let himself into the Royal Library and, as usual, it was quiet and still at this time of night, save for the soft chirping of the bats swooping around the arched ceiling above. Eli glanced at his watch. It wasn't quite time yet, so he took Humphrey out of his tortoise bag and set him down on the marble floor to have a stump about, his silvery light shining softly.

The minutes ticked by and Eli tried to take slow, deep breaths, but his heart continued to pound rapidly in his chest and his palms prickled with sweat. The meeting he was about to have was so very important. It had taken several pleading letters from Eli before the other person had agreed to it at all. Eli knew he only had one chance and couldn't bear to think about the consequences if he messed it up.

Finally, the allotted hour arrived. Eli picked up Humphrey and took his bunch of keys from his pocket. The one he wanted today was rather plain and ordinary – a small key to a small private library. He walked over to the nearest door, inserted the key and slowly pushed it open. The door swung forwards to reveal a cosy room, with bookshelves lining the walls, and a couple of armchairs placed beside a crackling fire. One of the chairs was occupied, and the man glanced over his shoulder to say, a little shortly, 'Well, come in, then. You're creating a draught.'

Eli stepped over the threshold and closed the door softly behind him. The Royal Library and the chirping of the bats disappeared, and Eli was in someone's home. He walked over to the fire, cleared his throat and said, 'Good evening, sir. I'm Elijah Cassius Dewey Fleet. It's . . . it's an honour to meet you, at last.'

He held out his hand, but the man in the armchair only looked at him with a chilly expression, until Eli slowly lowered his hand. Eli had seen pictures of the writer, but Lionel Gaskins was older than he'd expected – closer to fifty than forty, with greying hair and a piercing expression that made Eli want to fidget.

'You stole from me,' Lionel said flatly.

'I know. And I wish I could say I was sorry, only I'm not. I love Jeremiah more than you do. That's why I need you to give him back.'

'You don't seem to realise what you're asking. He's my livelihood.'

'But he's my family.'

'I've been trying for years to write that sequel,' Lionel replied. 'Jeremiah always seemed like such a real character in my mind, until all of a sudden, he wasn't. I couldn't find him on the page any more, couldn't hear him inside my head. And I never understood why – until I received your letter. You had no right to take him.'

'But surely it's the most wonderful thing that can ever happen to a writer?' Eli pushed on desperately. 'One of your characters actually came to life. Aren't you thrilled? Don't you want to see him thriving out in the real world?'

'I'm not sure that the real world is any place for Jeremiah. I don't see how he can fit in here.'

'But this is where he *wants* to be,' Eli said. 'That must count for something? He doesn't want someone else writing his adventures. He wants to create his own.'

'Look, this discussion is irrelevant. It's too late. The book has been submitted to my publisher. It will shortly go off for printing. I'm a writer. I write for a living.'

'Yes,' Eli replied. 'I know. And that's why I came to offer you a bargain.'

Lionel folded his arms over his chest. 'What sort of bargain?'

'You can still submit the book to the publisher,' Eli said. 'But perhaps you might ask them to include one last chapter?'

'What are you talking about?'

'I . . . I took the liberty of writing it myself,' Eli said, reaching into his bag and pulling out a pile of paper. 'Please take a look. I'm sure you'll want to rewrite it and that you can, um, say it all much better than me. It's very short, as you can see, just an epilogue, really. All I need to do is establish that a few years have passed and that Jeremiah is twelve years old again. Then I can bring *my* Jeremiah back out of the book.'

Lionel stared at him. 'Haven't you been listening to a word I've said? I don't *want* you to take him out of the book. If I made Jeremiah twelve at the end of the story, then I wouldn't be able to write about him any more. *My* Jeremiah is nine. I've already got some ideas for a third volume.'

Eli took a deep breath. 'Give Jeremiah back to me,' he said, 'and you'll write something different. Something even better. The kind of book you've always wanted to write, but never quite been able to.'

Lionel raised an eyebrow. 'And you know this how?'

'Because if you give me Jeremiah then I'll give you Cuthbert.'

Lionel snorted. 'Who's that? Some other fictitious character? He's not one of mine – I'd never name a character Cuthbert.'

Eli shook his head. 'He's not a fictional character. Look, what's the most important thing of all to a writer?'

'Coffee.'

'Even more important than that.'

Lionel looked blank.

'Inspiration,' Eli said.

He reached into his pocket and drew out a handsome grey rat. '*This* is Cuthbert.'

Lionel sighed. 'I like rats, but I'm not looking for a pet right now.'

'He's not an ordinary rat. He's an inspire-rat.'

'I beg your pardon?'

'He can sniff out inspiration,' Eli said softly. 'He'll lead you to the books, and places, and people that will help you write the best stories. All you have to do is follow him.'

Eli set the rat down on the floor. He immediately scampered across the carpet to run up Lionel's chair and on to the writer's lap, where he rose on to his hind legs and peered at Lionel with bright, curious eyes.

Lionel stared at the rat for a moment before turning his gaze to Eli. 'Are you telling me the truth? Such a creature would be incredible indeed, but I've never heard of an inspire-rat.'

'He's the only one of his kind, at least in this world,' Eli replied. 'I took him out of a book. I had to go through hundreds and hundreds before I found something good enough to trade. Will you think about it, at least? That's all I ask. Keep Cuthbert for a month and see what he can do, what stories and ideas he can lead you to. If you don't want him, then I'll take him back and ... and I'll never mention Jeremiah to you again. But if you want to keep Cuthbert, then all you have to do is add the last chapter to Jeremiah's book.'

Lionel was quiet for a long time. With one finger, he gently stroked Cuthbert's soft fur.

'Very well,' he said finally. 'One month.'

Eli took his leave, hoping that he had done enough. Now all he had to do was wait.

Barely a week passed before a parcel was delivered to Eli by special delivery at the Royal Library. Inside was no covering note or letter, merely a new copy of a manuscript Eli recognised. *The Further Seafaring Adventures of Jeremiah Jones*. He flipped through it with trembling hands. Every page and word was identical to the one he'd already seen – right up until the end, where a new chapter had been added.

It had been rewritten, and polished, and tinkered with since Eli handed it over, but it was, in effect, the same chapter. And all that really mattered was that

Jeremiah was no longer nine years old in it, but twelve instead. Eli gave a delighted gasp and looked up at the clock on the wall. There were still three hours until the end of his shift, but he knew he'd never be able to wait until then. So he paused only to scoop Humphrey up, then ran to the secret door behind one of the bookcases and made his way up staircases and ladders until he came out on to the library roof.

It was a space normally reserved for gargoyles and pigeons, and the one place Eli knew he wouldn't be disturbed. He set Humphrey down, placed his hands over the manuscript and concentrated with all his might. A few moments later, he heard the raucous cry of a sea phoenix, and a shadow fell across him. Eli looked up, and there he was, larger than life.

'My clever friend,' Jeremiah said with a grin. 'You really can do anything you set your mind to, can't you?'

He reached down to help Eli to his feet and then the two boys were hugging and laughing, and Eli could feel tears of happiness and relief on his cheeks. Humphrey stumped over too, and butted Jeremiah's ankle affectionately.

'I don't know how you did it,' Jeremiah said, clapping Eli on the shoulder. 'But right now I don't care.'

Eli smiled. 'I'm so happy to see you. I'll explain everything properly later, but for now just know that you're here for good this time. Your life is your own, to do whatever you want with. You said during the race you were worried that I'd outgrown you. Well, I think it will probably be the other way around – you're the one who will outgrow me. Eventually, you'll want to leave Harmonica and go off and do amazing things and have incredible adventures, and that's okay. As long as you're happy.'

Jeremiah gave Eli a nudge. 'Who knows? Perhaps I'll convince you to go on one or two of those adventures with me?'

Eli shook his head. 'I thought I might try to help a magical tree if I can,' he said. 'But after that I'm done with adventuring. I'm very happy where I belong, in the library.'

'Well,' Jeremiah replied, a gleam in his eye. 'We'll see.'

'Never mind about adventures right now,' Eli said. 'Once my shift finishes, there's something important we need to do.'

'What is it?' Jeremiah looked eager. 'Is it to do with shark fighting? Or a particularly dangerous rescue mission? Has someone been kidnapped by pirates?'

'No, no, nothing like that.' Eli drew a paper party hat from his pocket and then pointed at Humphrey, who was wearing an identical smaller one. 'We have a tortoise birthday party to get to.'

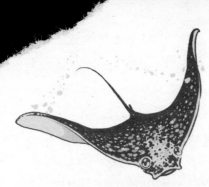

Acknowledgements

Many thanks to the following wonderful people:

My agent, Thérèse Coen, and all the people at the Hardman and Swainson Literary Agency and Susanna Lea Associates.

My editor, Jenny Glencross, and the lovely team at Faber.

My family.

All of the children's booksellers and teachers who take the time to champion books and nurture a love of reading in young people.

And, finally, to all of the children who have read and enjoyed my books. When you dress up as the characters, or write letters to me, or create things in the classroom, or share your amazing ideas at events, you remind me of what a special thing it is to be a children's writer. I hope you enjoy this book too.

About the Author

Alex Bell has published novels and short stories for both adults and young people, including *Frozen Charlotte*, *The Lighthouse* and the Explorers' Clubs series. She always wanted to be a writer but had several different back-up plans. After completing a law degree, she now works part-time at the Citizens Advice Bureau. She lives in Hampshire with her husband and sons.

About the Illustrator

Tim McDonagh's work has been used everywhere in every way, but he's perhaps best known for his epic Star Wars book series and his award winning *New York Times* Kid's section covers. Inspired by old comics, gig posters and tattoos, the depth in Tim's work is truly mesmerising. He lives and works in Brighton.